# UNSEEN

## THE UNSEEN SERIES - BOOK ONE

## GRETCHEL R. MORALES

Cover illustration and design by David Leahey.

Printed in the United States of America.

ISBN 978-1-7373802-0-7 (Paperback)


Flying Mantis Press
Los Angeles, CA
USA


Visit our website at flyingmantispress.com
Email us at flying.mantis.press@gmail.com

*For my husband, John.*

*This book would not have been possible without your support and encouragement.*

# Prologue

## December 16 – Sunday

It was a dark night. The quarter moon in the sky didn't reflect much light, but that hardly bothered the sullen man holding a bottle of whisky. He had swigged about half of its contents already as he pondered what had transpired earlier tonight. In fact, it was the recurring theme of his entire life. He was irked because he couldn't change the past yet still had to live with its consequences. So he came here to forget.

His silver Dodge Stratus was parked on the left side of a logging road in the middle of nowhere. He sat in the driver's seat, not minding the chill slowly invading the vehicle after he had shut the engine off. Loggers stopped using this road a long time ago. They must have harvested all of the trees in whatever area they were allowed to operate and then never came back, but the roads remained, albeit, in various states of disrepair. The trees remained too. They were thick like a fortress in many places, like a whole different world. These old logging roads were pathways into hidden places, which is why he liked to come out here sometimes, to this same spot where he and his wife would talk about plans. Talk about the future and how they would spend their lives together.

The man shook his head in disgust and then took another gulp of alcohol. None of those plans came to fruition. And all that was left were accusations. On the one hand, the longstanding, unspoken accusations from his father were like a childhood bully that you could just put to the back of your mind as you grew up. And when Dad died, it was easier to ignore the internal voice of paternal disappointment, but then *she* started accusing him of all sorts of failings. She wasn't blameless, but she sure acted like she had never done a wrong thing in this relationship. And the worst part wasn't that she left him. No. The worst part was that she left their daughter too.

The wind kicked up momentarily causing the tall trees to sway somewhat. Drafts of snow fell here and there from laden branches. The man's eyes had adjusted to the darkness so he could see the depression of the undriven road ahead in the snow. The white covering on the ground reflected the sparse moonlight, increasing visibility. It had snowed hard earlier today but the weather was calm right now. The weather could change suddenly though. If he were smart, he would sober up and drive back home. Instead, he took another sip of whisky.

His cell phone buzzed and he struggled to take it out of his winter jacket pocket. The stubby antenna on top kept getting caught in pockets. He was surprised that his flip phone was able to receive a signal up here. Cell phones generally didn't work in the woods.

The word "Mom" appeared on the tiny screen. He almost answered the call…almost. Mom had always been in his corner and, no doubt, she was calling to talk about the latest round of accusations, this time coming

2

from his own brother of all people. But he was in no mood to talk to anyone at the moment. He hit the silver button bearing the red cancel icon and put the phone on the passenger seat next to him.

He noticed his breath fogging up the windows somewhat, which was bothersome. He enjoyed looking out at the trees covered in snow. He liked thinking of the animals that lived out here, free to do *whatever* they wanted *whenever* they wanted. And whatever the animals did, the trees didn't judge. One animal slaughtered another for food and the next day was slaughtered in return. The trees saw it all and judged not. And whatever an animal did, whether it be a wolf, an owl, a bear, or a deer, it was done out in the open without malice.

I'm killing you because I need to eat or because you're near my cubs. Just something necessary for survival. End of story. They're just grateful that they managed to survive another day. The animals do what they do in plain sight and they don't hold grudges over it. Why can't people be that way too? Just be thankful we're all still alive. We survived another damn day. Maybe it wasn't a perfect day, or a perfect year, but, hey, we're all still here trying to live it.

*For crying out loud, I'm* trying, he thought.

The man felt some unwanted emotions begin to well up in his chest. Alone with his thoughts, sometimes he cried. He was taught that crying wasn't something a grown man should do, at least, not in front of others. This secluded spot shielded him from the patronizing gazes of his family. He didn't like to weep whether alone or not, but this was the only place he felt that he could mourn the life he had wanted to live. Loud gurgled

3

sobs emerged involuntarily from his throat. He tried to stifle them at first, but after a moment no longer cared. Who was here to see or to hear?

After a long while, the man was quiet, feeling some momentary peace after expelling the pent-up emotion. He even laughed a little at himself over how worked up he had gotten earlier this evening at his brother.

Absentmindedly, he heard what sounded like an owl in the distance. He smiled to himself and was glad of the company. A moment later, there was another long whooping sound a little louder than the first. He casually looked out at the trees lining the logging road, futilely scanning for that owl somewhere in the branches. After a minute, from the corner of his eye, he saw something emerge from the trees on the opposite side of the road about fifty to sixty feet in front of him. He focused his gaze on a shape, squinting to determine what it was. *Is that a man?* This was an old logging road and he didn't think anyone had used it in years. He laughed quietly at the thought of some cartoonish, big, hairy, logger out here at this time of night. *Scouting for timber, eh? But if I'm out here this late, why not someone else too?*

The man wondered where the other person had parked his car. He hadn't seen anyone drive by in the hour since he'd arrived at this spot. Perhaps the other person had parked closer to the main road and had walked up the logging road. Nighttime hikes weren't the strangest thing he'd heard of people doing.

The man squinted again to get a better look at the dark shape. Certainly, it was a big guy—wearing a bonnet and scarf maybe? And the figure seemed to be swaying from side to side, which was odd. *Why is he doing* that? *Is he dancing?* Again, the man half laughed to himself, but the longer he looked, the more uneasy he felt. Was it the effect of the alcohol? He abruptly felt very dry-mouthed.

Suddenly a strange, long scream cut the night. The scream was so loud that the man could feel its vibrations in his gut. This was not normal. Terrified, he dropped the bottle of whisky onto the car floor and instinctively popped the glove compartment open to grab the gun he kept there. The glove compartment light immediately illuminated the car interior. He fumbled a moment with the gun's safety switch—which he would have unlocked with ease had he been sober—then quickly slammed the glove box shut with a curse. He quickly looked up again, quietly upset that his eyes had to readjust to the darkness. Fortunately, he was able to spot the dark shape in the same location. The man's breathing was ragged as he firmly gripped the gun and pointed it at the figure through the front windshield, waiting.

A low-pitched growl emanated from the direction of the dark shape, slowly increasing in volume to some sort of a roar that penetrated the man's core. It was as if the car were emitting the roar at max volume and vibrating the seats.

*What is going on?!* thought the man in alarm.

Then the dark figure became silent, which strangely scared the man almost as much as the deafening roar. Unexpectedly, the already intimidating figure charged the car at an incredible speed. The man's eyes grew wide as he realized that the charging figure was unbelievably *massive* and frighteningly fast. In a matter of seconds it would reach the car.

    *That's not a man...*

# Chapter 1

## July 4 – Sunday

Jack swung his tall frame into the driver's seat of his Ford F-150 truck and shut the door. He ran a hand through his wavy, white hair and reached for the smart phone in his shirt pocket. He checked all of the text messages he had ignored during the lunch meeting that ended a few minutes ago.

Jack tapped the chat conversation labeled "NSI Farts" and scrolled up to read a message from Bill: "When are you getting to the party? Remember to bring my beer." *Yeah, yeah, Bill. I know the damn caterer couldn't get the swill you like to drink.* Jack scrolled to the next message in the chat from David: "How did the meeting go in Bonners Ferry?"

Jack typed, "Lukewarm response at lunch today…but got leads from them on other potential investors up here, maybe in Coeur d'Alene too. Will put together another lunch in a week or so hopefully. Will be at party around 3p – after I get BILL's BEER."

Jack moved to the next text chat from his ex-wife Ellen. It read, "See you at the 4th of July party. I'll be there early to help set up. Bill told me to remind you about his beer ☺." Jack grinned as he typed, "Got it.

Do me a huge favor and shove a bratwurst up his nose. Thanks! See you there."

The next chat message was from his niece Stefanie. "Uncle Jack, I don't know if we'll be able to talk much at the party today, and later I'm going to be busy getting ready for my survey trip in a few days, so I wanted to give you a heads up that lately I've been thinking of having Dad declared deceased. It's been 14 years and I just want to close that chapter and move on. If he ever actually shows up on our doorstep we can figure out what to do then, but you know my feelings on how likely that is. I'll see you later."

Jack sighed as he read the message. The thought of having Tom declared deceased was both shocking and logical. It's not the first time Stefanie had brought it up, but she'd never actually gotten around to doing it before. Stefanie had every right to do this and probably should, but part of him had always been bothered by the way things were left between him and his younger brother Tom. Not every discussion ended in a fight, but a lot of them did—toward the end there anyway. Jack regretted that. And declaring Tom deceased felt like it was closing off all hope of ever making things right. But if Tom were truly dead, then there would never be an opportunity to make things right between them—not in this life anyway. Jack shook off the ennui and typed to Stefanie, "Sweetheart, it's your decision and I'll fully support whatever you decide. But I do want to talk about it in person. See you at the party."

Jack opened the next message from Gina Lamb, Bill's assistant. "Jack, I can't find the big Northern Sun Investments banner. Is it still in your truck from the Chili Pepper Restaurant event? If so, please bring to Bill's today! Thanks!" Jack looked over his shoulder into the back seat of his crew cab. Yup, there it lay, rolled up on the floor like a scroll. He responded with "Yes, I have it in the truck. Will be at party in about an hour." Gina immediately replied, "Great! See you then."

Jack clicked his phone off and placed it on the truck's center console. It took about forty minutes to drive from Bonners Ferry to Bill's property in Everton—and he still had to buy Bill's beer. Jack started the truck and headed south.

Jack and his two business partners Bill and David enjoyed socializing with the various construction and design crews involved in the execution of their investment project: a new boutique lodge just outside of Everton, Idaho. This is why he and Bill had hosted a few events at their respective houses and at a couple of restaurants.

This last 8-week phase involved actual construction and installation, so the design, fabrication, and installation people would all be on site every day for about 3 months. Construction really needed to happen in any season *other* than winter. He, Bill, and David—the three founding investors of Northern Sun Investments (NSI)—had chosen a Grand Opening date of September 1 for The Grizzly Bear Lodge, and everything was on schedule so far.

The design companies that NSI had hired were based in California—Gibson Drake in Santa Monica and Eden Design & Fabrication in Los Angeles. Their design and installation crews were temporarily living in Everton, Idaho, during construction. Some employees had brought their families to stay with them since this phase was occurring in the summer months when school was out. Idaho was truly an outdoor vacation destination and Jack was banking on that very premise for this venture—there was a lot of natural beauty to explore in the Gem State.

Jack had been fiddling with different ideas on how to better utilize his family's land in Bonner County, Idaho, which was located in the northern panhandle of the state. After his father died in 1993, it was left to Jack to start handling the family's holdings, which equaled about two thousand acres of forest. There had originally been more land in the Evers Trust, but Jack's grandfather sold a lot of it to the Municipality of Everton when it officially became a city in 1917. In fact, so much of the city's downtown real estate had been established on the Evers Family property that the town was called Everton as early as 1913. Jack took his family's legacy in the community seriously and just wanted to bring more prosperity to the town of 8,000 people.

For years his family's land lay mostly unused except for two activities. The first activity centered around logging. Every 10 years or so, his father would arrange a timber harvest to create some openings in the forest canopy. They could clear out dead trees and make some extra cash. The other activity involved a decrepit campground with dilapidated wood cabins. The family hadn't rented those cabins out for a long time because the accommodations were, frankly, embarrassing. Jack himself would never spend the night in one of those things. Six cabins were built by Jack's grandfather Elijah Evers around 1946. Jack didn't know how much use they got back when they were new, but they certainly hadn't been fit for habitation for most of his adult life. Those six cabins stood there unchanged and without update for 75 years.

If any part of the land should be rehabilitated, it was that campground. The family had already paved a road leading up to it—named after his grandmother Beverly—when the cabins were originally built. Eventually, his own father Jeffrey Evers had some water, sewer, and power lines put in before he died. Jeffrey was trying to get that campground functional again and was actually up at the site with some surveyors when he suffered a fatal heart attack. His death halted all progress on the site. Jack was still living in California back then and had no interest in taking on such a project. His younger brother Tom, likewise, showed no intention of finishing the job.

The crux of the problem was that nobody in the family, except for Jack's father, really believed in the campground concept for that spot. Jack's brother Tom had his own crazy ideas about how to use the land—something to do with ATVs and motorbikes?—but Tom would never follow through. He seemed incapable of finishing the research and could never secure the funding, so how could Jack ever agree to any of these schemes?

When Jack eventually moved back to Idaho a little over a decade later, he felt the weight of doing something productive with the land. He realized that his father had already done a large chunk of the work in bringing water, sewer, and power up to the site. All that remained was to place something there that Jack believed in. The Evers Campground was situated in a great spot, not too close to town but not too deep in the forest either. It was literally just a ten-minute drive from the outskirts of Everton and only twenty minutes away with traffic from downtown. Yet, in that twenty-minute drive from downtown to the campground, it was like crossing over into another world. Most of the drive to the campground passed through meadows and tree groves, but the last three miles were *all* trees with dense undergrowth. These were thick forests of emerald giants guarding the hidden places and sheltering the amazing wildlife that lived there. Many trees grew over a hundred feet tall, creating a forest cathedral of serenity unseen by most people.

Jack intended to share that experience with others. He also wanted Everton to remain a successful city and to build a vacation destination in the woods that the town—and his family—could be proud of. Jack started Northern Sun Investments (NSI) in order to raise the funds to design, construct, and manage this project. It took years of planning and fundraising to get to this final stage. There were some moments when it looked like the project couldn't be done, but with the support of the Everton populace and city leadership, NSI was able to surmount the zoning and funding issues to finally make this place a reality. The Grizzly Bear Lodge would definitely bring more jobs to the area as well as boost local businesses with the increase in tourism. It was a win all around.

Jack heard his phone buzz on the truck console. He took a look at the notification screen when he was stopped at a red light. His son Bobby texted, "Happy 4th of July, Dad! Sorry we won't be there today, but we'll probably be able to visit next month. Maybe I can persuade you to go on a hunt with me this time. Talk to you later."

Jack smiled. That boy of his was always trying to get him to hunt. It's not that Jack was opposed to hunting, but rather that Jack got his thrills from doing crazy things like jumping out of airplanes or getting into bar fights. As a stuntman in Hollywood for a couple of decades, Jack had seen and done a lot of insane things. He had been away on film shoots so often that his marriage suffered for it. Raising kids by herself in California's San Fernando Valley while Jack was off to God-knows-where for who-knows-how-long didn't sit well with Ellen. Jack had no intention of changing careers, and since marriage counseling wasn't really a thing back then, he and Ellen got a divorce eight years after saying "I do."

Jack and Ellen had been high school sweethearts at Everton High School. Jack dragged her and the kids to California after he got back from Vietnam and became a stuntman, but she took the kids back to Idaho after the divorce. They never lost touch with each other because they had two children to raise, but after her second husband died of cancer a few years back, Jack and Ellen began to talk more often, especially when Jack moved back to Everton. It was an unexpected and happy development in Jack's golden years. They shared children and grandchildren together and Ellen was always easy to talk to. In hindsight—and three additional failed marriages later—Jack realized that he had been a fool to let her go.

Jack's phone buzzed again as he parked at the grocery store to get Bill's beer. It was not unusual for Jack to receive texts all day long. He was an outgoing member of the community and a businessman. Jack picked up his phone and checked the text. It was from Keith Carrera, one of the project directors for the Lodge construction. "Jack – good news – the animal elements will arrive at the Lodge next weekend. Including ROY. We can talk more at the party."

*Excellent!* Jack had insisted that the Grizzly Bear Lodge include life-sized, realistic animal props in the lobby and other common areas of the resort. The design people called these animal creations "elements" but Jack still considered them props in his own mind. The fabrication department had been running behind on those animals for reasons that didn't make sense to Jack, but this latest news was welcome indeed. Jack felt that once the grizzly bear element was in place in the lobby, seated on his throne if you will, that the Lodge would finally have a real personality.

Jack typed to Keith, "Can't wait to see him – good job!" Then he went into the store to finally buy Bill's beer.

*** 

Em squinted as the sunlight hit her in the eye. She sat in the front passenger seat of their Toyota Highlander while her husband Keith started up the vehicle. He punched in the address for the house where NSI was hosting a Fourth of July Party. The car's map system said it would take fifteen minutes to get there.

"Whose house are we going to again?" asked their daughter Margaret from the back seat.

"Bill Davis's house," Keith answered. "There'll be lots of food. And I think Bill bought some fireworks for people to light up."

"For *us* to use?" asked Jessica, seated in the back between her older siblings Jason and Margaret. They were all teenagers now and pretty much adult-sized.

Em laughed. "I know, right? We're not used to being able to buy fireworks and light them up in the street back in California." She glanced back at her three children and saw nonchalant expressions on their faces. Her oldest child, Jason, had his air pods on, listening to music no doubt. Strangely, Jessica, the youngest, and Margaret didn't have their earbuds in, but none of them looked eager to attend this event.

Em couldn't blame them. This was yet another one of Keith's "work" parties, which was really just professional schmoozing for the adults. Yes, there would be some other teenagers at the event, but so what? Em's kids weren't big on small talk with strange kids. Even Em had to mentally prepare herself to smile and engage in inconsequential conversation for the next eight grueling hours. Em calculated that if the party starts at 2 PM and sunset occurs at around 9:30 PM, and they need to stay until after the fireworks, then their family would be at Bill's house for roughly eight to nine hours. *Ugh.* Em forced herself to stop dwelling on how many hours were left until nightfall.

Maybe "grueling" was too harsh a word. There would be good food *and booze*, a great lubricant for the dullest of dialogue. To be fair, Em had met some interesting people from the community at these shindigs—many of them were senior citizens who formed a surprisingly close-knit and highly involved network in the city of Everton.

There was the party host Bill Davis, one of the NSI investors—a widower who never remarried. He was a local businessman who evidently had a toe in a variety of industries. Em only knew of three of his ventures: tourism, NSI, and whisky. Then there was David Eckert and his wife Leanne, also NSI investors. David was polite and quiet until you mentioned a topic that triggered an impassioned soliloquy from him, such as excessive government intervention in private enterprise.

There were many other senior citizens whom Em had met, and certainly they would be present at the party today, in addition to both of the design companies' employees. Naturally, Jack Evers, the third and founding NSI investor, would be there. Em liked Jack the most. He had lived an interesting life: served in the military, worked as a stuntman, spent some time as a fisherman, and married *four* times—yikes! He was in his seventies, but his energy seemed to rival anyone thirty or forty years younger. He also seemed to like driving around in his truck. If any delivery-type errand needed doing, like bringing signed papers to the Lodge, or picking up banners for the NSI events, or meeting potential investors in other cities, Jack seemed happy to volunteer for the task. And he always appeared pleased to be wherever he was. Em wondered if he really felt that way or if it was just the mask he wore in front of other people.

It was hard for Em to relate to that kind of temperament because she was naturally introverted. The misconception about introverts is that they don't like socializing with other people, but that's not the case at all. Introverts actually enjoy interacting with others, even strangers, and can be boisterous in conversation. However, the "good times" really need to have a hard stop for introverts, because after a certain threshold is reached, socializing suddenly becomes a huge drain on the introvert's energy. Whereas extroverts *gain* energy from interacting with others, introverts *lose* energy after a certain amount of time. The only exception to that rule is when an introvert is with an inner circle of people, like family or best friends. In that case, an introvert seems to also gain energy when in the company of intimate companions.

Alternatively, Em sometimes wondered if her aversion to these events had more to do with being over forty and therefore less patient with small talk. Perhaps it really was an age thing, not a personality thing. The counter to the age-argument was Jack Evers.

Jack was over seventy and certainly seemed to enjoy meeting new people and interacting with them. When Em first met him a few weeks ago, in the short amount of time they conversed, she learned a lot about his professional and personal life. Em wasn't surprised that he was still good friends with his first wife Ellen. She also learned that he had a couple of kids and several grandkids, had lived in California, and then moved back to Idaho when his mom fell ill. He smiled easily and liked to joke with everyone. Em's husband Keith liked Jack a lot as well. They'd had one argument about something at the Lodge, but it seemed to resolve quickly and neither mentioned it again.

"By the way, you might see some new faces at the party," Keith said to Em.

"Oh? Why's that?"

"We're at the stage where the artists can come in and work on the installations. The new people arrived yesterday."

"Okay, great. Do I know them?"

"Mmm...probably not."

*Ugh*, Em thought. *More new people to meet.*

"Wake up kids! We're here," Keith stated as he parked on Bill's street. Em looked in the back to see her kids rubbing their eyes and stretching from their surreptitious car naps. She wasn't too surprised that they fell asleep on such a short car trip since they were up till all hours of the night playing video games. There were about twenty cars parked on the street and the caterer's truck was in the driveway. The house was large—maybe 4,000-5,000 square feet?—and it was surrounded by a lot of land. The closest neighbor was a few hundred feet down the road.

The family of five walked up to the front door, which was open with no one to greet them. Em would never leave her front door open like this in Los Angeles. Em and the kids followed Keith as they looked for the host, but it was evident from the noise that everyone was in the backyard. They passed the kitchen bustling with the catering staff, who then pointed to the open French doors toward the back of the house. A large, white tent had been erected to shelter the tables and chairs outside. The entire backyard was bedecked in red, white, and blue, and there were four balloon columns standing in a row. A live band was playing on a small stage to the right. Many people were mingling with drinks in hand while waiting in line for the buffet. It almost felt like they were visiting a county fair.

Em and Keith spotted a portly Bill laughing about something with Andrew Colgan, who was the Project Manager for Gibson Drake Design—they were in charge of the architectural designs and construction for the Grizzly Bear Lodge. Keith's company, Eden Design & Fabrication, was in charge of designing, constructing, and installing the themed elements of the Lodge. These elements included rock climbing walls, mounted animal heads, antler chandeliers, and sculpted walls simulating alpine mountain cliffs. The highlight of it all would be the life-sized, realistic animal creations to be strategically installed in the lobby, restaurant, indoor pool area, and so on. It was all very exciting.

"The rock climbing vendor should be on site this week," Em heard Andrew say to Bill.

"Perfect," Bill replied. "I'm confident you two stellar project managers have everything in order. Keith said the animals should be on site soon too."

"Yes," Andrew replied matter-of-factly. "We're on schedule." Andrew wore a polo t-shirt emblazoned with a modest Gibson Drake logo on the chest. The guy always had an ironed look about him, nothing ever out of place. And he never spoke out of turn or had an emotional outburst.

19

Em always joked with Keith that she suspected Andrew was an android masquerading as an architectural project manager.

Andrew continued, "Keith also said his artists would be arriving this weekend."

"Yeah," Bill said, "they're over there." Bill gestured to another part of his backyard. "I can't wait to see what they do with the installations at the Lodge."

Em smiled at their conversation. She thought that all of Keith's work was amazing, but she felt that this particular alpine themed project was really stunning for its realism. There were many nights when Keith would call Em over to his computer to look at the drawings and concept art for the Grizzly Bear Lodge. She loved all of it, but the animal elements were especially impressive. There were many smaller elements too, but some of the larger ones included a moose, elk, and several grizzly bears. The main grizzly bear element—whom Jack and Keith had nicknamed "Roy"—was a towering figure measuring ten feet tall. Jack wanted Roy to stand in the lobby welcoming everyone into his Grizzly Bear kingdom.

Bill spotted Keith and Em and beckoned them over. Keith and Em shook hands with Bill and Andrew while the kids waved hello. "Kids, go ahead and get in line for the food," Bill instructed. "There's ribs, bratwurst, steak, you name it!" Jason, Margaret, and Jessica thanked Bill politely and headed over to the queue.

"Beautiful house, Bill," Keith commented.

Em echoed her husband's sentiment. "Everything looks great, Bill," she said with a smile. "I love the live band."

Anton and Angie Nielsen walked up to the group, having also just arrived at the party. They were contemporaries of Bill and owned a car rental business located in Everton.

"Well look who it is!" Bill announced. "I thought you two couldn't make it today," he said as he kissed Angie on the cheek and shook Anton's hand.

"Yeah, yeah," Anton said dismissively.

"I guess I should feel honored that you chose *my party* over your neighbor's," Bill teased.

"Oh we already went to the other party *first*, Bill," Anton said with a swagger. "This is our second party of the day."

"Bastard!" Bill laughed while Anton grinned like the Cheshire Cat.

Angie chided, "You know we love you, Bill, but our neighbor's dog has been missing for three days now. The family is losing their minds and we wanted to support them." Anton and Angie were avid dog lovers and owned two Great Pyrenees canines: Max and Lucky. These were large dogs weighing over a hundred pounds each and wearing a thick coat of white fur. Angie had informed Em at a previous party that they were an ancient breed of livestock guard dogs.

"Does their family dog have a habit of running off?" asked Em. In her mind, she was envisioning a 10-pound poodle ignoring its master's call just to scurry after a squirrel across the street.

"Well, you have to understand, their dog is a Caucasian Shepherd," Angie explained. "Like our dogs, it's a very large guard dog for sheep." Then, like a true dog-lover, she took out her phone to show Em photos of *their neighbors' dog.* "So, Argus—their dog—is out in the field with the sheep during the day."

"All by himself?" Em asked as she viewed pictures of a massive, bear-looking dog standing near sheep. There were also several photos of Argus lying down in the grass as he looked beyond the sheep to the forest, always alert.

"Yes, absolutely. These guard dogs were bred to make some decisions on their own about what constitutes a threat to their charges, or their pack. There is a wooden livestock fence around the property to keep the sheep from running off, but Argus never jumped out of the enclosure, not even to chase something off. I've seen him charge at wolves that were on the *outside* of the enclosure, but he wouldn't jump out and give chase."

"So, did he go missing while guarding the sheep?" Em inquired. She was very curious about how such a large animal could go missing— an annoying poodle getting eaten by a coyote happened quite often in Los Angeles, but what would make a large dog like Argus leave the sheep?

Anton said, "Yes, it was a routine day and Argus was out with the sheep. Sarah said she went to check on the animals around lunch time and found all of the sheep still in the enclosure but no Argus. I mean, no one is going to overcome that dog unless they've got a shotgun—and you better aim true before that dog gets to you!" Everyone else agreed as Angie held her phone out for all to see the photos.

"That dog is *huge*." Keith stated. "Was there any blood? Any signs of a fight?" This was sounding more and more like a murder mystery.

Angie and Anton were both shaking their heads emphatically. "None," said Anton. "That's what's so strange. We even brought our dogs over to sniff around for clues—I mean, they're not bloodhounds, but Max and Lucky know Argus. You'd think they'd smell something." Anton shrugged. "It was a long shot but we wanted to try. Our dogs just ended up sniffing inside the fencing. They didn't seem to like one spot on the wooden fence, but none of us could find any blood or scratch marks. We searched in the woods around their house too. Nothing."

"How close do they live to your house?" Em asked.

"About a quarter mile away, so, *yes*, we've kept a closer eye on our own dogs since Argus went missing," Angie said.

"*And* our goats, *and* our horses, *and* our grandkids," Anton elaborated with hands in his pockets, which seemed to be his signature stance.

"In that order?" Bill joked.

"Of course," Anton agreed, going along with the joke. "Anyhow, I don't think any wolves or bears were involved because there would have been a scuffle. We would have seen fur and blood on the ground—from *both* Argus and them."

"Maybe someone lured him out with a steak," Keith suggested.

"No," Anton said firmly. "Argus was a disciplined guard dog. He would never leave his sheep to go after food. Our dog Lucky on the other hand…" he grimaced jokingly. Angie poked Anton in the arm for making fun of her fur baby.

"Anyway, it's just such a shame," Angie said sadly. "Argus was a sweet, sweet dog. I mean, I'm praying that he comes home safely, but it really makes no sense."

Just then, Bill's sister walked over to the group with an exaggerated spring in her step. Angie was very excited to see the other woman as they hugged in greeting. Then Angie asked, "Did you get it?!"

"I did!! Look at my new knee!" Bill's sister almost squealed in delight as she performed some shallow squats to demonstrate how great her new right knee was.

Em was amused watching the two older women. Anton leaned over and held his hand up to his mouth so that no one else could hear him say, "Do you want to know how to avoid needing a new knee?"

"How?" Em asked.

"Don't get old!" Anton laughed. Em laughed too.

By now, Em noticed that Keith had stepped away to talk to Andrew and Bill about something else. When she turned back to the others, Anton, Angie, and Bill's sister were now engaged in some other discussion that clearly didn't involve her. Em didn't like hovering around Keith like a satellite while he talked shop, so she decided to look for her children.

Em scanned the enormous backyard and was amazed to see the trio seated at a table eating with some other teenagers. They even seemed to be talking to them! Well, Em wasn't going to interrupt *that* scene, so she got in line for food.

Em piled as much food as she could fit onto her plate so that she could try as many dishes as possible without getting back in line. Then

24

she looked about for a place to sit. She saw a round table that was only half full and headed over to it. She asked the woman seated there, who looked to be in her thirties, if they were reserving the other seats at the table for anyone else. The woman quickly said, "No, they're free," as she held a napkin to her mouth to cover her chewing. "Please sit!"

Em smiled and thanked her. As she sat, she introduced herself to the three people already at the table. "My name's Emmeline Carrera—I'm Keith's wife. Maybe you've met him."

"Yes, I think I met him briefly," said the woman. "He's from Eden Design, right?"

"Yup," Em replied.

"I'm Stefanie, Jack Evers's niece."

"Oh! Yes, I know Jack. Nice to meet you!" said Em.

"Thank you," she said jovially. "This is Cal Russo and Liam Rayburn…" Stefanie motioned to her companions and Em nodded hello to them.

"Are you guys also working on the Lodge?" Em asked Cal and Liam. In her experience, the people who were younger than forty at these events were usually employees of the two design companies.

Cal responded, "Actually, we live in Everton. I'm a reporter for *The Eagle Newspaper* and Liam is in charge of social and digital media for the paper."

"Oh, are you here to report on the party? Or just here socially?" Em inquired.

"Maybe a little of both?" said Cal. They all laughed.

"Cal is always looking for a story," Stefanie confided jokingly. "Careful what you say to him."

Cal straightened up in protest. "Well, hold on there," he said. "I always protect my sources."

Stefanie patted Cal on the shoulder, "All kidding aside, Cal is a great reporter. He also does live streaming reports in the field, so if you want to know what's going on in town, he's probably already on scene."

"Then I'll definitely look for you on the social media apps," said Em. "We've been renting a place on the outskirts of town so we don't really hear anything going on in the city. The rental house is on a big plot of land by itself—except for the owner, who lives in a smaller house about a hundred feet away. But there aren't any other neighbors to talk to really."

"Well, there are a lot of houses out here like that," said Liam as he shrugged. "People like to have space for their trucks and their animals. I ride motorbikes on the weekend and I own more than one, so I eventually needed the space to build a detached garage. A lot of other people have horses and sheep, and sometimes you don't want the animals living too close to the main house."

Em nodded. "Yeah, I've noticed that. There's a barn about thirty feet from our landlord's house. He's got two goats and a few chickens in there I think."

Stefanie chimed in, "It's the life here. Lots of animals, lots of space, lots of nature. I grew up running around in the woods with the other kids after school and all summer."

26

"Do you also work at the newspaper, Stefanie?" Em asked.

"No, actually I work for the US Forest Service, on forest inventory assessments. We study and record the types of vegetation currently growing in the national forests."

"That sounds very cool," Em said. "So you're out in the forest all of the time?"

"Yes! But, sometimes I'm working in the office for a week or two straight. It just depends on the schedule."

"Do you go out by yourself?" Em asked. She didn't like the thought of Stefanie hiking by herself in the forest. Em suspected it must be the mother in her to be worrying about this grown woman whom she only just met.

"Usually we go out in teams of two to four, depending on the area we need to cover," explained Stefanie. "We carry our equipment in backpacks and usually hike to the plot of land that we're assessing. But I've also had to access plots by horse or ATV—especially if we need to carry a lot of equipment, or if we need to stay out in the field overnight." Em could tell that Stefanie had gotten practice at explaining her job because she didn't have to stop and think of what to say next. Stefanie continued in an excited, teacher-like fashion, "While we're in the field, we measure the trees and record the kinds of plants that are growing there. Basically, we assess the overall health of the forest in both national lands and private property."

"Well, it sounds like you enjoy your job," Em commented.

"Definitely," Stefanie nodded emphatically. "I love it."

"Yeah, but you have to really be careful out there, Stef," chided Cal. "I check in with the city agencies all the time for the latest info," he explained to Em before turning back to Stefanie and saying, "and I heard from Animal Control that a lot of pets have gone missing lately. Maybe more predators are on the move right now, for whatever reason. So when you go out this week, I just really think you need to be extra alert." This sounded to Em like the continuation of a previous conversation.

Stefanie was about to respond, but then Jack appeared out of nowhere to sit down at the table. "How's everyone doing?" he asked boisterously.

"Heyyy! Uncle Jack!" Stefanie said as she got up to give him a quick hug. Em received a big hug from Jack as well. Jack nodded to Cal and Liam.

Keith arrived on Jack's heels with a plate of food. He sat down next to Em while she introduced everyone at the table to Keith.

Jack said to Em, "I found your husband wandering around the buffet line looking for you like a lost puppy." Jack mimicked a woeful canine looking around with wide, fearful eyes and trembling lips, almost about to cry—except that Jack moved with the stiffness common to most older folks. Em laughed.

"Wait a minute. It's not my fault I lost her," Keith explained in defense. "I was talking to Bill and Andrew one minute, and the next minute, I look around and Em's nowhere to be found." Em placed a hand on Keith's shoulder apologetically.

"Okay, okay," Jack placated. He then took a laminated, pale green card out of his shirt pocket and showed it to Em without explanation. Em, curious, took it from Jack and dropped her jaw. It was Jack's military ID from when he was just out of high school and joined the Army. The man in the picture was callow, but the eyes were the same—full of energy and eager to explore the world.

"Oh my goodness," Em said with delight as she showed her husband the ID. "Look, Keith."

Keith's eyes went wide. "Oh man, that's wild. Jack was actually young once!"

"I *gotta* see," Cal said. Em passed the ID card around the table and everyone was amused at how young Jack looked in the photograph. Seeing a picture of a person's younger self always made Em wonder what they were thinking back then, and were they so different from the person they are now.

After returning Jack's ID to him, Stefanie got up from the table and turned to Em and Keith. "It was nice meeting you both, but I actually have to head out. I have to start packing my gear for field work in a few days, and it kind of takes a while."

"I hope to see you again, Stefanie," Em said. Cal and Liam said some parting words to Stefanie as well.

"Stef," Jack said as he rose from the table too. "I wanted to talk to you real quick..." Stefanie nodded and the two of them moved off to speak privately.

"Keith," Cal started, "I was thinking of writing a piece on the Lodge's latest construction status. You know, how things are going, if you're still on track to have the Grand Opening in September, that sort of thing."

"Oh, hmm," Keith responded, quickly mulling over the implications.

"Don't worry," Cal said after seeing Keith hesitate. "I already proposed it to Jack yesterday. He was okay with the idea, but I just wanted to let you know now. I think we might want both you and Andrew Colgan for the interview, so we'd have representation from both design companies."

"Well, if Jack approves, then it's fine with me," Keith stated.

"Great," Cal said enthusiastically. "I'll connect with Jack about possible times to talk to the three of you—maybe next Monday. I was thinking of doing the interview at the Lodge so we can get some photos of the construction and the surrounding grounds."

"Sounds good," said Keith nodding. As he was looking at Cal, Keith must have seen someone he knew, because he beckoned that person to come over.

David Eckert meekly ambled into view and sat next to Keith. "Hello, everyone," David said politely. Em hugged him in greeting. It was nice to see people she already knew.

David was a retired accountant who, upon meeting anyone new, would explain that he was done with the "W-2 life." These days, he was perfectly content to watch sunsets and sit in boats pretending to fish.

"How are you guys?" David asked everyone.

"We're good," Keith answered. "Another beautiful Sunday."

Cal, ever the reporter, took the opportunity to ask David for an interview about the Lodge.

David put his hands up, "Oh I don't think so," he said mildly. "Jack is a good rep for Northern Sun. I'm retired from anything that remotely sounds like work."

"Are you sure?" Cal pressed. "It's always nice to get different perspectives."

"Jack, Bill, and I are all in agreement about the Lodge's progress. Jack can speak for us in the interview." David smiled.

After some more small talk, Cal and Liam left to go mingle—presumably with people closer to their own ages.

David and Keith then began talking about local politics, which Keith had started taking an interest in since NSI had to deal with many local agencies in order to move forward with construction. Jack and Bill had to have conversations with the zoning commission, the utility boards, the Sheriff's Department, and other local businesses. David was publicly silent on those matters. Turning down a chance to be interviewed by Cal was consistent with his previous behavior—but in private he had no hesitation in sharing his opinions. Em started zoning out on the current conversation and had to mentally slap herself to pay attention.

In short order, Bill and his assistant Gina came over to sit down. Bill plopped a whisky shot in front of Keith while Gina placed a Cadillac Margarita in front of Em.

"Ooo, thank you," Em said to Gina happily. The two of them shared a fondness for the cocktail, which they discovered during one of these events at a microbrewery a few weeks back. Gina was married and in her forties. She also had a couple of teenaged kids, like Em and Keith. Gina was just as outgoing as her boss Bill Davis, but that was probably a requirement for the job. When Em asked Gina where her husband was, she gestured to the makeshift bar area, saying he was talking football with someone or other.

"This is your whisky label, Bill?" Keith asked as he held up the shot glass.

Bill grinned with expectation. "Try it."

Keith drank half the shot to test the flavor. "Hmm...there's a hint of something—I mean, it's good—but what is that sort of buttery, warm...something..." Keith took another sip as he tried to determine what he was tasting.

Bill looked self-satisfied. "Peanut butter."

"Oh man," Keith said with surprise. "That's good." Em took a sip from Keith's shot glass and was also surprised to find that she liked it.

Jack returned to the table and sat down. "Bill," he started, "Good Lord, where are you keeping the dumpsters on this property? I was talking with Stef and all of a sudden a putrid stench washed over us."

"What?" Bill said incredulously. "Where?" Bill looked around his vast backyard and Jack pointed to a spot away from the house and crowds towards the forest.

Jack clarified, "See the tree stump where you cut last month to make more space? Over there."

Em looked to where Jack was pointing and saw a large tree stump beyond the party decorations and attendees, about a hundred feet away. The encroaching forest stood about thirty feet beyond the stump.

"There's no trash bins over there," Bill said. "Maybe you should have your nose checked—or maybe you farted. Better get that irritable bowel syndrome under control."

"Ha. Ha," Jack said woodenly while everyone else chuckled. "My nose is *fine*–and I haven't had IBS since Vietnam." Em realized these older gents never stopped joking, which is why it was fun to hang out with them. Jack continued, "I'm *telling you*, there's something rotting over there. Maybe you should check for a dead deer around the woods after the party."

Bill rolled his eyes. "Speaking of trash, Jack, can you please empty out your voicemail inbox? It's always full so I can't leave a damn voicemail."

Jack looked befuddled. "Uh, I thought older voicemails were auto-deleted after a certain amount of time."

Bill replied, "Yeah, but how many calls are you getting a day?"

"Maybe twenty?" Jack shrugged.

Bill looked around the table and said, "See, this is why I have an assistant. My inbox always has room." Bill held his shot glass up to toast Gina and then took a swig.

David chimed in. "I think ever since Jack has been spending so much time up at the Lodge, he's been missing calls because there's no signal up there. That's the real problem."

Everyone nodded in agreement while Jack's face took on a sour expression. "Okay, I'm working on it, people. Do you know how hard it is to get a cell phone tower built in the middle of nowhere?"

David held up a hand in reconciliation. "No disrespect, Jack. We all know the cell tower is a challenge."

"Uh huh," Jack grumbled. "Okay."

"Gina," Em said after a minute, changing the subject, "have you seen Jack's old military ID?"

"What? No," Gina said with interest.

"Show her, Jack," Em prodded, trying to defuse the conversation. Jack quietly handed the ID to Gina.

Gina's face lit up in surprise, just as Em anticipated. "Oh wow," said Gina. "So young!"

Jack's mood seemed to perk back up then.

"Yeah, yeah," Bill said, unimpressed. "He's been showing his baby pictures to *everyone* at the party."

After returning Jack's ID, Gina and Em started chitchatting about the party preparations while the others spoke about construction issues at the Lodge. Em could tell that Jack was particularly excited about Roy's anticipated arrival next week.

The rest of the evening was nice, but Em did get weary at around 8 PM and wished they could go home already. After all, a person can only eat so much apple pie à la mode before running out of things to do at a BBQ. She hung out with the kids at that point while Keith continued to talk to his co-workers. Jason, Margaret, and Jessica seemed to enjoy handling the sparklers and watching the other firework displays, which were set up in a large, separate area with gravel.

Em thought she caught a whiff of that garbage Jack had mentioned earlier. She looked around for a possible source, but they were in a totally different area than the tree stump that Jack had pointed out. Em's gaze swept over the backyard and the large house. She couldn't see any potential source for the smell in that direction. She then scanned behind herself toward the dark woods.

There was a stark contrast between the perimeter of the well-lit party and the mysterious tree line about thirty feet away. If anything were awry in there, she couldn't see it, and the partygoers and fireworks were pretty loud so she couldn't really hear anything other than the party celebrations.

Generally, Em found that she didn't like looking into the woods because it was so incredibly dark at night. Even at their rental house, she really didn't like gazing into the black shadows beneath the trees. At the moment, though, she felt particularly unsettled for some inexplicable reason. Em started to feel the hairs on the back of her neck and arms stand up and she couldn't shake the feeling of being watched from the trees. The feeling was so odd, especially when she was around so many other people.

After a while, she ushered the kids to a different part of the backyard, closer to the house. They left for home shortly thereafter.

# Chapter 2

Cal groggily opened his eyes. It was dark in his bedroom. Someone was talking. *Was the TV on?* No, it was the police scanner in the next room talking. He looked at his wristwatch—3:26 AM.

A woman was communicating with deputy patrol cars. "…Priest Lake. Indian Creek Campground area." She mentioned a police code to the deputies. Cal struggled to remember what the code meant. He knew it wasn't a burglary or a DUI, which were so common that he knew those numbers by heart.

If he really wanted to, Cal *could* get up and check his code list on the desk, which is where the police scanner sat, but he was much too tired after the Fourth of July party at Bill's house last night. He was definitely a bit hung over—but that peanut butter whisky of Bill's was pretty damn good.

Cal was a reporter, and his editor mostly allowed him to pick and choose what leads to follow. He was sure nobody had been murdered— he knew that code by heart too, and she definitely hadn't said that code.

Cal resolved not to get up. But the woman on the scanner kept talking. She kept saying the same code over and over again to several patrol cars. And they were acknowledging and repeating the code.

Cal got out of bed and slowly stumbled to the desk in the next room. He found the code list and searched for the number he had heard over and over again. After finding the code, he glanced at the words to the right of it: Missing Person.

Cal turned his attention back to the police scanner. Some of the cars were en route to the Indian Creek Campground up at Priest Lake, which was the "point last seen" for the person. It sounded like a male teenager was missing. Cal gleaned from the chatter that the teen was first noticed missing around 12:30 AM—about three hours ago.

Cal went back into his bedroom to put on some clothes. He went to the bathroom and splashed some water on his face. Before walking out the door, he grabbed his laptop bag, a handheld police scanner, and his press credentials.

A short while later, Cal entered the Everton Sheriff's Station to see an unusual amount of activity at 4 AM. They were obviously responding to the missing person call that Cal heard over the scanner. He walked up to the front desk and recognized the deputy on duty. Cal was able to strike up a brief conversation about the situation. She was willing to speak off the record, but Cal would have to wait for Captain Carlson to provide an official statement.

Cal learned that the Sheriff's Station in Everton had activated their Search and Rescue (SAR) Team and were performing an initial search of the area right now. Meanwhile, family members were being alerted and more information was being collected regarding the missing person's cell phone number and carrier. They were also looking at circumstances surrounding the disappearance and trying to get a photograph of the person for distribution. Hopefully this was all moot and the teenager would be found in short order. The sun's imminent appearance would dramatically improve the search conditions.

Cal debated whether to head up to Indian Creek now or wait for more information to trickle in at the Sheriff's Station. He had a good relationship with local law enforcement and knew they would give him information in order to solicit help from the public. To his knowledge, there hadn't been a missing person case in the backcountry for a few years, and even that very last one had resulted in the person being found alive the same day. If Cal went up to the campground, it would be harder to extract details from the search teams because they would be focusing on their jobs instead of answering a reporter's questions.

Cal asked the sergeant on duty when Captain Carlson would be available to make a statement. She didn't know that information, but she did volunteer that the Captain was headed to the campground right now. Cal thanked the sergeant and headed out the door. He knew Sean Carlson a little bit and figured he'd be able to get more information directly from him even if things were busy on the scene.

The drive would take a little over an hour. The campground was situated to the northwest of Everton on the east side of Priest Lake. Cal grabbed some coffee and a breakfast sandwich on the way out of town at one of the few places actually open this early. He also called Liam and his editor to discuss the social media posts they needed to prepare. They agreed that Liam should start heading over to the campground too. By the time Cal arrived at Indian Creek, it was 6:30AM.

Cal drove to the parking lot in front of the campground store, located across the road from the Indian Creek camp sites. Several emergency vehicles were scattered throughout the lot and uniformed personnel were moving about. Cal parked his car and looked for the SAR Team command center. Several Sheriff's deputies were gathered around the tailgate of one of their vehicles studying maps and GPS devices. They hadn't erected any crime scene tape to prohibit bystanders from walking up. Cal looped his press credential lanyard around his neck and walked to about ten feet behind them to try and hear any pertinent details without disturbing the discussion. There was chatter on their two-way radios about a current search taking place. Apparently they found a cell phone on the ground about forty feet from the campfire area.

"I'm heading over to the point-last-scene," said one of the men to the group. Cal realized it was Captain Sean Carlson.

"Captain Carlson," Cal called out, "Cal Russo from *The Eagle Newspaper*. Can I ask you a few questions?"

Captain Carlson looked at Cal and seemed to recognize him after a moment. "Cal. I have to get to the scene right now, but Sergeant Baker here can answer your questions." Captain Carlson walked off quickly without waiting for Cal to reply.

"How can I help you?" Sergeant Baker asked as he stepped toward Cal.

Cal opened a notes application on his phone and started to record. "Sergeant Baker, can I record our conversation?" The Sergeant held up a hand. "Actually, I can't speak on the record, but I'll answer your questions as best I can." So Cal turned off the recorder and proceeded to ask a series of questions about the situation. What he learned was that there was a group of twelve recent high school graduates from Everton High School who came up to the Indian Creek Campground on the Fourth of July—yesterday. Since all of the camping spots were full, the kids drove up a forest road they knew nearby. They were able to drive around the barrier gate that closed off the road and proceeded about a quarter mile further up.

The teens then parked their vehicles to the side of the road at a clearing which they had used before. They made a campfire, intending to remain there the entire night eating snacks and drinking sodas. At around midnight, one of the teens stepped away to urinate—a male teenager. At about 12:20 AM, the other teens realized that he had not returned. They admitted to being loud and engaging in horseplay while the teen was gone, so they didn't know if their missing friend had yelled out or made any noise during that time. None of them had heard anything unusual, but they admitted to loudly teasing one of the other teens about an incident at school, so they could have missed any calls for help.

When the teens realized that their friend was missing, they performed a cursory search of the woods, about ten feet in, but the moon was only a quarter full last night and the tree canopy was thick in the general area. They couldn't find him. The group then tried to call their parents and 911, but their cell reception wasn't good. Several of them got into one of the vehicles to drive back down to the campground store to try and get better reception. The other teens remained at the campfire calling out the missing teenager's name.

Within an hour of receiving the 911 call, the Sheriff's Station at Everton had mobilized, and an initial search team arrived at the point-last-scene around 3:30 AM. The team was in contact with family members and an official announcement would be coming soon.

Cal asked if he could visit the area where they were currently searching and Sergeant Baker said they wanted to keep non-critical personnel out of the area for now, but that if they didn't find the teenager soon, they would mobilize larger search teams. Journalists could visit the site at that point. The Sheriff's deputies were also still going around the Indian Creek camp sites asking campers if they had seen or heard anything. Once Search and Rescue had more information, they would make an announcement. Cal thanked the Sergeant, who in turn reminded him that all of that information was off the record, and that Captain Carlson or Sheriff Biggs would make an official statement soon.

Undoubtedly, the Sheriff's Department was also looking into whether any foul play had occurred. They probably didn't want anyone contaminating the area while they scouted for evidence that either corroborated the teens' story or refuted it. And who knew if the Sheriff's Station had actually been able to get a hold of the kid's parents yet to let them know what was going on. Cal valued his good relationship with the Sheriff's Office and wouldn't jeopardize it by publishing off-the-record information. Most people would probably be surprised at how much information a reporter could get from government sources as long as it was off the record. People just like to talk. However, at this point, the most Cal could say publicly was that there seemed to be a missing person in the area.

Cal started walking back towards his car while scanning the parking lot and mulling over what to post online. A middle-aged man wearing a fishing vest and a teenage boy similarly attired—father and son perhaps—were just getting out of their truck, ostensibly to buy something at the campground store. They were eyeing the law enforcement presence in the parking lot and seemed hesitant about going to the store. The man saw Cal walking by and asked, "Hey, is everything okay at the store? We were going to buy some fishing supplies."

Cal stopped and nodded. "The store is open, I think. The Sheriff's deputies are actually here for a Search and Rescue mission," Cal said sadly. "Last night someone went missing near here."

The man looked shocked as he shook his head. "That's terrible news. Do they know anything yet?"

"Well, I'm not sure what exactly they know. I think there'll be an official statement soon. I'm a reporter so I'm waiting to hear more information myself." Cal knew better than to repeat any unofficial details that were provided by Sergeant Baker. Cal continued, "Are you camping at Indian Creek? The Sheriff's Office has people asking campers if they have any information."

"Really?" the man said. "Nobody visited our site…at least, not yet." The man didn't leave to go into the store. He and the teenager both seemed disproportionately disturbed by the news. Cal sensed that the man wanted to say more, but was weighing the benefit of doing so.

"Did you see something last night? Or this morning?" Cal prompted in a light, conversational tone. He knew from experience that people tended not to volunteer information if they felt pressured into making definitive statements.

"Well…" the man said. "I didn't *see* anything specifically—and I don't know if it's related—but we might have been followed in the woods last night." He shrugged as he closed the truck door and the teenager came around the truck to stand next to him.

"Really?" Cal asked curiously. "What happened?"

"Well," the man continued thoughtfully, "we were coming back to the campground from fishing at the creek yesterday. It was around eight o'clock, before sunset, but it was already getting dark so the trout weren't going to be out anymore. We were hiking back to camp when we heard someone following us—which isn't really that strange since other people had been fishing at the creek too, and maybe they were heading back at the same time we were—but what made it strange is that every time we stopped walking, whoever was following us stopped walking too. I looked behind us to see who it was, but I couldn't see anything in the trees. We stopped two or three times to listen, and each time we stopped, the other

44

footsteps also stopped. I mean, why would anyone try to hide from us? Unless they meant us harm. We high-tailed it out of there without stopping anymore at that point. It was getting pretty dark by then and I just didn't feel safe encountering anything out in the woods at night."

"You were at Indian Creek?" Cal clarified.

"Yep. It's about three or four hundred feet behind the campground store, in the woods." The man gestured to the west, beyond the store and into the forest.

"Whoever it was, did they follow you back to camp?" Cal asked intently. This seemed like important information. Maybe there was a deranged person in the woods who was up to no good.

The man shook his head. "Honestly, I stopped trying to listen for whoever it was and just wanted to get back to where other people were."

The teenager spoke up, "Well we were kind of running with our fishing poles and buckets," he said, then slowly realized that perhaps the admission made them seem cowardly. He quickly rephrased, "We were making a lot of noise so I couldn't hear the footsteps anymore either way." The teenager shrugged and shook his head. "We looked back after we broke out of the trees near the store, but I didn't see anyone come out of the woods. I mean…" He looked at the man for confirmation.

The man grimaced then nodded, "My son's right. We looked back at the woods for about five minutes from the road right there," he pointed to the road next to the parking lot, "and nothing came out after us. That doesn't mean whoever it was didn't follow us all the way to the tree line.

He could've just stopped in the trees." The man and his son were very serious.

"What made you think someone was following you?" Cal asked. "I mean, what exactly did you hear?" As a reporter, he wanted to make sure he clearly understood what people had experienced.

The father said, "You could hear twigs breaking like they were being stepped on, like they were snapped from someone walking. We were pretty tired because we'd been fishing for a few hours. We just wanted to get back to camp for dinner, so we weren't talking. You couldn't miss the sounds of someone following us...maybe thirty or forty feet behind us." He looked to his son for consensus.

"Yeah, that sounds about right," the son confirmed glumly.

"Did you hear someone follow you immediately after you left the creek? Or was it sometime after?" Cal asked.

The father and son looked at each other trying to remember. The father said, "I don't think I heard anything at the creek. Did you, Kevin?"

"I wasn't paying attention at the creek," Kevin replied. "I think it was halfway back to camp when I noticed it."

Cal knew he'd have to take these two over to the deputies to relay what had happened to them yesterday, but he first wanted to extract every bit of information from them before doing that, because he knew he'd lose access to them at that point.

"And you're positive you didn't see anything when you looked behind you? Was it maybe more than one person following you?" Cal probed.

The father answered, "It was getting pretty dark when we were walking back. When I looked behind us, it was just too dark to see anything separate from the trees and brush, but I don't think it was more than one person. They'd have to coordinate their steps, which seems unlikely."

Kevin concurred. "It sounded like just one person to me. Maybe a big guy. I couldn't see anybody in the trees, but the way the twigs were crunching, it sounded like a big, heavy guy to me. Like, there was *a lot* of crunching when the guy stepped on the ground."

"Yeah," the father said, "if it had been a deer or a wolf, it would've been quieter. And it definitely sounded like someone walking on two feet."

Cal felt that he'd gotten a good amount of information from the two and reached in his pocket to give the father his business card. "My name is Cal Russo. I'm a reporter with *The Eagle Newspaper* in Everton. Can I contact you in the future to further discuss your experience here?"

The father studied Cal's business card, "Um sure."

"Great," Cal said. "Can I get your name?" The father seemed to hesitate, so Cal rushed to allay his fears, "I *promise, I won't* use your name or anything you've said without your permission. I would just like to be able to contact you if your experience here turns out to be connected to the missing person situation." Cal looked sincerely at the father.

"Well, okay I guess," the father acquiesced. "My name is Abraham Johnson." Cal was able to get the man's house phone number, which was probably the number the family used to screen phone calls, but it was better than nothing. Then Cal convinced the man to walk over to the deputies to repeat the story to Sergeant Baker.

Cal watched the deputies escort Abraham Johnson and his son to a position between two patrol vehicles where Cal could no longer hear the conversation. Eventually, Sergeant Baker and two other officers walked with the Johnsons to the spot where they exited the woods yesterday. The officers proceeded to place orange cones around the spot along with some crime scene tape to cordon off the area. By this time, a Deputy Patrol SUV drove up and Captain Carlson emerged from the vehicle to join the Johnsons and Sergeant Baker. After some discussion, the four of them went into the woods, leaving an officer standing at the entry spot.

Cal decided to call Liam to provide an update on what type of social media post they would be publishing. Liam was still about half an hour away. As they were talking, Cal watched another Deputy Patrol SUV drive into the parking lot. Sheriff Dwayne Biggs came out of the vehicle and began speaking to the other personnel. The officers began setting up a press conference podium with the Bonner County Sheriff's Seal on it.

Cal inquired from another sergeant when the press conference would happen and he informed Cal that it would take place at 7:30 AM, in about twenty minutes. Cal decided to livestream a preliminary post about the missing person report and the upcoming press conference. He opened the video recorder on his phone and started recording himself.

"Hi, this is Cal Russo reporting from Indian Creek Campground on the east shore of Priest Lake. Last night at about 12:30 AM, a report came into the Bonner County Sheriff's Station in Everton about a missing

48

person at Indian Creek Campground. We are currently waiting for an official statement from the Bonner County Sheriff, which is scheduled to happen at 7:30 this morning. We will livestream the press conference, so please stay tuned to our channel. I was told that either Sheriff Dwayne Biggs or Captain Sean Carlson would be making a statement at that time. All Search and Rescue efforts in the backcountry are headed by the County Sheriff's Department. I'm told we'll have more details in about twenty minutes. Again, we'll be livestreaming at that time. This is Cal Russo reporting on scene for *The Everton Eagle*."

Cal shut off the recording and checked to see that the video had posted correctly to social media. Other journalists and TV reporters began arriving at the parking lot. He hoped Liam would get here soon since he was the one with the good video camera and microphone.

***

Em couldn't sleep in past sunrise these days despite the fact that she didn't need to get up for work. The sun rose pretty early in the summer—around 5 AM—which made it hard for her to stay asleep. Keith had left for the Lodge site at around 7 AM and Em had gotten up to make him coffee and breakfast before he left. It was a holiday Monday—due to the 4th of July falling on a Sunday—but Keith and Andrew needed to manage something at the Lodge to stay on schedule. They only had a few people on site with them today.

Em was currently sitting at the kitchen table of their rental house in Everton. The kids were all still in bed of course. *Those teenagers could probably sleep through the sinking of the* Titanic, she thought.

Em sipped her coffee as she perused social media on her laptop. She stopped scrolling when she saw a livestream by Cal Russo in her feed. She had actually started following his account during one of the lulls in the party last night, when she wasn't talking to other people.

The headline of the livestream post was "Missing Person at Priest Lake." According to the time stamp on the post, he had just published this video fifteen minutes ago, and the press conference would be happening in another five minutes.

Em knew Priest Lake was fairly close to Everton. In fact, she and Keith had discussed visiting the lake at some point during their stay, but there was so much work to do at the Lodge that Keith didn't have much time or energy on the weekends to go hiking or kayaking, or whatever. That didn't seem to bother the kids. Regrettably, they preferred staring at their smart phones and laptops even in the midst of all this natural beauty. Em intended to break them of that habit somehow. Unfortunately, the only way seemed by enforced edict. Em sighed.

She searched for a map of the local area on her web browser while waiting for the press conference to start. Apparently, if you traveled on US Highway 2 West to Idaho State Highway 57 North, it would take a little over an hour to get to Priest Lake from the rental house. Em toggled the map to satellite view so she could see what the actual terrain looked like from above. The entire area around the lake was blanketed in various shades of green, unlike Los Angeles which was a sprawl of grey and tan cement from above.

Just then, Cal's livestream came on showing the Sheriff's podium with various microphones sticking out of it. Cal came into view briefly to explain that he was at the Indian Creek campground store at Priest Lake, and that Sheriff Dwayne Biggs would be making a statement about the missing person situation. Then the camera feed returned to the podium which was attended by several uniformed personnel. Some were from the Bonner County Sheriff's Office and others looked like employees of the Idaho State Parks.

Sheriff Biggs stepped up to the podium. "Thank you, all, for coming to the press conference this morning. I'm Sheriff Dwayne Biggs of Bonner County. Behind me are representatives from the US Forest Service, Idaho State Parks, and the Idaho Department of Lands, or IDL. At approximately 12:30 last night, a call was made to 911 reporting a missing person in the vicinity of Indian Creek Campground here at Priest Lake. Our office immediately mobilized to get a Search and Rescue Team up to the area as quickly as possible. We also communicated the missing person report to the Idaho State Park, Forest Service, and IDL so that they could render assistance in the search. Since the report was made by friends of the missing person, we first needed to contact the person's family—the parents—to notify them of the report, and second to confirm where this individual was supposed to be last night. The parents confirmed that the missing person—their son, Steven Mahakian, 18 years old—went out with a group of about eleven friends last night to celebrate one last time together before they went their separate ways for college and jobs. The group of teenagers initially went to the Indian Creek Campground to check if any camp sites were available, but it being the Fourth of July, no spots were available. The teenagers knew a place just up a service road that they'd used before, so they drove to that spot and made a campfire. At some point during the evening, just before midnight, Steven stepped away from the others to use the bathroom. After about fifteen minutes, the others in the group realized he hadn't come back, so they performed a preliminary search of the area themselves as best they could in the dark, but couldn't find him. That's when they called in the report of a missing person." The Sheriff was very clinical and matter-of-fact in his statements.

Em shook her head as she watched the livestream. It was especially heartbreaking to hear that the missing person was a teenager close in age to her own children. Her son Jason was 17 years old. She imagined Jason in the same situation and felt sympathy for the parents.

*Steven Mahakian. Why did the last name sound familiar?*

Sheriff Biggs continued. "We're employing search dogs and we plan to dispatch a helicopter this afternoon. We just completed an initial search of the area on foot by the Sheriff's Department and we'll be using volunteer Search and Rescue groups for additional sweeps this morning. We've been interviewing the campground employees, as well as guests using the Indian Creek Campground, for any information they might have.

We did receive a report about one of the campers being followed in the woods last night by unknown persons, which we are currently pursuing as a possible lead to Steven's disappearance. If anyone has information that they think could be related to Steven's disappearance, please contact the Bonner County Sheriff's Office. We'll be releasing a photo of Steven at the end of the press conference, as well as the phone numbers to contact if anyone in the public has information about Steven's disappearance. If you'd like to volunteer to search for Steven, please call the Sheriff's Office…"

Em wondered if maybe she and the kids should help search for Steven. Em picked up her cell phone and texted Keith: "Hon, did you hear about the missing person news this morning? A teenager named Steven Mahakian up at Priest Lake. Why does his last name sound familiar?"

Em wrote down the phone number for the Sheriff's Office when she heard one of the deputies recite it on the livestream.

After about ten minutes, Keith texted back: "Bill just called Andrew and me. He and Jack wanted to know if anyone from Eden or Gibson wanted to help search. He said NSI wouldn't hold it against us if we lost a couple of days from the schedule to help look for the kid today—and tomorrow if necessary. As far as the last name sounding familiar, Andrew reminded me that we met a guy named Jarod Mahakian at one of the NSI parties. He's on the Everton Zoning Board. This might be his kid? ☹"

Em replied: "I think I want to help search. Maybe get the kids to help too, although not sure they'd allow anyone under 18 years old to volunteer."

Keith: "Yeah, agreed. I'm not sure if I can go, but definitely some of the crew here want to help."

Em: "Okay, I'll keep you posted."

Em looked at the time. It was just after 8 AM. She called the Sheriff's Office and found out how to volunteer for a search group, but as she suspected, they wouldn't allow anyone under 18 years to participate. Her own children were 17, 15, and 13 years old—all too young. If Em went up to the lake by herself, she'd have to leave the kids alone at the house with no transportation and with no real knowledge of the area. There were no neighbors to run to except the elderly landlord Martin Green, and in Em's mind he was still a stranger. He was nice enough, but that alone didn't warrant trust with regard to her children.

Em decided she couldn't join any search effort, but she could at least ask her own kids if they knew anything that might help the Sheriff's Office. She went into the kids' rooms and told them what was happening.

"Steven?" Jason repeated groggily. "I think I met a kid named Steven at one the parties we were at. He was cool."

"Did he or any of the other kids you met talk about plans for the Fourth of July weekend?" Em asked. His sisters were in the room across the hallway and Em had opened both of their bedroom doors to explain it to everyone at the same time.

Margaret sat up slowly in bed. "I think they were talking about going up to a lake for the Fourth of July, but I don't know anything more than that," she said somberly. Evidently, the kids had no additional information on Steven's whereabouts.

54

"I don't know why anyone would want to go out into the woods at night anyway," Jessica commented as she curled up on her side in bed. "The woods are scary at night."

That statement piqued Em's curiosity. Em trusted her children's sensibilities. She never told them they were imagining things in the dark when they were scared, because she truly believed that sometimes people sensed things beyond the material world. Em never dismissed things as crazy until she'd at least reviewed the reasoning and evidence proffered.

"Why do you say that, Jess?" Em asked.

Jessica shrugged. "I just get a bad feeling sometimes when I look at the trees at night."

"Where?" Em probed. "At Bill's house?" She mentioned Bill's place because that's where she herself experienced uneasiness looking at the woods.

"There…and here sometimes," Jessica said.

"Around the rental house?" Em clarified. The tree line actually stood only about forty feet away from the house. The security of her family was of prime importance to Em, and she was keenly aware of the possibility that intruders could easily sneak up to the house through the trees without detection.

Jessica nodded in response, then she looked at her mother and said, "It feels like something is watching me…sometimes even during the day." Jessica clammed up at that point because just talking about it was unnerving to her apparently. Em knew that Jessica liked to sit outside on the patio and listen to music with her headphones on. Jess could totally get lost in her own world when she did that. Who knew what oceans of emotion she was diving into these days since she hit puberty. The main problem with that situation was Jessica's oblivion to her immediate environment.

Generally, Em and Keith didn't like the kids wearing earbuds or headphones because they were usually rendered unaware of their surroundings. Not only was it annoying as a parent trying to call your kids for dinner and not getting any responses, but it wasn't safe. There could be a fire raging in the house or someone could sneak up on them with ill intent, all while these kids were oblivious.

Em pondered her daughter's statement about feeling watched before saying, "Okay…well, if you get that feeling again, let me know."

Jessica just nodded.

Em looked at her two older children. "Either of you get that feeling too?"

"I don't spend time outside if I can help it," Jason stated matter-of-factly. "So, no."

Margaret sheepishly grinned and said, "Same."

"Well," Em started, "either way, this is a good reminder that we need to be aware of our surroundings all the time—especially in the forest or in places we're not familiar with. Even in the city. And for goodness sake, if we're in a woodsy area, don't go off by yourself. Even if you have to pee, have someone go with you. Let people know you're leaving the group." The kids agreed, although she could tell that Jason and Margaret didn't think they would find themselves in that situation since they had no intention of going into the forest voluntarily.

Em continued firmly, "And if you're wearing headphones, *please* don't turn the volume up so loud that you can't hear anyone talking to you."

"Got it," Jason said. Margaret and Jessica similarly agreed.

Em looked over at Jessica who was still curled up in bed. No matter how old her youngest child was, Jess would always be Em's baby. Jessica was always receptive to affection from her parents in spite of the onset of the cranky teen years. Em went over to kiss Jess on the forehead and give her a bear hug. Em never took her family for granted.

The rest of the day was spent relaxing for the four of them. Keith might be working, but this was, after all, a summer vacation for everyone else.

# Chapter 3

July 8 – Thursday

Em grabbed two of Keith's reading glasses along with her purse as she headed for the front door. "Kids," she shouted, "I'll be back in about 45 minutes."

A chorus of "Okay, Mom!" rang throughout the house from various locations.

Em added, "Cell phone coverage might be bad at the Lodge, just FYI."

Another obligatory chorus of "Okay, Mom!" came back in response.

At 8:15 AM this morning, Keith had texted Em to ask her if she could please drive his reading glasses up to the Lodge. In fact, Keith owned several reading glasses which were scattered around the house, in the cars, and at the job site. Unfortunately, he'd inadvertently brought all of his glasses home from work and his rental car over the last couple of weeks. It was not uncommon for Keith to be searching the house for the reading glasses that were actually hanging from his t-shirt crew neck.

Em got in her SUV and was on the road by 8:40 AM. It would take about fifteen minutes to get to Keith. Thankfully, there was never any traffic between the rental house and the Lodge—but by Em's standards, there was never any traffic in all of Everton, even in downtown. It was one of the nice things about small towns that Em could definitely get used to.

The drive itself was, of course, beautiful. Sometimes Em would spot a bald eagle flying overhead or a group of deer on the side of the road. Sometimes the road was lined with towering trees, but at other points along the way, the path was framed by wild brush and meadows. Eventually, though, the route to the Lodge entered the forest proper, and it was just walls of hundred-foot trees stretching to the sky for the rest of the drive. This change occurred almost immediately after turning onto Beverly Road, which wound into the woods for about three miles.

Em was always struck with awe at the immenseness of nature when she drove up to the Lodge, but she could also imagine how dark and unnerving it would be to drive this same road at night. Beverly Road was a wide, two-lane asphalt thoroughfare with very little shoulder—none, in some places. There were no streetlights lining the road at all, but there were some road signs indicating how many miles left to the Lodge. Thankfully, the road didn't wind too much, so you could see a good portion of the path ahead of yourself.

At unexpected moments, Em would spot a dirt path branching off of Beverly Road into unknown parts. She wondered if those were the ubiquitous logging roads that ribboned about the hills and mountains of the forest. Had anyone driven those paths in recent memory?

Em occasionally glanced upward as she drove. The way the sunlight hit the tree canopy from above was inspiring, but in many places the canopy was incredibly thick, allowing little sunlight onto the forest floor. These were dark places on the way to the Lodge that Em imagined would be a nightmare to walk through. Leaving aside the creepiness factor, she didn't think a person could move very quickly through such an area with dead bushes and bramble clawing at your clothing. She also wasn't sure about the bug population in Northern Idaho. It was summer right now and who knew how many fleas, ticks, and whatever were waiting to jump on you as you walked by.

Em's thoughts then turned toward the missing teenager, Steven Mahakian. Today was the third day since he disappeared. Was he struggling to get through untamed wilderness? Did he suffer any injuries? Had someone tried to kill him?

Em had spoken to Leanne, David Eckert's wife, about Steven yesterday when they'd bumped into each other at the grocery store. Leanne was a practicing nurse at Everton General Hospital, so she knew about the types of injuries Steven might sustain in the forest. She also seemed to know a lot about who Steven was from talking to other people in her extensive network. Steven's father was indeed on the Everton Zoning Board. Steven had been on the Track and Cross-Country teams in high school. He was physically fit and uninjured on the day he went missing. In fact, he had been accepted to the U.S. Merchant Marine Academy in New York, and was due to fly out there on July 6 with his parents. They had planned to arrive a couple days early to go sightseeing around Manhattan before dropping Steven off at the Academy at Kings Point, NY, to start their version of boot camp.

Em couldn't begin to imagine the hell that Steven's parents were going through right now. She had caught a couple of reports from Cal online providing updates about the search, which was still ongoing. Cal had mentioned that the weather in summer was very hospitable at the lower elevations in Northern Idaho, especially near water. There were also plenty of creeks and streams that Steven could take advantage of in terms of staying hydrated and possibly following the river to a populated lake. Most missing people instinctively head downslope when trying to get back to civilization. Steven went missing in an area that was roughly 2,500 feet in elevation. The area around Priest Lake was about 2,400 feet in elevation, and the town of Everton sat at around 2,220 feet. To return to populated areas, Steven would just need to travel downhill, either to Priest Lake in the west, or toward Everton to the south. The Pend Oreille River—pronounced *pon'-doh-ray*, Em learned, which is French—lay to the south as well. In fact, Everton sat on the northern banks of the Pend Oreille River. Any way you looked at it, if Steven could just head downslope towards the west or south, he would eventually run into the lake or one of the towns on the Pend Oreille. It was less likely that Steven would head upslope toward the north or east, which could reach peaks of roughly 4,000 feet or more.

One other interesting piece of information that Cal reported was that the Search and Rescue Team discovered Steven's cell phone in the area he was last seen. They didn't elaborate on any possible clues that the phone could provide, but it definitely made the search more difficult because they wouldn't be able to ping his phone to see which cell towers the signal passed through.

Cal was also able to livestream footage of the clearing where the teenagers parked that night to make a fire and hang out. The video depicted a long turnout on the side of a forest service road surrounded by a thick stand of trees. Cal said that the clearing measured about fifteen feet deep and roughly thirty feet long. It ran lengthwise along the road so that the teens could park their two cars on one end of the turnout, while making a campfire toward the other end. Steven wouldn't have had to walk very far to get some privacy to urinate. In fact, the other teens stated that he walked toward the parked cars, which were unoccupied at the time.

If something had caused him to run off, why wouldn't he run *toward* the campfire and his friends? Why would he run *away* from them? Or, had someone abducted him?

Nobody said out loud what many at least considered a possibility, that some foul play may have been involved. However, if it were foul play, no one could figure out a motive. Steven didn't have enemies. There was no girl he was fighting over and no known drug use. His grades were excellent and he was actively involved in sports and church. He was a strait-laced kid who had a bright future ahead of him. Allegedly, two of his best friends since grammar school were there at the campfire when he went missing, so he wasn't with strangers who didn't care about him. It didn't make sense.

Steven was still missing after three days and that didn't bode well for his recovery in statistical terms—about 85% of all lost people are found within the first 12 hours, and 97% are found in the first 24 hours, according to Cal's report. The search time had exceeded those markers, but the fact that Steven was young, athletic, and healthy were favorable factors. Additionally, because it was summer, the temperature and weather made the woods survivable right now. The weather could get up to 90° Fahrenheit during the day and around 48° Fahrenheit at night this summer. These conditions made survival tenable even without shelter. As long as Steven found drinking water and berries or some other food sources in the wild, there was still a pretty good chance he could be found alive. And Steven knew the area. He'd grown up all his life in Everton. He knew the basic layout of the mountains, lakes, and towns. According to the Sheriff's statements, Steven's family had gone camping numerous times over the years in the surrounding forests and Steven was familiar with the wildlife. If anyone had an excellent chance of surviving this situation, it was Steven Mahakian.

In the ensuing days, Em had seen local social media posts explaining that the Search and Rescue Team employed search dogs, drones, and helicopters, but the trees were thick all over, decreasing the chances of spotting him from the air. Em was curious to know what the dogs had discovered, but the Sheriff didn't go into details about that. Em heard that many people from the community were volunteering to search—fifty to a hundred people at a time—but nothing of substance had been found yet. They were widening their search grid and spoke of containment measures, wherein they would station searchers at specific areas of the terrain where Steven was more likely to end up such as hiking trails. Still nothing so far.

Em finally arrived at the Lodge parking lot. Work crews were present everywhere with all sorts of construction equipment. The concept of the Grizzly Bear Lodge could already be seen even in this early stage. The log cabin feeling permeated the entire two-story building, but the centerpiece of the structure was clearly the front entrance. It boasted two-story high windows that were encased in granite-like stonework, reminding the visitor of the granite Selkirk Mountains to the north. The stonework looked as though nature herself shaped it from wind and snow—Jack had wanted a rugged and majestic facade to reflect the local mountain ranges. Large windows were placed in every guest room so that occupants could constantly enjoy the green outdoors from the inside. It reminded Em of one of their family trips to Hawaii. The resort they vacationed at was practically made of glass so that they could enjoy the view from every side of the building.

With the exterior mostly complete—the windows and doors were in place and the Lodge structure was covered in logs and stone—construction could now focus on interior elements such as drywall, completing the wiring, installing fixtures, creating the rock-climbing column, and installing the mountain faces. The next phase after that entailed interior work on paint, wallpaper, furniture, antler chandeliers, and installing the animal elements. It was all very exciting to see it come alive.

Em checked her cell phone for a signal. Of course, there was none, which irked her because she hated being out of reach if her children had an emergency. She exited the vehicle and headed over to Keith's office trailer. There were several mobile office trailers in the parking lot, along with bathroom trailers and a kitchen trailer with microwaves and sinks. Em knew that sometimes the companies would pay a food truck to stop by and provide lunch to the crews since there were no eateries nearby.

Em opened the trailer door and found Jack talking to one of the crew leaders. Jack stopped his conversation to give her a hug. The crew leader said he needed to talk to one of the other team members and excused himself.

"So, my dear, what brings you to the Lodge?" Jack asked.

"Keith forgot his reading glasses," Em replied. "Do you know where he is?"

"Hm, no, but uh…" Jack looked around the office for a second and then picked up a walkie talkie from its caddy. "We can call him and find out. I just need to find the right frequency." He consulted a list on the wall and tuned the walkie talkie to the appropriate code.

"Hey, Keith, this is Jack. Are you out there? Over." Jack waited for a response.

"Yeah, Jack. What's up?" Keith returned.

"Your beautiful bride is here at the office," Jack stated. "Better get over here before someone snatches her away." Jack winked at Em and she chuckled.

"Agreed," Keith said. "Be there in a second."

Jack put the walkie talkie back in its cradle and asked, "How's your stay been so far? You and the kids having fun?"

"Well, we're enjoying the rental house—the grounds are really wonderful—but we kind of wanted to do the outdoor activities with Keith and he hasn't had the time yet."

"Hmm, well you don't want the whole summer to go by not having done *anything*." Jack paused to think. "What about huckleberry picking? That's an easy thing to do and it'll get you out in nature."

"Oh," Em said enthusiastically, "That sounds like fun. Where would we do that?"

Just then Gina Lamb entered the office to pick up some papers for Bill. Jack handed her a folder then said, "Gina, you've gone huckleberry picking, right?"

"Yeah, last year," Bill's assistant confirmed.

"Do you know where Em could take the kids to pick some this year? I heard the season is starting early."

"Sure!" Gina replied. "Actually, a friend of mine with little kids also wants to go this year and I said I'd take her to the same place I visited. You could come with us, Em."

"That would be awesome," Em said. "When are you thinking of going?"

Gina said that they could go as soon as the next day, which was fine with Em. Then Gina looked at her cell phone for the time. "I gotta get these papers to Bill but I'll text you later today. We should probably all meet at my house and go from there," she explained.

Keith entered the office right as Gina was stepping out. He looked at Em with gratitude. "Thanks, hon."

"I brought two pairs," Em said as she held them out.

"Getting to be an old man, huh?" Jack quipped.

"Okay, wise guy," Keith retorted, "I'm holding my own."

Em told Keith about the plan to go huckleberry picking the next day with Gina, which was a Friday. He thought that was a really great idea.

"By the way, Jack," Keith started, "the guys are placing the security cameras around the exterior of the Lodge right now, so you'll be able to check the video tonight from your house or your phone—as long as the internet holds up, of course. Otherwise, it won't upload the video to the cloud."

Jack shook his head in disappointment. "We should have had security cameras installed sooner, but the internet up here doesn't work for crap. Reliable internet or not, the Lodge is going to be up and running in about six weeks and we need the cameras on the premises."

"Cell coverage ain't the best either," Keith added.

"I know, I know," Jack said. "I've been complaining to the internet and cell carriers that the signals are bad up here. They provided devices that boost the signals, but it's still spotty. I'm thinking we'll need a landline installed just to have dependable communications with the outside world. Sometimes there's nothing you can do about the terrain and the trees, though."

"Well, it just makes it a little difficult to get things done with this internet," Keith said. "I know Andrew was trying to download some big

CAD files yesterday and actually had to drive down to the coffee shop about ten minutes away to use their Wi-Fi."

"Look," said Jack, "I get it. I'm talking to the Everton Zoning Board about zoning for a possible cell tower on my property nearby, but that's all gonna take some time. As for internet, the current company I signed with says they'll run a new line up here at some point, but I can tell there's no motivation on their part really. Frankly, there's slim pickings for internet up here, as you can imagine. I looked into satellite internet but I hear that they suck worse than DSL—these tall trees present a problem getting enough of a view of the sky. And if there's bad weather, then forget it. There ain't gonna be a signal."

"Well, it is what it is," said Keith, "and we'll make it work during construction if Andrew and I have to drive down to the coffee shop twice a day for downloads and uploads, but as far as the security footage goes, someone will just have to check the hard drives onsite for the surveillance video if it doesn't successfully upload to the cloud."

"Yeah, but I figure we'll have a 24/7 staff presence here once construction is complete, and they'll be able to check the hard drive footage as needed. There's gonna be a security manager and probably a contracted night guard at that point too, you know."

Keith shrugged. "As long as you, Bill, and David are aware that, during construction, if some fools come around to vandalize the property after everyone has clocked out for the day, the only thing we have is the security footage. And if the internet is unreliable, then we won't see the footage until somebody drives up here in the morning."

"Right. *During construction,*" Jack pointed out. "Listen, I think the odds are pretty low that anyone will come up here for monkey business. Maybe some vagrants used to sleep in the old cabins before we tore them down, but they never really did any damage to the place. They'd just leave their empty beer bottles and some trash in the cabins. As far as I know, that was the extent of it."

"Were there any lights up here back then?" Em asked, thinking again about how dark it would be to drive up to this site at night. "In the cabins, I mean."

"Naw," Jack replied. "My dad had just gotten power lines extended to this spot before he died in '93. He was *planning* to put lights in the cabins—probably toilets too since he got water and sewer up here as well. But, no, the lights never got put in."

"Oh," Em said. "Well then, do you plan to install streetlights on Beverly Road? I imagine it's awfully dark driving up here at night."

Jack and Keith both chuckled, and Keith said emphatically, "Uh yeah, it's *dark*. Especially if there's no moon."

"Well, then surely, if this is going to be a tourist destination, there should be some lights on the road leading up to the Lodge?" Em reasoned.

"I'm thinking about it," Jack said. "Let me put it to you this way: it'll cost a good chunk of money. I'm trying to get more investors on board, but some of these improvements just have to wait a bit. And, really, it's only a three-mile drive in the dark." Jack shrugged dismissively. "I mean, there aren't any cliffs to fall off of. Anyway, doesn't it make the drive charming and romantic?" Jack laughed his signature raspy laugh.

69

Andrew came into the office at that point and Em decided to excuse herself and get back to the kids. She said her goodbyes to Keith, Andrew, and Jack and drove home.

# Chapter 4

## July 9 – Friday

Em had just finished putting away the breakfast dishes and was calling the kids to get ready to go meet Gina at her house for huckleberry picking. Margaret and Jason yelled back that they were getting their shoes on upstairs. Em waited to hear a response from Jessica but didn't get one.

"Margie? Jason?—Is Jess up there with you?" Em asked.

"Um…no," Margaret called back.

"When did you guys last see her?" Em inquired up the staircase.

"Uhh, breakfast?" Jason responded.

Puzzled, Em walked around the first floor looking for Jessica and calling her name.

Nothing.

Now Em was getting worried. She opened the side door and went out to the fire pit on the patio, but Jessica wasn't there either. A mild panic started to creep into Em's chest as she ran around the corner of the house to check the other side.

As she turned the corner, Em nearly ran into Jessica, who was clearly surprised herself. Em was incredibly relieved and also very upset.

Her daughter had earbuds on and clearly couldn't hear anything going on around her.

"Jess!" Em shouted. Jessica removed the earbuds. Em continued, "What did I tell you about wearing earbuds and not being aware of what's going on? I've been calling you for five minutes!"

"Sorry, Mom," Jess said sheepishly. Em rubbed her face in exasperation and escorted Jessica into the house for a proper scolding.

"Jess, why didn't you tell anyone you were going outside?" Em chided once they were in the kitchen. "We *just* discussed this the other day! Especially with that teenager missing! We don't know the people here. We don't know what kind of animals roam around here. You need to tell me when you're going outside!"

"*Okay*," Jessica said in a sulk. "I'm *sorry*."

By this time, Margaret and Jason were also downstairs watching the drama. Em decided that this was the perfect time for a three-minute lecture on safety. "Look, guys, this house is beautiful and peaceful, but also kind of remote. We have no neighbors except for the landlord Mr. Green and his dog. I really need you to cooperate with me here. You need to pay attention to what the other people are doing in the house *instead of being focused on your cell phones*! You need to *care* about what is going on with each other. For crying out loud, look up from your laptops once in a while!" There was no mistaking that Em was a little incensed at Jessica's lapse in judgment and Margaret's and Jason's lack of interest in what was happening with their younger sister.

To Jessica, Em said emphatically, "Tell me *every time* you walk out that door. Do you understand?"

"Yes," Jessica replied. "Sorry, Mom."

Em cooled off quickly after venting her frustration. She continued more calmly, "We're going to leave in five minutes, so everyone just go to the bathroom or whatever and get in the car." The kids quietly dispersed.

Em had already packed four cinch backpacks with water, granola bars, wet wipes, and plastic bags for trash and whatnot. She'd also gone to a dollar store yesterday to get buckets for collecting berries. Em was really a boy scout when it came to preparedness. She hated being caught without the proper supplies or tools in any situation.

The kids piled into the car with Jason riding shotgun and the girls in the back. Em drove them to Gina's house and saw Gina's friend Lydia waiting in her car with her two younger kids, both of whom were napping in their car seats.

Gina got in her own car with one of her teenage sons. The three cars formed a motorcade to a service road off of a highway to the southwest of Priest Lake. There was plenty of room to park on the side of the road next to a small clearing with younger trees and a lot of bushes. This area had probably been cleared of timber in the last couple of years.

Gina checked the shrubs near the roadside for berries because the huckleberry bush grew best in areas where they could get sunlight—near roads, in burn areas, or in recently logged areas.

"I don't see any huckleberry bushes here," Gina said. "Let's walk a little further into this clearing—watch out for bears," she stated nonchalantly. "They like huckleberries too."

*Um, what?* Em thought. At that warning, she looked around the surroundings like a meercat. She slowly scanned the clearing but didn't see any animals. Meanwhile, Gina had spotted some berries and gathered everyone else around to show them what to look for and how to pick the fruit off of the branches. The kids all tasted some of the berries and agreed that they were pretty sweet, but very small. It seemed like a lot of work to collect them when there were only two or three berries in a cluster, and you had to look under the bush leaves to find them sometimes.

Everyone seemed to settle into their own spots to pick berries. Gina and Em began chitchatting while they picked. "How are you liking Everton so far, Em?" Gina asked.

"It's nice," Em responded. "So many stars at night without the city lights." Em omitted the part about being generally uneasy at seeing the vast darkness just beyond the porch lights at night. Em had always lived in either the city or the suburbs of Los Angeles. Even in the suburbs, the neighbors were only about ten feet away on either side, so everyone could hear the next-door family squabbles. People lived in close enough proximity so that everyone could be equally annoyed at the one house with a party raging past midnight on the weekend. Neighbors were still in each other's faces even if they stayed in their own walled backyards. But here, there was space enough to not be seen or heard *by anyone*.

"The Grizzly Bear Lodge is looking *beautiful*," Em volunteered as she changed the subject. "I love the whole theme."

"Oh I *agree*," said Gina. "Jack has really put a lot of thought and effort into this project. You know, the land that the Lodge is sitting on belonged to his family since forever. He's leasing it to the investment company—and it's not even all the land that his family owns, just a bit of it."

"It must be weird that the town you live in is named after your family," Em mused. "They must have owned a lot of land here."

"Well, most of downtown Everton was sold to the town by the Evers family," Gina explained as she picked. Then Gina's face took on a conspiratorial expression. "I don't know if you know this, but Jack's younger brother Tom went missing more than ten years ago. He just drove off one night after a fight with Jack and never came back."

"Really?" Em said quietly.

Gina continued, "It was kind of a big deal at the time. People still wonder if he's alive in some place like the Bahamas, smoking weed and lounging in a shack on the beach, or…if he's…" Gina raised her eyebrows with finality "…if he's dead."

"Gosh, that must be hard for their family," said Em. "Did Tom have any kids?"

"Yeah—Stefanie. She was at the Fourth of July Party at Bill's," Gina said.

"Ah, I met her," Em said softly. "That's so sad." Em liked Stefanie and hadn't detected a scent of tragedy on her at the time. Em decided that

Stefanie must have had to put such things aside to a certain degree in order to function on a day-to-day basis.

Em looked around to do a headcount of her children and the others to make sure that none of *them* were missing. Everyone was staying in sight mostly. Lydia was the farthest away from the group with her kids—about fifteen feet distant. Em looked at the tree line to check for bears when she noticed that some tree trunks to the north had been snapped in half with the top portion bent down to the ground at a sharp angle. The snaps in the trees seemed to be at a height of about six or seven feet up the trunks.

"Gina," Em started, "Why are those trees broken over there?" Em pointed just beyond Lydia and her kids to a group of three trees about thirty-five feet away. The trees weren't super thick—maybe about four or five inches in diameter from what Em could guess at this distance—but she wondered if some sort of storm had damaged the trees like that. The trees stood a little apart from the rest of the wood line.

Gina looked to where Em pointed. "Oh," she said, "huh, I don't know. Maybe a bear snapped it down?"

"Like *that* though?" Em asked as she continued to study the sharp angle of the breaks. "Do bears do that?" Em knew bears could stand up to ten feet tall on their hind legs based on the animal elements that Keith was creating. But, could they physically break a tree in this manner with their bear paws at that height?

"Well…" Gina trailed off with uncertainty as she looked at the trees.

76

"Hey…is there any way to tell if a bear is nearby?" Em said with some concern. "Aside from seeing one, do they make a certain warning noise or something?"

"Hmm," Gina started, "I don't know. I think we just need to periodically look around."

Em and Gina continued to look at the trees as Lydia took her kids by the hands and guided them around bushes and shrubs back to Gina's position.

"Gina," Lydia said, "I can't take the smell over there anymore. Whenever the wind blows a certain way, I start smelling something like uh…like a skunk or something. Anyway, I'm not finding too many berries anymore. Maybe we need to check out other spots."

"I agree," Em said for different reasons. "Maybe we should find a different spot."

Gina had no objections, and the teenagers really didn't care one way or the other. They all loaded back into their cars and drove to another spot a few miles down the road. There they were able to pick several pints of huckleberries. Gina remarked that the season started early this year, and that they could pick berries again all summer long. Everyone had purple fingers from handling the berries.

Back at the house that afternoon, Em started searching online for more local activities that she and the kids could do without Keith— basically, activities that Keith didn't really care for. She found that Everton actually had a small museum downtown. Em didn't expect such a trip to blow their socks off, but it was something to get them out of the house, and she could entice the kids by offering frozen yogurt or ice cream afterwards.

She checked her social media accounts and saw another livestream update from Cal a few hours ago. He had recorded it up at the Search and Rescue staging area for volunteers. She clicked the play button and he began talking about the search for Steven Mahakian near Priest Lake. This was the fifth day of searching and they were still no closer to finding him. Em wondered where Steven could be. Was it possible that they had been near him while out huckleberry picking today? It seemed unlikely, especially since Gina took them to the opposite side of the lake, but Em still felt a tiny bit guilty for going on with their lives while this teenager was still missing.

It made her think of Stefanie Evers going on with her life after her father Tom disappeared. Em couldn't imagine being able to live a normal life ever again if Keith or one of her children went missing. Yet, Stefanie seemed to be filling her time with worthwhile activities like working in the forest. Em wondered if Stefanie's desire to spend time in the forest had anything to do with her father's disappearance in a subconscious way. Em didn't know the details of Tom's disappearance, but it wouldn't have surprised her if he somehow went missing in the woods, and Stefanie's desire to spend time there was her subconscious need to either be close to him or to somehow stumble upon clues to his whereabouts.

Or, *maybe, just maybe, Stefanie simply likes the forest,* Em chided herself.

The livestream was still playing and Cal was now talking about missing pets. "…and we have reports that twenty pets and domesticated animals have now gone missing in Everton in the last five weeks," Cal stated as he moved to his right, bringing into view, of all people, Anton Nielsen. Cal continued, "This is Anton Nielsen, a longtime resident of Everton. Now, Anton, I understand you live in the Emerald Terrace area, which is situated in the northern part of town."

"That's right, Cal," said Anton, standing in his usual pose, hands in his pockets.

"And you found out a day ago that one of your goats was missing?" Cal prompted.

"Yes," Anton confirmed. "My wife and I have three goats that we keep on the property at home. They stay in this fenced space next to the stable, and in the back of their enclosure is a wood shelter for them to sleep in, or to get out of the weather if it's raining and so on. Well, yesterday morning, I went out to feed them as usual, around 6:30 AM, and our billy goat was gone. The two nannie goats were still there—they didn't seem to be injured. And the gate to their pen was still closed."

"Did you perhaps hear anything strange outside in the early morning or the night before?" Cal asked.

"No, nothing. And our dogs didn't bark during the night either—we keep them in the house with us," Anton clarified.

"Well, what do you think happened," Cal asked.

Anton sighed. "Well, obviously I can't say for sure," he started, "but I don't think it's a human taking these animals. Like, for instance, our

79

neighbor's dog is also missing—been missing over a week now. He's a large Caucasian Shepherd and, barring the use of tranquillizers or guns, nothing should have been able to take him off of the property. It's just extremely strange. And I think that whatever got our neighbor's dog also took our goat."

"Was there any evidence of predators stalking your goats? Paw prints maybe?" Cal suggested.

Anton frowned and shook his head. "I didn't see anything. The Sheriff's Station sent a patrol over to inspect the area as well—they view it as a theft. They didn't see any tracks, but remember, the ground is pretty hard and dry right now. There really aren't going to be tracks or footprints."

"Well that's really unfortunate. If anyone out there has information on the Nielsens' missing goat, or their neighbor's dog, please contact the Sheriff's Station. I know that they'll take anonymous reports as well. Now, Anton, I understand you're here today at Priest Lake to help search for Steven Mahakian," Cal pivoted.

"That's right. I think it's terrible that this has happened in our community, and I want to help in any way I can. I was part of a search group two days ago looking for Steven. I know his mom and dad. His dad works on the Everton Zoning Board, and their family is one of the bulwarks of our community. So I'm going to help search as much as I can."

"Well we certainly need people like you volunteering their time to help search. And, on the missing animals issue, what would you say to the people who have domesticated animals or dogs and cats?" Cal asked.

"I'd say to keep your animals locked up in a shed or a stable," Anton advised. "We have horses too, right next to the goat enclosure, but they were in a stable with closed doors, so maybe that's why they weren't bothered. Our goat shed didn't have a door on it, but I put a couple of wooden pallets together to make one the same day our goat went missing. We lock the goats up at night now. And we keep our dogs inside at night. If this is a predator coming down from the mountains, then just do as much as you can to keep your animals safe at night, which is probably when these predators are hunting."

"Okay, thank you, Anton," Cal said as he moved away from the older man to finish his report. "Again, we don't know what's taking these animals, just as we don't know what made Steven leave the campfire where his friends were gathered five nights ago. The best advice is to keep your animals inside at night, either in your house or in a closed shed or barn with a door. Please, everyone, stay safe. As always, I'll continue to provide updates on the latest developments in the Steven Mahakian case. I'm Cal Russo for *The Everton Eagle*. Thanks for watching." The video ended.

Em thought it was interesting that Cal juxtaposed the missing animals with Steven's disappearance. She felt that it must have been deliberate on his part as she remembered back to the Fourth of July Party when Cal was imploring Stefanie to be careful in the forest these days. He clearly thought that there were more predators migrating to the city this summer, although Em herself hadn't seen one yet.

Em heard Jason hook up his electric guitar to the amplifier in the living room. A moment later he started strumming chords. Em could also hear Margaret upstairs talking to her best friend on the phone. Em decided to check up on Jessica, whom she could see sitting outside at the patio table. This time, Jessica had specifically told her mother that she would be at the fire pit listening to music.

"How are you doing?" Em asked her daughter as she pulled up a chair next to the cold firepit.

"I'm alive," Jess responded dryly as she removed her earbuds.

"Did you have fun picking huckleberries today?" Em asked.

"Yeah," she replied with a half grin.

Em could tell that Jess was making an effort to be congenial, which was encouraging, but she also wanted to know what was really going on inside her daughter's head. "No creepy vibes from the trees today?"

Jessica looked up at the forest nearby. "Not really. I don't know why sometimes it feels strange and other times it doesn't. It's like…" she seemed at a loss for words, then just finished with "I don't know."

"Well," Em said, "That's okay if you can't fully describe it. Like I said before, just let me know if you get a strange feeling. And just come inside the house if that happens again. You might somehow be sensing a mountain lion or something. Better safe than sorry, right?"

Jessica nodded.

"You feeling okay these days? I know you've said before that sometimes you feel sad and don't know why." These conversations predated their time in Idaho. Jessica had really been on an emotional roller coaster once she hit thirteen. Keith and Em had hated going through Jason's and Margaret's puberty, and it certainly was no picnic with Jessica. Yes, it's tough for the kids, but honestly it's hell for the parents too.

After a minute, Jessica responded. "Sometimes I feel okay, and then an hour later I'll feel sad and depressed. I don't know why." Jessica was looking down at her sneakers.

"You know," Em said, "growing up can be confusing. You're starting to feel emotions that are strange and complex. You're also becoming more independent but at the same time you're still a child. I get it. I went through it too. I was really grouchy for about three years there." Em laughed to herself. "Oh man, was I cranky all the time. And I don't even know why."

"Really?" Jess said with surprise.

"Oh definitely," Em continued. "Everything my parents did annoyed me. I also perpetually wore headphones listening to CDs on my Walkman."

"What's a *Walkman*?" Jess asked.

Em laughed again. "It was a portable device for playing CDs. You know what CDs are, right?"

"Yes, *I do*," Jessica replied indignantly.

"Hey, I have an idea. You wanna do a fire tonight and make s'mores?" Em proposed.

Jess's mood lightened up. "Yeah, that sounds good."

"We'll make Dad start the fire when he gets home for dinner."

"Okay," Jess said smiling.

"You know," Em said after a bit, changing the subject, "I experienced something weird at the Fourth of July Party last weekend."

"Really?" Jess said.

"Yeah," Em continued. "It was after dark, when we were lighting the sparklers at that gravel area…do you remember that?"

Jessica thought back to the party. "Yeah, I remember. We were on the edge of the party, kind of close to the trees."

"Yeah." Em started to get goosebumps just thinking about it. "Well, I felt like something was in the woods. And I also smelled something, like, rotting in that area."

"Oh," Jess said suddenly, "I thought I smelled that there too. It smelled like a stinky wet dog to me." Her face scrunched up as she recalled it.

"Really?" Em asked. "Did you see anything? Or hear anything?"

"No," Jessica said as she shook her head. "I just tried to ignore it. But I was glad when you made us move to a different spot. Then I didn't smell it anymore."

"Did you smell anything strange when we were picking huckleberries today?" Em inquired curiously.

Jessica thought back to this morning. "Where? At the first spot?"

"Yeah—or either spot," Em responded.

"Maybe a little bit at the first place we stopped. But not a lot. I thought it might just be a stinky flower—you know, like the type that grandma likes?"

"Paper whites? Or gardenias?" Em asked.

"Yeah, one of those," Jess said. "I just figured I was smelling some strange flower out there."

"I don't think it was a flower," Em said. "And it can't be garbage because there wasn't any trash laying around in either place. Not at Bill's. And not in that brush where we stopped for huckleberries. But Lydia, Gina's friend, said she couldn't take the smell anymore at that first spot— that's one of the reasons we moved to a different area. She said it smelled like a skunk."

"Oh," said Jess. "I thought we moved because there weren't many berries there. It seemed like someone had already picked a bunch of them."

"Well…true, we also moved because Lydia said she wasn't finding any berries," Em clarified, "but what makes you think someone had already picked them?"

"Because there were a lot of empty stems," Jess explained. "You could see that there used to be berries there, but someone else had already picked them. I was talking about it with Margie. Didn't you hear us?"

"Sorry, no," Em said. "I wasn't listening to you guys because I was chatting with Gina. I didn't really notice if it was like that on the bushes near me either. I guess I was kind of paranoid about bears sneaking up on us so I was too busy watching the trees."

Jessica giggled. "Poor Mom," she said sympathetically.

Em smiled.

They stayed outside for a few minutes longer. Then Margaret poked her head out of the side door to ask Jessica if she wanted to join Jason and her in one of their online games. Jess was keen to do that, so Em went inside too.

Em tried calling Keith at the Lodge to tell him that he would be on fire-pit duty tonight, and maybe he should get more wood on the way home, but his cell phone went directly to voicemail.

"Darn cell phone." Em shook her head in displeasure and then went about making dinner.

# Chapter 5

"So, are there any questions?" Jack asked the three people seated at the table. He was pitching Northern Sun Investments over lunch in Bonners Ferry again. He could tell that two of the people—a retired married couple—were ambivalent about the project, but the third guy in his fifties, Dan Meeks, seemed interested in learning more.

"I'm just not sure that this is our cup of tea," said the reticent husband as his wife smiled politely.

"That's fine," said Jack. "I only want people to invest if they're really sure about it." He thanked the couple for coming to lunch, but Dan stayed on to ask more questions.

"I know these woods, Jack," said Dan. "I see the potential myself. Sure, we already have some established tourism for skiing, hiking, and the resorts at Pend Oreille Lake and Priest Lake, but we don't really have a themed lodge in these parts—not like what you're working on."

"Exactly," Jack said enthusiastically. "There's definitely a niche there to fill. I worked in Hollywood for twenty years and I saw the kinds of magic that they create. People *want* to be awed. They *want* to be courted." Dan seemed eager to hear more, so Jack continued. "You know, sure there are some tourists who want the 'authentic' experience of going to that hole-in-the-wall restaurant that only the locals know about, or going to the, you know, 'hidden grotto' that only the locals know about, but a lot of times those places are crap—can I be honest here?"

Dan was nodding emphatically. "Yup."

"Maybe the food is delicious at that hole in the wall, but you end up sitting on beat up folding chairs, eating on a wobbly table, and staring at the water stains in the ceiling!" Jack made a look of incredulous disdain. "And maybe that swimming hole that the local kids go to is just a glorified mud pit! All I know is that when *I* travel, I want to spend time at a place that *wows* me. And that's what the Grizzly Bear Lodge is all about. We're starting with sixty rooms—a mixture of suites and single rooms, et cetera—but we'll have the microbrewery restaurant, the indoor pool," Jack was counting the items off on his fingers, "the rock climbing walls both *inside and outside* eventually, bicycle trails in the woods, creek fishing nearby, and that's all just to start. Bill has lined up some activity packages for zip lines, rope courses—the works!"

"Well, that all sounds good to me," Dan reiterated. "I especially like the part about the life-size animal props around the Lodge. Those'll be perfect picture opportunities for tourists. Have you thought about animatronics?"

"Yup, we already have a limited application of that technology planned for the Great Room," Jack said, "We're starting small because I really want to guard against this becoming kitschy. It's possible to do animatronics in a classy way, but I just think that the line is kind of blurry where you cross over from aesthetically pleasing to campy and gaudy. I've been in the entertainment industry, and I've seen it go both ways. You just have to be careful and I'd rather err on the side of caution here. And we can always add more once the Lodge gets some cashflow."

"Okay, yeah, I see that," Dan replied. "Also, I was wondering if you'd had any trouble with wild animals in that area lately?" Dan inquired. "I mean, with the missing teen at Priest Lake, and um, I hear that a lot of animals have gone missing in Everton...have you *seen* anything, any predators or bears, up at the construction site?" Dan probed.

"Um, I haven't heard that there's any problems on that front," Jack said. "If there were any bears and wolves, I would think that all of the construction noise and lights would scare them away honestly. You know, the Lodge is located right up Beverly Road. Not too far from town actually."

Dan suddenly got quiet, as though he were pondering something serious. "Um, did you say Beverly Road, Jack?"

"Yeah, exactly—you know where that is, right?"

Dan started scratching at his jaw and chin in an uncomfortable manner. "Jack, I think I'm gonna have to sleep on this decision."

"Okay," Jack said in some bewilderment. *Wasn't Dan eager to get on board just a second ago?* "What are we talking about here, Dan? You need more financials or something?"

"No, it's not that. I just...I just can't right now...um..." Dan looked incredibly unsettled.

Jack was baffled. "Well, at least tell me what the issue is. Maybe I can put your mind at ease."

Dan was rubbing the back of his neck for some odd reason, and he looked like someone had just walked over his grave. Jack continued to look at him expectantly.

Finally, Dan said hesitantly, "Um, remember when I told you I was a surveyor back in Everton way back when…"

"Yeah," Jack nodded.

"Well, I didn't realize it until you described the property location just now, and I just hadn't thought about it because it was over twenty years ago, but…*I* was actually the junior surveyor in the group that was with your dad up at the campground…when he had that heart attack." Dan studied Jack's face for a reaction.

Jack was a little stunned. His jaw dropped a little, as though he wanted to say something, but nothing came out.

Dan decided to provide more details. "I must have been around twenty-four or twenty-five years old at the time. There were two other surveyors on site who were much more senior than I—they were the ones mostly talking to your dad in arranging the visit. I was mainly getting trained during that time, being new on the job and all."

"You don't say," Jack said weakly.

"I'm sorry to bring this up, but you did ask," Dan said apologetically. "But we don't have to talk about it any further if you don't want to."

"No," Jack said quickly. "It's just…it's just a surprise…I haven't thought about it in a while myself," Jack said with a smile, trying to put Dan at ease. After a moment, he said, "I'd like to hear what happened from your point of view, Dan. I only heard about it from my mom over the phone. I never talked to the other surveyors who were with him…I was still living in California at the time."

Dan nodded. He continued slowly, "Well, it was a spring day if I recall correctly. Beautiful drive up to the campground, but you could tell right off the bat that the cabins were pretty dilapidated."

Jack grinned, "Yeah, those cabins have always been a mess."

"Well, your dad was really excited about rehabilitating them—I remember that," Dan said. "He wanted to add a bathroom facility with showers. He might have wanted to build a few larger cabins too…? And then, obviously, upgrade the existing ones. He said he hadn't been there in about half a year himself, so he went around visually assessing the cabins while we were setting up our equipment…the tripods and all."

Jack was nodding as he listened. It caught him by surprise how the mention of his father made him weak all of a sudden. He didn't understand why he was being so emotional about it now, especially since, at the time, he hadn't really felt any deep sorrow. Maybe it was because in the time since he lost his dad, he'd also lost his brother, and finally his mom. And it was all hitting him at once. Jack was the last one left from his family. Yes, he had his children and his grandchildren—and his ex-wife Ellen even—but of his parents and his brother in their nuclear family, it was just him now.

91

Dan kept talking, "Well, your dad had been gone a while—maybe twenty minutes—and the other surveyors sent me to go look for him. I'm sure you remember, but the way the cabins were situated, you couldn't see all of them at the same time because they were somewhat spread out, and there were stands of younger trees growing between them—especially at that point, because no one had cleared any vegetation there for a long time."

"Right," Jack agreed. He could envision the campground as Dan was describing it. It was almost as if Jack was walking beside a young Dan as he looked around for Jeffrey Evers from one cabin to the next.

"I called out to him—you know, 'Mr. Evers? Are you there?' and wasn't getting a response. Around the fifth cabin, I actually took a peek inside since the door was wide open, I saw some empty beer bottles in a corner, and some large branches piled up in another corner."

"Branches?" Jack repeated. "The hobos might have been using it for a bed, I guess?"

"Maybe," Dan said. "The branches seemed new, though, because they looked green and the branches smelled fresh—although there was a weird, rancid smell in the cabin too. I thought it might be mold or rot so I backed out real quick. But as I backed out of the cabin, that's when I heard your dad sort of cry out faintly. It wasn't like a shout. It was faint, like he struggled to get it out but was too weak."

Jack continued to nod stoically.

"I ran around the back of the cabin and saw your dad lying on the ground clutching his chest." Dan stopped at that point. He seemed to be considering what to say next. "Then I ran over to him and asked him what had happened. He seemed to say 'Help,' but it was very weak. I yelled at the other guys to come over because your dad had been hurt or something. I just shouted anything to get them to come over quickly because I didn't want to leave your father on the ground by himself. The three of us carried your dad back to the car and we drove straight to the hospital from there, but he seemed to lose consciousness a few minutes into the drive. They tried to revive him at the hospital, but…"

Jack nodded again. After a minute or two, he said, "Thank you for telling me. I'm glad he wasn't alone when it happened."

After a minute, Dan looked at Jack pointedly and said, "There's something else." Then Dan paused as though he were having an internal debate, but then continued. "Now, I never mentioned this to anyone else because I wanted to keep my job, and I didn't think anyone would believe me. And after your dad passed, it seemed like no one else was going up to the campground anymore anyway…"

"Yeah?" Jack asked. It was rare to see someone taking this long to confess something, which made Jack wonder if Dan had anything to do with his father's death. He kept his cool, though, because he didn't want to scare Dan off from saying whatever it was he needed to say.

"I think I know what triggered your dad's heart attack. What I didn't tell you before is that, after I saw your dad lying on the ground, I looked up because I saw movement in the trees beyond your dad, and…*I saw it.*" Dan seemed nervous and unsettled again.

"What do you mean?" Jack prompted when Dan didn't say anything else. "Was someone else there with you?"

"Not some*one*...some*thing*," Dan said emphatically as he shuddered.

"You're not making any sense, Dan," Jack stated. *So it wasn't a person? It was a thing? What does that even mean?* thought Jack.

"It was a dark shape..." said Dan. "It was too hard to tell what it was because it was behind a tree, but it was *huge*, and I saw *the eyes*. Terrible, terrible, yellow eyes—like hate. I froze. I couldn't move forward to your dad. *I was terrified*," Dan said quietly so as not to attract anyone else's attention in the restaurant. Dan's breathing seemed a little erratic now. "It was only after the thing ran off into the woods that I was able to run to your father. And even then, I kept looking up at the trees to make sure the thing didn't come back."

Jack put his hand over his mouth as he thought. He didn't even know how to respond to this information. *Was Dan crazy?* Dan seemed like a completely logical and intelligent human being this whole time up until discussing the thing with the terrible eyes.

Dan spoke again, "Look, I *know* how this sounds—but I had to tell you what I saw. Your dad struck me as a no-nonsense, tough guy. But this thing in the woods...I was about twenty-five years old at the time and I could barely handle what I saw. Your dad was in his seventies? Eighties? It's no wonder he had a heart attack. Maybe it even came at him—I don't know. But if I saw that thing again now? *I'd* probably have a heart attack," Dan admitted fervently.

Jack was still silent. He really didn't know what to say.

Dan said defeatedly, "Look, I don't want to gunk up your works, and you don't have to believe me. You can call the company that sent us out to do the survey at the campground—they're still around. They'll tell you I went on that trip. I haven't told anyone else about this, and I don't plan on starting now. I only told *you* because it was your dad, and I felt I owed it to him to tell you what he encountered that day. If you say there's nothing up at that construction site now—today—then I believe you, but I can't be involved in this project after what I saw."

"I'm really not sure what to say, Dan," Jack said. "I mean, was it a wolf? They can have yellow eyes."

Dan shook his head languidly. "No, Jack. It wasn't a wolf. It...it ran on *two* legs. That much I saw." Dan was staring right into Jack's eyes.

Jack looked away after a minute.

"Look, Jack, thanks for lunch. I wish you the best of luck on this project." Dan sighed as got up abruptly and walked out of the restaurant without waiting for a reply.

Jack sat there with mixed feelings about what had just transpired. He really liked Dan. The guy seemed like someone Jack could work with as a partner in NSI, but that other stuff just came out of left field. *A thing in the trees?* The sane thing to do was to put aside all of the loony stuff that Dan had just mentioned.

And yet, could Jack just dismiss it? It's true that his father was a strong, tough guy. Could a surprise encounter with *something* have shocked his dad so deeply as to trigger a massive heart attack? *Dad* was

95

*seventy-two at the time*, thought Jack. He was a strong man even then, but still no spring chicken.

Jack looked at his watch. It was 1:30 PM. He had told his daughter Jenny that he'd visit her and her family in Coeur d'Alene this afternoon, which was about an hour and a half away from Bonners Ferry. Jack paid for lunch and left the restaurant.

Once he was in his truck, Jack texted Jenny that he was getting on the road now. As he was driving, he remembered everything about the day his father died. Jack recalled the phone call from his mother. She was heartbroken. He'd never heard her so worn out as that day on the phone. Jack himself was in shock upon hearing the news. It didn't seem real.

At the funeral, his brother Tom was in genuine mourning. Jack wasn't sure what exactly the state of affairs was between his father and Tom at the time. Their relationship had always been turbulent, mainly because Jeffrey had such high expectations of Tom, which Tom resented and always rebelled against. Truth be told, Tom was a little bit of a mama's boy. There was a seven-year difference in age between Jack and Tom, so they were never really peers.

Jack remembered the Evers Campground and what it was like during the times he had visited it. It was no secret that he didn't like that area, but Jack had always thought it was because of the rundown state of the cabins. Additionally, his father didn't have the trees cut back very much around the campground, so it never received much sunlight. The place felt damp, dreary, and unloved. Could it be that Jack's dislike for the place was based on more than the ruined state of the structures? Was there something else there to dislike?

Jack told his phone to call Ellen as he continued driving south.

"Jack," said Ellen. "What's going on?—Are you driving?" He and Ellen had known each other their entire lives and really didn't stand on any formalities.

"Yeah, I'm heading to Jenny's right now, but I just finished another NSI Investor lunch…anyway, it turns out that one of the people at the lunch was at the campground when Dad had his heart attack. Says he saw something that may have triggered the heart attack."

"Oh, geez, really?" she said. "Who is this guy?"

"A guy named Dan Meeks. A former surveyor in Everton—he would have been around twenty-four years old at the time," Jack explained. "Anyway, the main thing is…" Jack paused and thought, *Um, how to put this?*

After a minute of silence, Ellen said, "Are you still there?"

*Aw, to hell with it.* Then Jack blurted out, "He said he saw something creepy…something in the woods that might have scared Dad so bad that he had a heart attack."

"Creepy? Like what?" she asked. "Like a ghost?"

Jack frowned. "I don't know. He just said it was big, dark, and had—and I quote—'terrible yellow eyes of hate.'" Strangely, the more Jack thought about it, the less absurd it sounded.

"Terrible yellow eyes of hate?" she repeated.

"Yeah. What do you think about that?"

After a second, Ellen said, "Ahm, I don't know. Does he seem credible to you?"

"I liked him when I met him," Jack explained. "He seemed really smart and was enthusiastic about the Lodge. I was all set to send him a prospectus, but then he just dropped a bomb with how he saw Dad on the ground, and he would've run over to him sooner except that he saw this big, dark shape in the trees with terrible yellow eyes of hate…and he froze. Then the thing ran off into the woods."

"Well, if it ran off, then it doesn't sound like a ghost," Ellen offered. "Is he sure it wasn't a bear?"

"Honestly, I didn't ask him any details because it just sounded so outrageous—and part of me was wondering if I was being pranked—is that the word they use these days? You know, I mean 'fooled.'"

"I know what you mean," said Ellen. "But, why didn't he say anything before? Back then?"

"He says he was afraid of losing his job," Jack explained.

"Hmm…" Ellen mused. "I guess he's got a point."

"Alright, I want your opinion, Ell. Should I listen to the guy?" Jack almost pleaded. "Or is he crazy? I mean, you've been up to the campground a couple of times when the cabins were there. What did *you* think of the place?"

"I agree, it *was* creepy," Ellen stated firmly. "I never wanted to stay up there. It definitely had um…bad juju."

"You would have told me if you saw something, right?" Jack asked.

"*Of course*, but I never *saw* anything. It was just…the place felt wrong…" Ellen struggled to express herself for a second. "It was like…like something was watching you. So maybe this guy really did see something. Maybe your dad *did* see something."

Jack was silent for a while as he drove and thought. It was not unusual for there to be quiet lulls in their conversations, but neither he nor Ellen were uncomfortable with them.

"Give me that guy's name again," Ellen said, "I'm at my laptop. Do you remember the company he worked for?"

Jack provided the relevant information while Ellen searched the internet.

"I see Dan's profile on the professional networking sites. On paper he looks legit," she said.

"Do you think it was a mistake for me to put the Lodge on the old campground?" Jack asked, experiencing a moment of doubt about the whole endeavor. "You've been up to the construction site at least once. Did you get any creepy feelings then?"

"No, I felt fine the last time I was there. I don't think it was a mistake to put the Lodge on the old campground," Ellen said confidently. "You tore down those awful cabins and opened up the space to a lot of sunlight. The aura is totally different there now. It's a good thing what you're doing with that place."

"Okay," Jack said. "I just needed to get my head clear on it."

"Are you still going to partner with Dan?" Ellen inquired.

"Actually, he backed out after realizing it was the place where he had that experience…"

"Oh."

"Hey, Ell, I'm coming up on some weird traffic here. I gotta get off the phone. But thanks, I'll talk to you later."

Jack signed off and concentrated on driving. He felt better after hashing it out with Ellen, which was good because he decided he didn't want to bring it up with his daughter Jenny. He just wanted to forget about it for a few hours while he spent time with his grandkids.

Several hours later, Jack was walking back to his truck escorted by his daughter. The sun had set already and Jenny walked out with him. Jack had had a great time at dinner joking with his grandkids who were all baby adults now. They were leaving the nest in stages and becoming their own people. Jenny and her husband John didn't seem to be suffering from empty nest syndrome even though they teased each other about it a lot. It gave Jack a sense of satisfaction that his kids turned out okay, and that they in turn had children who were going to be alright.

"Dad," Jenny said, "Are you sure you don't want to sleep over? You know the guest room is always available."

"I'll be fine, Jenny," Jack replied. Anyway, everyone knew he liked to drive. It gave him time to think about things.

Jenny sighed since she saw it was hopeless to debate. "Fine, but let me know when you get home."

"I will, I will," Jack promised as he gave her a hug. "I love you, little girl."

"I love you too, Dad," she said. No matter how old she got to be, Jenny would always be his little girl. *Goodness, wasn't she in her fifties now?* Jack thought. Two of Jenny's kids were in college and the oldest one was trying to start a fishing business on the lake, but they were all home this weekend, which is why Jenny suggested that Jack visit.

Jenny walked back inside after Jack started up his truck. It was about 9:30 PM and the drive back to Everton from Coeur d'Alene would take about an hour. Jack didn't mind. He loved his truck and it was no chore to spend time on the road.

Jack saw that Keith had sent him a text earlier today around 3 PM. "Jack, I'm here at the Lodge and the animal elements just arrived. I'm having some of them placed in the lobby and the rest in the Great Room for now. It'll be a bit crowded here for a while, but we'll make it work. Roy's in the lobby 🐻"

*Yes!* Jack was elated at the news. He had been waiting to see Roy for months, if not years, counting back to the day he first came up with the idea. It was pretty late, and it would take an extra twenty minutes to get to the Lodge, but Jack didn't care. He'd just gotten an injection of adrenaline at reading Keith's text and wanted to see Roy *tonight*.

While on the road, Jack got a call from his son. Jack put him on speaker. "Hey, Bobby, how ya doin'?" Jack asked.

"Hey, Dad, so I'm looking at coming up from Boise on Saturday, August 14th. How does that sound? I'm taking a week off from work."

"Lemme guess. Deer season starts the next day up here." Jack laughed with a phlegmatic cough. Allergies seemed to be the bane of Jack's existence.

Bobby also laughed. "Dad, I'm truly hurt by that accusation. *No*, deer season *does not* start the next day…but elk season does." They both laughed. Bobby continued, "Hey, can't I do two of my favorite things at the same time? Hunting *and* spending time with dear old dad?"

"Yeah, yeah. Glad I made the Top Ten," Jack joked. "Who's coming? Just you and Anabel?"

"Jake wants to come too. He didn't want to miss out on the meat."

"Well, maybe I should put some antlers on my head so my boys will actually hang with me more often," Jack joked. His grandson Jake inherited a love of hunting from Bobby. It was their thing.

"Now, Dad," Bobby chastised teasingly, "This early in the season we're only allowed to hunt antlerless elk, so wearing antlers wouldn't make a difference."

Jack laughed. "So sad."

"So, Dad," Bobby said. "Can I count on you to come with us on the hunt this time?"

"Bobby, you know that's not my thing," Jack said.

"Gah, fine, Dad, then just be ready to make some elk enchiladas. You want some of the meat, right?"

"Of course," Jack replied. "You know I don't turn down meat."

"By the way, how's the Lodge looking?"

"It's looking so great, Bobby," Jack said. "There were times when I really thought things were going south, and maybe this was all a big mistake, but the place is looking beautiful. In fact, I'm on my way to the Lodge right now to look at the animal props—or, um, *elements*—whatever. They just arrived this afternoon."

"Dad, isn't it kind of late to be doing that? It's nearly 10:30," Bobby argued. "Can't it wait until morning?"

"Now, Robert, your old man has been a big boy for quite some time now," Jack chided. "I'm fine. Besides, I'm too excited to wait until morning. I'll be there for like twenty minutes and then go home, okay?"

"Alright, Dad, since it's obviously futile to try to dissuade you," Bobby said in disappointment. "Stay safe."

Jack said goodbye to Bobby as he started up Beverly Road. The drive was really dark since there was no moon to speak of, which made Jack think he really needed to get those streetlights going sooner rather than later. It didn't really feel charming at all to be driving in the backcountry with only your headlights illuminating the way. Jack switched to high-beams. Strangely, seeing more of the trees artificially lit up made them look even spookier if that was possible.

Occasionally an old logging road would intersect Beverly. Some logging roads were recorded on official maps, especially if they eventually became Forest Service roads. On the maps, the logging roads almost looked like rivers winding through the land, taking the most convenient route through the terrain, sometimes crossing each other or main roads.

Seeing the dirt turnoffs made Jack think he should check them out more often. It was his family's land after all. Shouldn't he be aware of any goings-on around here? Sometimes backroad enthusiasts took their off-road vehicles down trails on private property—without permission. He knew that some of the roads looped back to reconnect with Beverly Road but hadn't traveled any of them in a while. He realized he didn't want tourists getting lost around here. What if someone got stuck on a logging road that was in severe disrepair? Better make a map of these byways—and build a locked gate on some of these offshoots.

*One more thing to add to the to-do list*, Jack grumbled to himself.

In contrast, Beverly Road was well-maintained and easy to navigate. The two-lane byway was fairly wide and mostly straight, but in some places, the trees came right up to the asphalt. Jack didn't know why, but he had a bad feeling about being in the forest tonight. The feeling seemed to come out of nowhere as he drove up the road.

Everybody on the Lodge project worked during daylight hours, clocking out around 6 PM. So the summer sun was still in the sky at dinner. Jack only went to the Lodge during the hours that the work crews were there. He tried to think back to the last time he had been in the forest after sunset, and he couldn't remember any such time in the last decade. Jack didn't camp and he certainly didn't hunt, so he had no reason to be.

Jack breathed a sigh of relief when he saw lights illuminating the road ahead from the Lodge's parking lot. Jack wove around the mobile office trailers and parked in one of the spots closer to the Lodge. It was still a good forty feet from his parking spot to the Lodge doors. The Lodge itself, unlike the parking lot, was only dimly lit by some temporary area lights placed on wooden poles or affixed to the Lodge's exterior walls. The work crews had removed the safety fencing around the perimeter once the Lodge facades were all in place and all of the doors and windows were installed with locks. Signage, custom lighting, and landscaping were the remaining elements to be completed outside.

Jack exited the truck and started walking toward the front doors, then stopped while he was still under the parking lot lights to search for the Lodge's front door key amid the jangle of other keys in hand. After identifying the correct key, he looked up to the Lodge again and saw one of animal props positioned next to a stone column near the front entrance. The prop could only be Roy since it was pretty big and standing on two legs. He'd insisted that Roy be a standing grizzly.

"Damn it," Jack cursed. "I thought Keith said he was putting them all inside," he complained out loud to himself. *And of all the props to leave outside—Roy? Really?*

Jack started walking again more briskly toward the large figure, which was backlit by a dim area light behind the column. The parking lot lights didn't reach far enough toward the Lodge to see any detail on Roy. As Jack came within fifteen feet of the large, dark prop, time seemed to slow down and he inexplicably felt a wave of trepidation. Before he could even ask himself why, the prop suddenly moved its shoulders, freezing Jack in place. Jack felt his stomach bottom out and a cold ripple of terror traveled up his spine. It was horror that gripped him as he realized that he had been walking towards something *alive* and *massive*. He could see hair outlining its silhouette and he could hear it taking huge breaths into its cavernous chest. Jack stared with mouth agape as the thing tilted its head down an inch and Jack saw red eyeshine focus on his own smaller frame.

Jack thought reflexively, *I'm dead.* Before Jack could react, the dark figure turned to its left and walked off into the woods in a matter of seconds, gliding like a ghost, looking back once before entering the forest.

The figure's disappearance into the trees seemed to unfreeze Jack, and he bolted back to his truck, fumbling with the keys for a few seconds before unlocking the door and swinging himself inside. He locked the doors and started up the vehicle. Quickly glancing around the lot, he screeched out of his parking spot and sped down Beverly Road towards Everton, praying the whole time that he wouldn't see anything on the road.

# Chapter 6

## July 11 – Sunday

Jack tapped Ellen's name on the Recently Called list of his cell phone. It was 6:12 AM but Jack really couldn't wait any longer to discuss this with someone. He didn't want to call his kids because he feared getting lectured about what an old man he was and that he shouldn't have been out so late at night anyway.

Jack woke up in a bit of a fright this morning. He was dreaming about a dark figure looming over him with red eyes, getting closer and closer. He tried to run but his feet were glued to the ground. He was stuck watching it steadfastly approaching, feeling the horror rising…

"Jack?" Ellen said when she picked up—her voice startled him back to reality. He'd been seeing the dream in his mind as he waited for her to pick up. She sounded like she was already awake actually.

"Ellen," Jack returned. "I'm sorry to call you so early, but something happened last night and I really need to talk to someone about it."

"Okay, what happened?"

"After I left Jenny's, I headed over to the Lodge because Keith had texted me earlier that the animal props had arrived that afternoon."

"Okay," she said.

"It was late, around 10:40 or something. I got to the parking lot and was walking up to the front doors when..." Jack stopped because he started to get chills up the back of his neck. Jack was surprised at how traumatized he was over the experience.

"Yes? What happened, Jack?" Ellen suddenly sounded very concerned.

"I saw something standing there...outside—in front of the Lodge." Jack was rubbing the back of his neck to make the chills go away.

"Go on," Ellen prompted when Jack went silent.

"At first I thought it was one of the props that Keith had left outside. I thought it was Roy and I was upset that Keith would do such a stupid thing to leave him outside like that." Jack breathed a couple of times before continuing. "But after a second or two, as I got closer...it moved."

"Uh...was it a person?" Ellen asked.

"No," Jack said abruptly. "Ellen, it *wasn't* a prop...and it wasn't a person."

"Then...what was it, Jack?" she inquired.

"*I don't know.* But it was alive. It looked at me," Jack was struggling a bit to get the words out. "And...it had red eyes."

"Oh, Jack," Ellen said softly. "Was it a bear possibly?"

"*No.* It wasn't a bear—*it walked on two feet.* Ellen, I was damn afraid," Jack admitted. "Even in Vietnam I was never that afraid."

"And you don't know what it was?" she asked.

"*No—I don't,*" Jack said in exasperation. "It was black. It seemed to have hair all over its body. I couldn't see any other details really...other than it was *huge*...and it had red eyes, like red eyeshine. I tried to access the security footage online but the damn video never uploaded!"

"Is this...is this maybe the thing that the guy saw when your father had a heart attack?" Ellen asked.

"I don't know, but sure, why not, right?" Jack ran a hand through his hair. "What the hell am I going to do? Am I crazy?"

"No, Jack," Ellen said. "You're many things, but crazy isn't one of them."

"I gotta go back...I gotta go back there and check the footage on the hard drive, Ellen," Jack stated.

"If you're going to go back there, you need to bring other people with you. Maybe even some deputies."

"Yeah," Jack sighed. "But what am I gonna tell them? I saw a giant thing with red eyes hanging around?"

"No," Ellen said. "You tell them you saw...a...um...an *intruder.* You say there was a suspicious person at the Lodge and you didn't hang around to find out what they'd been up to. Let *them* figure out what it was. Play the video footage for them."

"Yeah," Jack agreed as he considered it. "Maybe I need to bring David and Bill up there too."

"Yes. They ought to be told since they're invested too." After a moment, she continued. "Did that thing do anything to you, Jack? Did it hurt you?" Ellen asked with concern.

"Me? Naw, other than scare the heck outta me!" Jack laughed in his usual raspy way.

"Jack," Ellen said, "What if that thing has been there all this time, and nobody has said anything because they're too scared people will think they're crazy?"

"Huh," said Jack curiously.

"I mean, that guy who told you about the thing with yellow eyes—Dan, right?—he said he was afraid to lose his job, so he didn't tell anyone anything. Could it be that other people have seen something during construction? And they just kept quiet?"

Jack pondered that for a minute. *Had people seen something? Would they have told anybody? Would they have told Andrew or Keith?* It was definitely worth looking into.

"That's a good question," he said. Jack really wanted a sanity check, so he asked, "Ellen, *what did I see?* Is my mind playing tricks on me? Tell me something that makes sense, and I'll believe you."

"Jack," she started, "I've never seen anything like what you've described, but I know people who swear they've seen something out there. They say they've seen some sort of man-ape in the woods, and it was the scariest thing they've ever encountered. And that's the truth."

Jack sighed. He really wanted her to give him some mundane explanation to cling to. Ellen was always interested in the truth, whether it was pleasant or not. She didn't gossip and she didn't exaggerate. He trusted her judgment on a lot of matters.

"Jack, there are a lot of things in this world that we know nothing about," Ellen said. "Ancient sailors used to talk about giant squid in the ocean, but proof wouldn't come until hundreds of years later. And we now know there's an even bigger squid out there—the colossal squid. So, if you're asking me if I have a hard time believing that, um—and I'll just say it—that Bigfoot could exist in the woods? No, I don't have a hard time believing in the possibility."

Jack was a little stunned by Ellen's statement, and also a little disappointed that she wouldn't be providing a plausible, ordinary explanation for what he saw.

"Well, hell, Ellen."

"Look, it was Ben, okay? Ben saw something in the woods when he was camping as a kid. It was just a head peeking out from some bushes when they were on a hike, but he said it scared the living daylights out of him. It was huge and dark, and it ducked down out of sight after a couple of seconds. He said he never told anyone else but me, but I believe him."

So, Ellen's second husband had seen this thing. Jack didn't know the guy too well when he was alive, but he had seemed like an honest person with no reason to tell stories.

"Either way, Jack," Ellen continued, "be careful when you go back up there—maybe bring a gun."

"Maybe," Jack said as he considered it. He certainly owned a gun, as did most people in rural areas. "Listen, Ell, I'm gonna call Bill and David now. Then I'll head out to the Lodge. —I won't go alone, and there's *no way in hell* I'm going after sunset. I'll let you know what I find."

After hanging up with Ellen, Jack called Bill and David and asked them both to meet him at the Lodge this morning. He told them he saw an intruder on the site last night. Since it still hadn't uploaded to the cloud, Jack said that they should review the surveillance footage at the Lodge together with law enforcement. They readily agreed.

Suddenly, Jack was feeling much better about the situation. He had gotten people to investigate the issue without telling them the real story. Without a doubt, if he had mentioned anything about a big, hairy monster loitering around the Lodge, he would have been ridiculed silently if not outright. Jack wanted people to look at the issue without prejudice when they showed up at the Lodge. If the video showed some sumo wrestler in a fur coat ambling around the Lodge doors, then fine. So much the better. But if it didn't—if, in fact, it revealed something out of the ordinary—then at least everyone else will have seen it on the video too.

Jack arrived at the Grizzly Bear Lodge around 9 AM. The drive to the site was rather pleasant when the sun was shining and the birds were singing. The trees were happy and the sky was blue—all of nature acting as if nothing unusual had happened last night. Jack pulled into the parking lot and parked a little farther off from the Lodge so as not to disturb any potential evidence.

Before getting out of the vehicle, Jack did a 360° scan of the parking lot and the surrounding tree line. Nothing seemed amiss. He debated whether to enter the Lodge now and wait for the others inside or stay in his truck. Before he could decide, the issue was moot as he saw David drive up and park beside him. Jack exited his vehicle.

David got out of his car and asked with concern, "Jack, are you okay?"

"Yeah, I'm fine, David," Jack replied. "I just want to get to the bottom of this."

"Me too," David agreed.

Just then, Bill drove up in his truck. "Well, gents," said Bill as he got out and closed the truck door, "I hope there aren't any hoodlums coming around the Lodge. We don't need the hit to our insurance over vandalism." Although Bill was a caring guy, front of mind for him was always the financial cost or benefit to any new development.

"Look, guys," Jack started, "I haven't searched for any clues yet around the front door. I haven't gone inside at all yet. I just realized we should stay out here so we don't destroy any evidence that might tell us what's going on."

"Well, I kind of want to get inside and see the video," said Bill pointedly. "But okay, that makes sense. When are the Sheriff's deputies getting here?"

"They said as soon as possible, but who knows when that'll be," Jack replied.

"Tell us again, what exactly happened last night," David said.

"It was late—after 10:30—and I parked a little closer...over there," Jack pointed to the spot, "and as I was walking toward the Lodge, I stopped to find the right key for the front door—and let me tell you guys, it is *dark* around the Lodge at night with just these little area lights. The parking lot is well lit, but *not the Lodge*. I know we're in the construction phase, but I think we need better lights at night for security. –Anyway, I started walking toward the Lodge again and saw the uhh…*the intruder*. I don't know what it—I mean, *he*—I don't know what *he* was doing before I arrived, but after I saw uh…*him*, then *he*—uh—moved his shoulders. I stopped walking at that point. Then, um, *he* walked off to the trees over there." Jack pointed to the eastward tree line, trying to distract the other two from his discomfort.

David and Bill looked at each other, ostensibly to read if the other was buying this story as God's honest truth. They then turned back to Jack.

"Okay, that was painful," quipped David. "I wasn't aware you had so much trouble with pronouns, Jack."

"Jack," Bill started, "why do I get the feeling you're not telling us something?"

Jack nonchalantly put his hands in his pockets and shrugged, "Guys. Someone was here last night. Someone who probably shouldn't have been. *That's* the truth."

"Mmm yeah," David chimed in sympathetically, "I believe that much, Jack. But it feels like you know something more than what you're telling us."

Just then a Deputy Patrol SUV arrived on scene, to Jack's immediate relief. "Look, guys," said Jack, "let's just have the deputies do a walkaround first, and then we can all view the video inside at the same time."

Neither Bill nor David looked satisfied with that response, but there was nothing to do but follow Jack's suggestion. The deputies did a preliminary search of the outside areas that Jack pointed to and found nothing unusual. They also walked a perimeter around the structure.

"Could anyone be inside the building?" asked one deputy when they returned.

Jack shook his head, "Naw. I talked to Keith this morning before coming over. He was here until about 5 o'clock yesterday, and he locked up as usual. Today's a Sunday, so nobody should be in the building."

The lobby doors were intact and no forced entry was evident. The deputies entered the building with hands on their holsters. Jack and the others stood a few yards away outside and were somewhat startled by the deputies' reaction to stepping in the Lodge.

"Oh man!" said one. "For a minute there I thought we were going to have to call Animal Control!" he blurted with obvious relief.

"Sheez," said the other deputy as he shook his head and laughed.

Jack, Bill, and David entered behind the deputies and saw what had initially alarmed them—several life-sized animal elements were sitting in the lobby, exactly as Keith had texted yesterday. Bill, David, and Jack marveled at the animals. The elk and coyotes were so life-like—especially the eyes. Then Jack looked to the side and towering above them all was Roy—utterly magnificent. Roy turned out better than Jack had hoped, powerful and majestic. Roy was not there to intimidate the guests. He was there to welcome and inspire them.

Jack gestured to Roy and said, "Long live the king." David and Bill nodded in approval.

The deputies then instructed the three older men to stay in the lobby while they did a cursory sweep of the building. This took a while since it was a lot of square footage to cover, but not all of the interior doors were installed yet, and none of the furniture was in place, so the sweep didn't take too long.

"It looks clear," said the one deputy. "The place is still under construction, but we didn't see anything that could be construed as damage. We didn't see any evidence of intruders either."

They all proceeded to the Security Office, which had some computer desks and chairs already in situ. A wall of monitors had been installed along with the computers and external drives. You could see the system cycling through video feeds from each camera on the property.

Jack logged into the system and searched for the appropriate camera and video, searching by time stamp. At approximately 10:42 PM the front door camera showed Jack's truck arrive and park in the brightly lit parking lot in the distance. This occurred in the periphery of the camera view. So far, nothing strange appeared on the video. Unfortunately, the area around the Lodge was dimly lit, with light progressively dimming the further away from the structure you looked.

Jack realized, however, that the real problem with the footage was the fact that the camera had been placed so that the stone column on the left was probably going to occlude most of the strange visitor's movements from last night. The front door camera had been positioned

116

mainly to capture faces of people walking up to the doors. Everything beyond the stone columns was in shadow and grainy, except for the parking lot, which had its own lighting. Additionally, the camera footage was from a fisheye lens, so the relative size of everything was skewed in order to capture more area.

As the video continued, everyone watched Jack walk toward the building head on, then stop to look for keys. At that point, something dark and large moved from the left periphery of the screen to behind the left column so that the camera was only capturing the figure's left side sticking out—an arm and shoulders, perhaps? It was plain to see that *something* was standing on the other side of the left column—where the camera couldn't see—but what was it?

The deputies made some "Hmm" noises when the unidentified figure appeared on screen. One of the deputies leaned forward as everyone watched Jack start toward the building again and then suddenly stop about forty feet away from the camera. Jack had been wearing a light-colored shirt so that his movements could be tracked fairly easily on the video. The dark figure seemed to shrug its left shoulder. Suddenly, Jack's form became visibly startled. On screen, Jack seemed to cringe for a second and then defensively bring his arm up to chest level. After another few seconds, Jack turned his head to watch something move off to the camera's left, but whatever Jack had been watching was too far out of the light to properly identify.

Jack watched himself on the monitor turn and run back to the truck, fumble with the keys, scramble inside the vehicle, and peel out like a crazy man. The deputies replayed the segment a few times. Then they rewound the video to about an hour prior to see if anything had happened earlier. In methodical fashion, they fast-forwarded the video to a time stamp *after* Jack had driven off to see if the intruder returned later. Nothing else came into view.

Jack was relieved and disappointed at the same time. On the one hand, the video confirmed that something had positively come to the Lodge last night. On the other hand, the video didn't provide enough definition to say it wasn't just a really, really big guy dressed in dark clothing. The stone column on the left was probably about twelve feet from the camera, and everything was pretty dim beyond the column.

"Well," said one of the deputies, "since nothing seems to be stolen or destroyed, we'll just take a report of a suspicious individual on the premises. We'd like a copy of the footage, if that's okay, so we can include it with the report." Jack nodded.

The other deputy suggested hiring a night guard for the remainder of construction. He explained that most vandals and vagrants don't want to deal with uniformed personnel patrolling the building, even if the guard is unarmed.

"It'll take some time," continued the deputy, "but you might want to have someone review *all* of the footage you have stored here to see if there was any previous behavior. I know these security companies say they watch your video feed real-time, but that strategy only works if the video is actually *accessible* in real time. It sounds like the internet up here is unreliable."

"Yeah," Jack admitted unhappily.

"Lastly," said the deputy as he pulled out a small notebook and pen, "we're gonna need a description of the intruder."

"Oh...right," said Jack. He cleared his throat, "Well, it was dark, but from what I could see, the guy was about seven feet tall...or more."

The deputies raised their eyebrows. "Okay," replied the one, "so can you guess a weight?"

"Um," Jack said. "Upwards of...400 pounds maybe? He was muscular. Big shoulders."

The deputy cleared his throat. "Are we talking about a man here or a gorilla?"

"I'm telling you what I saw with the amount of light available and from about fifteen feet away from the guy. You can believe it or not. I didn't see any facial features." Jack just decided to omit the red eyeshine from the description at this point. The deputies were already skeptical enough. *Thank God that thing was recorded in some fashion on the security camera*, Jack thought.

After the deputies left the Lodge, the three NSI investors stayed to discuss what had happened. Nobody spoke right away, but eventually David broke the silence.

"So what did you really see, Jack?" David gently prodded. "*I saw how scared you were on that video.*"

Jack took a moment to collect his thoughts and then decided on full disclosure. "Bigfoot maybe?" He shrugged. "Something that scared the hell out of me. Something that could have killed me in a heartbeat, no question. When I saw how massive it was? I thought I was *dead meat*. Dead as the deer carcasses my son brings back from a hunt."

Neither Bill nor David scoffed or laughed in derision.

"Well," Bill said, "It's no wonder you held back some details. Now, I'm not going to tell you what you did or didn't see, Jack, but what I want to know is, are we dealing with something dangerous? Is this thing going to throw a monkey wrench in our operations?"

"Beats me," Jack replied. "I've never seen one of these things before...crap," Jack suddenly remembered that he was supposed to brief David and Bill on Dan Meeks' account of his father's heart attack. If this thing was here twenty years ago, and showed up again yesterday, maybe it had no intention of leaving the area.

Jack then explained about the investor lunch yesterday, and how Dan Meeks admitted to being present when his father had a heart attack, and seeing a large creature in the trees that might have triggered the heart attack. Even then, neither Bill nor David seemed shocked.

"I have to say," Jack started, "I'm surprised that neither of you is ridiculing the whole Bigfoot thing."

"Well," David said, "I worked for Dixon Timber for about thirty years, and although I was in the office all the time—being the accountant—I *did* hear talk amongst the other employees. You know, sometimes there were tracks around the equipment of something large. Other times, smaller equipment was pushed over on its side when crews returned in the morning." David shrugged. "Nobody said anything out loud of course, but we were all thinking it. Some people wondered if it was maybe extreme environmentalists, but these were such remote areas, and some of it was on private land where we'd harvest so infrequently that you'd have to be an employee to know where they were harvesting that day. Terrorism just didn't seem likely."

"Did these creatures ever destroy equipment or hurt anyone?" Jack asked.

"Other than possibly pushing things over? No, not that I'm aware of," David replied. "But work crews never stayed long in one place."

Jack looked at his other business partner. "Anything to add, Bill?"

Bill shrugged. "I've never seen anything personally, but my grandmother was part Nimiipuu Indian and she *definitely* believed there were big, hairy, man-like creatures running around the woods. But, you know, I just figured it was a myth...or a story to keep kids from misbehaving."

Jack harumphed. "Well, that was no myth on the video playback from last night."

"Agreed," said David.

Jack continued, "At the minimum, I think we ought to add a night watchman during construction. I know we budgeted for that to start a week before the Grand Opening, but I think it's worth it to start a couple of months early."

"You know me," Bill said. "Whatever this thing is, we need to protect our investment, so I support getting the night guard."

"I just don't want anyone to get hurt," said David, "so I agree we need more of a deterrence on site. We don't know what this thing is capable of, but like I said, I've never heard of anyone getting injured by…um…Bigfoot. Even if it's real, at most the creature pokes around the Lodge then leaves. Maybe after a while it'll stop coming around."

Jack hoped David was right, but he had a bad feeling about this. Jack had seen the thing with his own two eyes and had been terrified. He couldn't imagine parents with small children having a different reaction upon bumping into such a creature in the parking lot.

Bill then declared that he would arrange a guard on site with their current security company. It gave Jack a sense of relief that David and Bill took this issue seriously—David more for everyone's safety, and Bill more to protect their investment—but still, it was a weight off of his shoulders.

Jack reminded the other two about his interview with Cal Russo the next morning regarding current progress on construction. He assured them that no mention would be made to the reporter of the unknown visitor.

"Great," David said, "but we need to tell Andrew and Keith. They need to be aware of the situation." Jack and Bill agreed.

The three men decided to walk around the exterior of the job site together to see if anything was out of place. Jack imagined his father doing the same kind of inspection of the dilapidated cabins all those years ago. This was the very same ground where his father had had a fatal heart attack. Jack had somehow blocked off that connection in his mind, but now it almost made him sick to think about it. He hid his revulsion from David and Bill as they travelled the perimeter of the site and scoured the tree line for any movement.

Nothing unusual presented itself to the trio, but Jack had a sneaking suspicion that this issue wasn't going to just fade away. He hoped he was wrong.

# Chapter 7

July 12 – Monday

Jack arrived at the Lodge around 8 AM Monday morning. Yesterday, he, David, and Bill agreed that they should review the surveillance footage from the prior seven days—from all of the cameras on site—but Bill and David frankly didn't want to spend the rest of their Sunday on that task. Jack sensed that his two partners viewed this intruder as some sort of animal, and that it could be controlled or shooed away in the same fashion as a bear or a moose. Thus, there was no huge hurry to review the remaining surveillance footage. Jack saw no harm in adopting that view since no one had been injured so far. He would have stayed to watch the video alone, but couldn't bring himself to stick around the Lodge since he started to feel unwell after inspecting the grounds one last time.

This morning, however, watching the work crews clamoring around the Lodge like ants on an anthill, it was easy to break the site's connection to the old campground. In contrast, yesterday, the stillness of the forest and lack of human activity made it all too easy to mentally travel back in time to the unpleasant feelings Jack had associated with this area his entire life.

This was the same place that depressed him every time he visited it growing up. His mind recalled broken down cabins under an unsettling green canopy. It always felt damp and stale here, like wind couldn't break into the area. That's what it was like before.

In the present, the area had been clear cut to create more than double the usable space of the previous campground. None of the original trees were left on the Lodge site. Any alpine landscaping needed for the project would be brought in from nurseries.

There was a breeze here now. It smelled clean, fresh, and inviting. If you wanted to see the older trees, you needed to walk out to the wood line a few hundred feet beyond the Lodge structures. Jack wanted the site to be reborn with none of the taint of its previously failed endeavors, but, as of this weekend, he suddenly felt like the site was fighting against him—that it did not want the disinfecting power of the sun, and it didn't want anyone to see what happened here.

Jack walked over to Keith's office trailer. He found the two project managers chitchatting as they waited for him to arrive. He had texted both Andrew and Keith yesterday that he needed a meeting with them first thing Monday morning.

"Hey, Wolfman Jack," Keith said in greeting.

"Hey, Jack," said Andrew with more reserve but just as pleasant.

"Morning, guys," Jack responded somberly. He closed the office door behind him and slowly sat on the edge of a nearby desk. He crossed his arms as he thought about how to explain the last two days.

125

In the ensuing silence, Keith commented, "Wow, Jack, it feels like you've got some serious news."

"Okay, guys, I need to tell you what happened this weekend on the job site," Jack started. "Now, I was all giddy to get up here on Saturday to see Roy and the other props after reading Keith's text that they'd been delivered. But I was already in Coeur d'Alene visiting my daughter and grandkids that afternoon, so I couldn't come until the evening. And I didn't want to wait until Sunday morning, so I drove up here late and arrived around 10:40ish Saturday night."

Keith and Andrew were nodding their heads in acknowledgement.

"So," Jack drew a deep breath, "when I got here that night, I saw a large intruder on the grounds, right in front of the lobby doors."

Andrew's and Keith's expressions suddenly became more serious.

"Intruder?" Andrew restated, almost spilling his coffee.

"Yeah," Jack said, "I'll show you the surveillance footage after we're done talking here, but it was big. And it scared the crap outta me. I didn't make it into the Lodge. I hauled ass as soon as I could get my legs to work again."

"*It?*" Keith asked. "Don't you mean *he*? Or *she*?"

"Guys, at this point, I'm just going to go with *it*," Jack said.

Andrew and Keith looked at each other quizzically.

"Now," continued Jack, "I told David and Bill what happened on Sunday morning, and we met up here with a couple of Sheriff's deputies to search the Lodge and review the video—which never uploaded to the cloud damnit. It's not super clear on the video who the intruder was, but it was walking on two legs. I still need to review the footage from the prior seven days to see if there was activity before Saturday on the site. Since there was no damage or stolen property, the deputies just submitted a report of a suspicious person on the premises."

"Okay," Andrew interjected, "but just to be clear, you're saying it wasn't a person? But it walked on two legs? So what was it? A bear?"

"Well," said Jack, "the word 'Bigfoot' comes to mind." Jack was done playing word games.

"Are you *kidding?*" asked Andrew incredulously.

"Nice joke, Jack," said Keith laughing as he wagged a finger at Jack. "I'll admit, you *actually* had me for a minute there!"

Jack shook his head and said seriously, "I wish I *were* kidding, Keith. Come on. I'll show you the video." Jack walked out of the trailer, leaving Keith and Andrew staring at each other in disbelief. After a few seconds, they followed Jack to the Security Office in the Lodge.

Jack played the video for the two project managers, neither of whom seemed so confident that Jack had lost his marbles anymore. Keith even volunteered to review the unseen footage for a while to check if there had been any other visitations to the Lodge. Jack asked them if they'd seen any unexplained disruption to the equipment or work areas in the last few weeks—neither of them had, but this didn't convince Jack of anything. He still wondered if people just hadn't reported it and determined to go around the site today asking people if they'd seen anything strange.

Eventually, Keith had to stop reviewing the security footage because people were asking him about other tasks around the Lodge.

Andrew had left the Security Office fifteen minutes earlier to finish some other business before Cal arrived for the interview. Jack instructed the two of them to say nothing of this during Cal's visit. Jack knew that Andrew and Keith weren't sure one way or the other what was on the video, but they certainly weren't going to blab about it to anyone outside of the project.

Cal arrived a little before 10 AM with Liam. They wanted to scope out the best place to have the interview without a lot of construction noise. Andrew suggested sitting near the Bike Shack structure on the south side of the parking lot. It was away from the main lodge building and its exterior was already finished if any photos were taken. Keith rounded up four folding chairs and placed them in a semicircle. Liam seemed busy taking photos of the construction activity and the surrounding woods to post along with the article.

"Thanks for sitting down with me today," Cal said after everyone was seated. "Is it okay if I record this conversation? I'll refer back to it when I'm writing the article."

"Uhh, sure, that's fine," Jack said ambivalently. "I don't want the actual recording posted anywhere though."

"No no," Cal replied, "it's purely for my use as notes. I won't post it on the internet or anywhere. Scout's honor."

"Alright," Jack said.

"So," Cal started, "I know there's a lot of family history here, Jack."

*Oh boy*, Jack thought. *Maybe this interview was a bad idea.*

Cal continued, "There used to be a private campground here—Evers Campground—that fell into disrepair over the years. What made you decide to put a lodge up here now?"

Jack cleared his throat. "Well, truth be told, I never really liked the old cabins. They were old, no bathroom facilities, no electricity at all, and the vegetation was rarely cut back so it was very overgrown. My father decided to rehabilitate the cabins and add water, sewer, and power, but as you know, he passed away before he could finish that endeavor. At the time, neither I nor my brother Tom were in a position to finish the project, so the cabins fell into a progressively worse state. Additionally, I was still living in California, so the timing was just off for all of this. When I moved back to Idaho to take care of my mom, the idea of using the campground site kept nagging at me. After a couple of years, the idea of the Lodge started taking shape, and I casually researched how to fund such a big project. Well, everything just started falling into place—Bill Davis and David Eckert joined in on funding with Northern Sun Investments—NSI. I found Gibson Drake Architecture from old contacts in California—Andrew here is their Project Manager for the Lodge. Gibson Drake then pulled Eden Design into the mix for the specialized theme construction. Of course, Keith here is the Project Director for Eden. The final hurdles were zoning issues, but even that got settled fairly quickly. It's been a wild ride."

"Yeah, the community really supports this project," Cal said. "I've talked to many residents who feel that the Lodge will bring more jobs and more business to Everton. Now, Andrew, can you tell me how Gibson Drake developed the current design for the Lodge?"

The rest of the interview passed without controversy. When Cal originally pitched the interview, he never mentioned talking about Jack's father, so when Cal said the words 'family history,' that got Jack's hairs up. Fortunately, nothing came of it.

It struck Jack during the interview, as Andrew and Keith were answering questions, that tragedy was always tangentially associated with this place. His father Jeffrey had a heart attack here. He and his brother Tom would argue about what to do with this place—and then his brother went missing. Even talking about the Everton Zoning Board had tragedy laced in it because board member Jarod Mahakian's son Steven was still currently missing in the woods.

"Well, that's great," Cal said, pulling Jack out of his thoughts. "I think that's all I need for now, but can I get a picture of the three of you for the article? Maybe get a couple of shots with the Lodge in the background, and then some with the natural backdrop of the forest?" Cal ushered Jack, Keith, and Andrew to a couple different spots to take photos and then Keith and Andrew headed back to work.

After Cal and Liam left, Jack decided to wander around the site and talk to people on their breaks and to those who weren't engaged in any dangerous tasks. Jack had asked Keith and Andrew earlier if anyone on the crews had reported suspicious activity or evidence of any tampering with equipment. Neither had heard anything on that subject from their employees, nor had they seen anything themselves.

Most of the workers Jack approached shook their heads saying they hadn't seen anything. Jack then realized that after the various phases of construction were completed, works crews would rotate out while others rotated in for the next phase. The people Jack was talking to today were not all the same people that were here a few weeks ago. Jack decided to find Frank Tiller, who was the Construction Manager for Gibson Drake, and ask him about it. Frank would have been on site the entire time.

"Hmm," said Frank as he searched his memory, then his eyes lit up. "Oh, well there was one thing that was strange…a few weeks back, a couple of panels from the safety fencing were pulled down onto the ground—looked like someone had cut the links holding them to the adjacent panels—and the windscreen on the panels got torn up."

"The windscreen on the *inside* of the chain link fence?" Jack clarified.

"Yeah," Frank confirmed. "I mentioned it to Andrew that maybe some thieves came up here and wanted to see if there was anything to steal. The fencing was six feet high so it's not like most people could just look over the top. You'd have to be really tall, right? Like a basketball player. That's why I figure whoever did this just wanted to see what was in here."

Jack's brow furrowed. "Okay, so you're saying you think some thieves came up here to scope out the construction site and ended up damaging the fence? Was anything stolen or broken?"

"Well, no," Frank said. "I guess they didn't see anything they wanted—or they were just teenagers doing dumb stuff. We didn't have surveillance cameras on the property back then because the internet was no good—though I guess that's changed now?" Frank said.

"Guess again," Jack said unhappily, "but continue…"

"Well, it was cost prohibitive to have a guard come up here for a walk around during the off hours, so nobody witnessed what happened."

"Well, how exactly was the windscreen torn up? How much of it?" Jack asked.

Frank was nodding to himself. "Yeah, a good five-foot portion of it had been torn off of the grommets."

"You wouldn't happen to have the fencing still around somewhere?" Jack hoped as he looked around the area.

"Sorry, Jack," Frank said. "We sent the fencing back to the rental company when we took it down. But uh…" Frank took out his cell phone and started swiping this way and that. "I did take a couple of photos of the damage."

*Thank the Lord*, Jack thought. Frank showed him five pictures of the torn windscreen and two fence panels lying flat on the ground. The green windscreen wasn't just torn off in one large swath either—it was shredded in tatters on the ground. Furthermore, the links holding the panels together looked a little stretched, like they were pulled open, not cut with bolt cutters, but it was difficult to say either way. It wasn't hard evidence of anything, but it was certainly suspicious.

Jack thanked Frank and asked him to text him the photos. Jack looked at his phone and saw that it was around 12:30 PM. He had to head over to Bonners Ferry to see Dan Meeks again this afternoon. On short notice, Dan had agreed to meet for lunch, which Jack was definitely running late for.

On Sunday night, Jack had discussed with David and Bill that Dan had decided against investing in Northern Sun Investments, but that Jack still really wanted to get more details surrounding his father's death. Dan might even have additional information about the creature that could be relevant to understanding it all. Bill insisted that Dan be told nothing about recent events because they weren't sure what was going on at the Lodge. In fact, they should hold off on any more fundraising invitations until they had real facts in hand. David cautioned Jack to be careful with his words at the lunch.

On the way to his truck, Jack caught Andrew and asked him about the damaged safety fence that Frank had just told him about. After jogging his memory with some of the details, Andrew finally remembered the conversation with Frank and apologized profusely to Jack. He explained that various levels of vandalism happened at practically all of their projects, and since it was only the one time, it hadn't occurred to Andrew to mention it to Jack.

"It's okay, Andrew," Jack said. "Just please let me know if any other weird thing happens around here." Andrew readily agreed.

On the way to Bonners Ferry, Jack recalled his conversation with Dan Meeks two days prior, which felt like a month ago after all of the continuing revelations—Saturday night, seeing the visitor, Sunday morning, reviewing the video, and today, hearing about the damaged fencing. It reminded him of the time he found out that his house was infested with termites, except that those buggers had been inside his house for months before he'd seen any evidence of them. This situation felt the same way, except that the 'infestation' went back decades.

Jack couldn't help but wonder if this entire project might turn out to be one gigantic failure, just like the campground before. It was too late to back out now damnit. The structures were built, the animal elements were on site, and they'd already started taking reservations! But could Jack, in good conscience, have tourists coming up to that spot knowing that there might be  unfortunate encounters with something dark and hairy? And was Jack destined to suffer a heart attack or a nervous breakdown from dealing with this mess? Jack reminded himself that he'd seen that thing in person, and he'd survived it. This gave him some small comfort.

At lunch, Jack was very conciliatory towards Dan. When they parted ways a few days ago, Jack was pretty speechless at Dan's firsthand description of his father's final hours, not to mention hearing of a frightening creature in the woods. Jack's attitude had probably come across to Dan as being offended, so Jack made an effort to let him know that his previous silence was mostly shock at new information.

Dan assured Jack that he harbored no ill will. Dan couldn't recall any more details about the experience twenty years ago, but he did want to emphasize that he had never been so frightened of anything in his life before, or since, seeing that creature.

"Jack," Dan said, "In all my years of surveying in these parts—I've seen bears, wolves, moose, you name it—I was never as scared of any animal as I was of that *thing*."

"And you can't tell me anything more about it? It was during the day—you couldn't see what it was clearly?" Jack gently prodded.

"No, it was standing behind several trees so that only the head and a shoulder were visible." Dan shuddered and tried to shake it off. "It was leaning out to look at me...it had hair, or fur, that was dark—almost black—with a reddish tinge on the ends...but I was mainly drawn to the eyes." Dan shuddered again. "I couldn't look away. And..."

After a beat, Jack asked, "What?"

Dan looked at Jack and said, "Is it possible to feel hate from another thing so clearly? That was the most jarring thing of all. It paralyzed me." Dan shook his head and took a deep breath. "So when you told me that no one had seen anything during construction at the old campground, I was so relieved. Whatever that thing was, maybe it was just passing through."

"You said you saw it run off eventually," Jack persisted. "You must have seen more of it then—what it looked like as it was running off."

"Well, remember, those woods were *thick*. It ran off behind more trees and brush. I never saw it out in the open. I mainly saw the head, and when it turned to leave, it was gone in a millisecond." Dan snapped his fingers. "That fast. But it definitely ran off on two legs. The way it moved when it ran off, I could tell. And I could *hear* it running on two legs—the footsteps, it wasn't like a four-legged creature, not like a dog."

135

"And the eyes," said Jack, "you said they were yellow. Were they actually yellow? Or was it eyeshine of some sort?"

"No," Dan shook his head, "It was daytime so it wasn't eyeshine. Its eyes were actually yellow...maybe a little amber. Like an owl's eyes, but they were *huge*. It was damn creepy."

"Hmm," Jack said absentmindedly as he tried to reconcile Dan's experience with his own. After his encounter with the creature at the Lodge, Jack had done some research online about eyeshine in the dark. Eyeshine color didn't necessarily indicate what color the iris was. Eyeshine occurred when the pupil was dilated in the dark—and it only applied to creatures with a tapetum lucidum, the reflective tissue layer in the eyes of some animals to improve night vision. Jack even learned about the sclera, which is the part of the eye around the iris—in humans, the sclera is white. Interestingly, some animals have black sclera.

Since Dan's experience was during the day, he was actually able to see the color of the iris. Could Dan's creature from almost thirty years ago be the same one Jack saw? Maybe the creature that Jack encountered was a younger one? Jack didn't think he had enough information to make that determination.

"Jack," Dan said pointedly.

"Hmm? Yeah, Dan?"

"You *did* say that there have been no recent encounters at the construction site, right?"

*Oh crap*, Jack thought, and immediately berated himself for believing he could interrogate Dan about the creature and not have the guy get suspicious. *Think quick, Jack.*

"Right," Jack said confidently. "But, I recently found out there's been possible…vandalism…on the site. You know, either thieves or rowdy teenagers. That sort of thing that, um, one of my project managers said is very common to construction sites." *Yes—that's not a lie.*

Dan exhaled in relief. "Well, I'm glad."

"Listen, Dan," Jack said changing subjects. "Thanks a lot for meeting me again to talk about what happened to my dad. It's a hard subject for me, but I'm glad you told me. I appreciate it."

"Sure thing, Jack. Glad to be of help." Dan smiled genuinely.

Jack was satisfied that he had parted on good terms with Dan as he left the restaurant. Jack decided to run a few errands while he was in Bonners Ferry, as well as visit a couple of people. He always had a lot of business and social dealings going on. Jack figured he probably wouldn't head back to Everton until tonight.

\*\*\*

Em heard Keith drive up to the house as she stood at the stove finishing the mashed potatoes for dinner. She looked at the clock on the wall and saw that it was almost 7 PM, which was later than usual for Keith to arrive home. Em was thankful that the summer sun was still out. It felt as though it weren't so late in the day and that they had plenty of downtime left with Keith before retiring for bed at night.

"Kids!" Em walked over to the stairs and shouted, "Dinner will be ready in five minutes! And your Dad's home."

"Okay, Mom!" answered the familiar chorus.

Em returned to the stove as Keith strolled into the house carrying his laptop and some binders. "Hello, honey!" he said with a smile as he planted a kiss on Em's lips.

Em smiled back. "Something happen at work today? You're home a little later than usual."

"You could say that," Keith said as he put his laptop and other items on a side table in the kitchen. Then he came over to Em and said quietly, "I don't want to talk about exactly what happened in front of the kids, but I'll tell you right now that something was hanging around the Lodge on Saturday night, and Jack saw it."

Em gasped slightly. "Was it a bear? Is Jack okay?"

"It wasn't a bear," Keith said shaking his head. "The security footage caught some of it, but it was too dark to really tell what it was. Now, *I* saw the footage *myself*, and I couldn't say for sure what it was, but it definitely walked on two legs..." Keith paused.

"Yeah...?" Em asked expectantly, wondering what the big deal was. Criminals usually walked on two legs—or else they were crouching to avoid detection.

You could hear the kids upstairs start to rouse themselves for dinner so Keith just blurted out, "Jack said it was Bigfoot." Then he glanced toward the stairs to see if the kids had reached the bottom yet.

"*What?*" Em asked emphatically.

"Look, I don't want to say that in front of the kids, but I do want them to be aware that there might be some predators—or maybe a psycho—running around the woods. The point is, we don't know what is going on here, so we need to all be vigilant," Keith explained. "I don't want you and the kids going huckleberry picking anymore. Just go to places where there are a lot of people when you're sightseeing—and absolutely no one is going out into the woods at dusk or at night. *Capiche?*"

"You don't have to tell *me* twice, but I want to discuss *the real story* more later," Em whispered as the kids spilled into the kitchen and sat at the table.

"Fine," Keith replied, then greeted the kids. After telling their father hello, the kids seemed to resume some conversation about a blogger getting canceled for saying something controversial.

When they were done, Keith sat down and started talking. "Guys, I wanted to let you know that I just found out this morning there was some kind of intruder at the Lodge on Saturday night, after dark. The Sheriff's Station sent some people over on Sunday to look around and take the report. Nobody was hurt and there was no damage, but I just want you all to be aware that this happened, and that we need to be aware of our surroundings, and we shouldn't go into the woods alone or at night. Not even at sunset. Okay? I don't know if it's pranksters or bears or what, but there's still a missing kid, and the authorities still don't know what happened to him. So this is serious."

"There are missing pets too," Jessica added.

"That's right," Keith affirmed.

"No worries, Dad," Jason said, "I have zero interest in going into the woods for my entire life." Everyone laughed.

Margaret echoed, "Yeah, Dad, I'm not outdoorsy either. If we're in the woods, it's only because Mom forced us to be." Everyone laughed again.

Keith looked at Jessica. "Understand, Jess?"

Jessica nodded. "Yes, Dad."

As Em was placing dinner on the table, she remembered that their landlord had offered to show them the blueberry patch on the grounds. "Oh, what about picking blueberries with Martin near the house? I just remembered that we're doing that tomorrow morning—at least, Jessica and I are. The other two troglodytes want to stay in the cave."

"Well," Keith said, "I guess if it's on the grounds, and at least two of you are going with Martin during the day, then it's fine. Just keep your head on a swivel."

"Listen, I'm already paranoid about grizzly bears," Em said as she sat down, "We *are* picking berries after all, which is, you know, one of their favorite foods."

Everyone wolfed down dinner, except for Margaret who always ate extremely slowly. Then Keith suggested that they all watch another episode of a new science fiction series that everyone was totally addicted to. Keith and Em tried to get in as much family time as possible with their children because the kids were growing up so fast. Jason would be going away to college next year and they just didn't want to waste any of their time together right now. It was another reason for bringing the whole family out to Idaho during this project. They didn't want to lose any time.

During the show, Em thought she heard police sirens outside in the distance. While everyone was still watching, she got up from the couch and looked out of the family room windows. The sun had already set and the last red rays were fading in the sky. She looked to where the dimly lit main road skirted the property and saw no vehicles. Then the siren sound stopped. Em wondered if maybe there was another road nearby that she couldn't see from this window.

"Trouble?" Keith said as he paused the show and got up to stand next to Em.

"I thought I heard police cars," Em said.

Keith looked outside. "Maybe it was background noise in the show?"

"We're not watching a cop show," Em countered. "They're shooting lasers and traveling in spaceships, not chasing serial killers on the 405 Freeway."

After a few more seconds of silence, Em and Keith were about to sit down when the siren started again, but this time a little louder and more elongated, like an air raid siren. Both of them looked outside but saw nothing. Puzzled, Keith went to the patio sliding glass door and scanned the dark woods. To Em's dismay, he then opened the door and stepped out onto the covered patio. She quickly followed him outside. The kids got off the couch and poked their heads through the doorframe.

Outside, the siren noise was noticeably louder and you could tell that it was coming from the trees across the main road. Em didn't think there was a road located in that area. She stepped over to the edge of the patio to look at Martin's house. The lights were on and Martin also seemed to be looking out the window toward the trees.

Suddenly the siren noise stopped. Em didn't know whether to be relieved or not, but before she could decide, a loud whooping sound erupted from the woods somewhere beyond Martin's house. Em couldn't tell what was making the noise, but she'd never heard anything like it in the weeks they'd been living here. She looked at Keith and said quietly, "What is that?"

Keith didn't answer. He seemed to be concentrating on the noise— studying it. Em scanned the surrounding darkness. There was the dimly lit main road in the distance to the east, and in between that road and the house lay a grassy field with some brush. To the north, about fifty feet away, stood Martin's smaller house where he lived with his terrier Frisco, and beyond him was the barn and more trees. The west and south sides of the house had views of the forest which stood at varying distances away. Except for Martin's house, everything else was dark. There was no moon out tonight, making the experience especially unsettling.

Em found that all of her children had followed them out onto the patio. This made her very uncomfortable, but at the same time she felt that they should be aware of what was transpiring. They were becoming adults and shouldn't be kept in the dark about everything. Jason had his phone out and seemed to be recording the sounds.

The whooping noise from beyond Martin's house finally ceased after a few minutes. Then a separate, lower-pitched whooping noise came from the area where the 'police sirens' originated from previously, in the trees across the road.

At this point, Keith ushered everyone back into the house and locked the sliding glass door. "Em," he said, "close and lock all of the windows around the entire house. I'm checking the doors." To the kids he said, "Stay in the family room." Before leaving the room, he pointed to Jason and said, "You. Keep your eyes open."

After Em finished closing all of the windows, she met Keith at the foot of the stairs. The whooping noises had not stopped. As she listened, the whoops seemed to be answering each other, but Em couldn't tell if they were moving.

"I wish I'd brought our gun," Keith muttered. "I didn't want to deal with the hassle of driving with it through Oregon and Washington, but maybe that was a mistake."

"Well, we can't change things now," Em said.

Jessica came up to them then. "Mom. Dad. What is that?" she asked. She was clearly spooked as she looked at the windows. "What kind of animal is that?"

"I don't know, honey," Em responded as she hugged her daughter. "We just need to stay inside."

Keith returned to the family room window to look out. He opened the window about five inches to listen to the strange calls. A second later, what sounded like a woman screaming tore through the night.

"Holy shit!" Keith blurted out. Em was just as stunned. Jason and Margaret were sitting on the couch, clearly worried.

Then, suddenly, the noises stopped. Keith and Em went to the upper floor to look out of the windows with a better view of the surroundings. It was too dark to see anything that didn't walk directly under a streetlamp.

"I don't know if we should call the police or not," Em said in confusion. "This seems abnormal, but what would we report?"

Keith took out his cell phone and dialed Martin's number. After a second he said, "Hi Martin, it's Keith Carrera. Sorry to bother you, but did you just hear that noise coming from the woods?"

Keith put the call on speaker so Em could hear the conversation. Martin said, "Yes, I did."

Keith continued, "Do you know what it was? Have you heard this type of thing before?"

"Well," said Martin, "I don't think I've heard this exact kind of noise from the woods before. But Frisco is cowering under the table right now, so he doesn't much like whatever's making the sounds."

"Look, Martin," Keith said, "we're city folk. Should we be concerned about this? I mean, it sounded close."

"Sometimes mountain lions will make a noise that sounds like a woman crying..." Martin responded, "so maybe there's a mountain lion out there."

"But what about the other noises?" Keith pressed.

"I would just say to keep your windows and doors locked, and don't go outside until morning," Martin replied. "But it seems to have stopped now."

"Okay. Thanks, Martin," Keith said. "Again, sorry to bother you."

"That's quite alright. Goodnight," Martin replied.

Keith hung up his cell phone and Em commented, "So he doesn't know what it is either."

"I don't think I'm getting much sleep tonight," Keith stated glumly.

That night, all of the kids decided to sleep in the same room. They never finished watching their science fiction show, but no one mentioned it. Everyone was too busy wondering what the hell was in the woods.

# Chapter 8

Jack was in a pretty good mood as he drove south on Route 95 back to Everton. After lunch with Dan Meeks, he made a social call to a friend who owned a printing business in the area. Then he visited a few local stores that carried some specialty items that he could only get in Bonners Ferry. After that, he had a business dinner with a guy trying to pitch Jack on promoting his boat charter business at the Grizzly Bear Lodge.

By the time Jack hit the road, it was about 9:30 PM. He was a little tired but didn't mind the drive. It was already dark outside and few cars were on the highway at this time. Jack started to daydream a little bit when he noticed movement on the road up ahead. Jack reflexively took his foot off the gas to slow the car and squinted a little to get a clearer idea of what it was.

Jack braked a bit more as he watched the movement carefully. He saw white shapes on the ground reflecting his headlights. As he got closer, he realized that the white reflective material was actually the backs of two sneakers—someone was walking on the right side of the road. Jack exhaled in relief. After all of the drama of the last few days, he was afraid that this would be another episode in a series of unfortunate events. But it was just some crazy guy walking around on the highway at night.

Actually, that was *not* normal.

*Maybe the guy's car broke down somewhere?* Jack thought. Jack realized he was somewhere near McArthur Lake. He slowed the truck until he was about ten feet behind the person and saw it was someone wearing jeans and a torn, red, lightweight jacket. He could see some of the jacket stuffing coming out of tears on the side. The person's jeans had dirt and mud all over, and even a few tears here and there. Jack slowed the truck to a crawl right next to the person, but the pedestrian didn't seem to notice the big truck driving next to him. In fact, the guy seemed to be walking like a zombie—sort of ambling in a distracted way.

*Please, God, don't let this movie turn from a creature feature to a zombie flick*, Jack thought. He'd been in plenty films doing stunts as all sorts of monsters, and lately he'd started to feel like a washed-up, aging film star in a B-Movie.

As Jack studied the guy, he realized that he had scratches on his face. Jack rolled the passenger side window down about six inches and said, "Hey, are you okay? Do you need help?"

The guy didn't respond and kept walking forward slowly, so Jack shouted out, "Hey! Guy! You okay?"

The person finally stopped and slowly turned to look at the truck in confusion. It was as if he had been sleepwalking and was now suddenly awake. Jack could see that it was a young man, probably a teenager, who'd obviously been through something rough.

147

The teenager abruptly placed his hands on the passenger window and said in desperation, "*Sir!* Please help me! I need to find my parents! *Please!!*"

"Did your car break down or something?" Jack inquired.

"*No, sir, please!* My name is Steven Mahakian and *I'm trying to get home,*" the kid shouted as he tried to open the truck door.

*Oh crap!* Jack thought as he unlocked the door. "Get in, kid."

Steven was already in the car before Jack could finish the sentence. Steven quickly locked the truck door and scrunched down into the seat.

"Steven," Jack said, "get your seatbelt on and then I'll take you to Everton." Steven didn't move. He just stared ahead at the road. Jack touched Steven on the arm to get his attention. Steven flinched and drew back from Jack.

Jack put his hands up and said, "Steven, put on your seatbelt." The teenager complied this time. Jack found a bottle of water and handed it to Steven, who downed the whole bottle in a minute. Jack poked around his console and found a granola bar. He opened it and handed it to the kid and then started moving the truck again. Steven devoured the granola bar. The kid was gaunt. Who knew the last time he'd eaten anything?

Jack started driving again. He glanced at Steven and saw that he was shell-shocked and exhausted. How many days had he been missing? Jack counted from last Monday—a week. "Steven, everyone's been looking for you. Where've you been?"

After a second, Steven said, "In the forest…I was with my friends near Indian Creek. I just went off to take a piss and…I was done and about to go back to the campfire…"

Jack was all ears and really needed to know what happened—to see if this was related to what happened at the Lodge. "What happened, Steven? Why didn't you return to the campfire?"

Steven started to get upset, "Something…something was there…in between me and my friends. I couldn't get around it…" Steven started shaking and crying. The kid was losing it.

Then Jack felt like a heartless bastard for questioning the youth who was clearly afraid and at the end of his rope. "It's okay, Steven. You're safe now." Jack settled for driving back in silence.

"I don't know," Steven said raggedly. "They wouldn't leave me alone."

"Who?" Jack asked. If the kid wanted to talk, he wasn't going to stop him. "Who wouldn't leave you alone?"

"*Them*," Steven answered quietly at first. He was still breathing kind of hard. "They watched me," he muttered as he hunkered down in the seat. "Their eyes…red…yellow…I could see them in the dark…*watching*." Steven's breathing was becoming rapid. Then in frustration he said, "Then they were screaming and I had to run. I could hear them chasing me in the trees! Throwing branches and rocks at me. I couldn't rest…wouldn't leave me alone. *They're monsters*."

"Who? Were they men? Bad men, Steven? Who was it?" Jack half-pleaded.

Steven shook his head. *"They weren't men*...I never...never saw them, but I heard them so close...growling and screaming...and I *had* to run..." Steven put his hands over his ears as if to stop hearing a noise that was playing in his head.

"It's okay, Steven," Jack repeated. "You're safe now."

"No..." Steven said wearily. "They're everywhere..."

"Did they hurt you, kid?" Jack asked with concern.

"They...they herded me...like I was an animal!!" he shouted in anger. *"They're the animals.* I hate them!"

"Listen, kid, you're alive," said Jack. "You beat them. You won. You made it."

Steven slumped a bit then as he stared ahead blankly. Eventually his breathing became more even and he fell asleep.

Jack drove straight to the Everton Sheriff's Station and arrived around 10:15 PM. Steven was still asleep and Jack didn't want to leave him alone, so he parked in the lot and picked up his phone. Jack called the station desk, telling them he'd found Steven on Route 95 and they were currently parked outside.

Several deputies rushed to the truck to take Jack and Steven into the station. An ambulance was called for Steven while Jack gave an account to the deputies of what had happened. Everyone at the station briskly carried out their tasks, but you could feel a positive energy in the air.

Steven was alive and had been found.

# Chapter 9

Em and Jessica met their landlord at his house after breakfast. Considering the previous night's strange screams, Em wasn't sure about going to the blueberry patch today. But when the sun came out this morning, it seemed to wash away the sense of danger that had settled on the family last night. Keith and Em decided that morning that blueberry picking near the house was an acceptable activity during the day.

Their landlord Martin Green was a pleasant older gentleman who walked with a cane. He was probably in his eighties and his dog Frisco seemed to be the equivalent age in dog years. Martin first led Em and Jessica behind his house to the barn to grab some blueberry harvesting baskets. The barn housed several hens and two nannie goats. The hens had their own chicken coop in the barn and were separated from the goats by wooden fencing.

"Martin," Em asked, "what do you use the goats for?"

"Oh, they're really good for clearing brush around the property," Martin said. "And they fertilize as they go!" They all laughed.

"And do the hens provide a lot of eggs?" Em inquired, quietly wondering if she could have a few since people seemed to rave about fresh eggs back in the city.

"Oh, not anymore unfortunately," Martin said with regret. "These hens are all older, around seven years or so. They stopped laying eggs a couple of years ago. They're mostly just pets now. I can't bring myself to eat 'em." Martin handed the harvesting baskets to Jessica and Em, then added, "I used to have a rooster too, but, you know, roosters go charging at any threats to protect the hens. Yeah, he got eaten by a wolf I suspect— or something similar. I just heard a big dust up out here when I used to let the chickens roam around outside near the barn. I'm not so fast anymore— now that I use a cane anyway. By the time I got out here with my shotgun, old Freddie was gone. Just a couple of his feathers laying around and the hens all hiding in the coop."

"Oh, that's sad," Em said, thinking it was years ago. "When did that happen?"

"Hmm," Martin thought a minute, "April? Or May?"

"Oh! Just a couple months ago," Em clarified.

"Yeah," Martin replied. "Freddie was a good old bird."

After Em and Jessica fixed the basket straps to their waists like fanny packs, Martin led them to the fenced blueberry patch, which was located about twenty feet behind the barn. All of the structures on the property had been built in a mostly straight line apparently. Martin had three rows of blueberry bushes inside the fencing. It reminded Em of rows of grapevines.

Once inside the gate, Martin showed Em and Jessica how to pick the blueberries, which was different from picking wild huckleberries. In the wild, the huckleberries grew mostly as single berries along the branches, so you had to pick each berry individually. However, this type of blueberry bush produced clutches of berries in a group of ten or more. Since the berries ripened at different rates, the best way to pick only the ripe ones was to use both hands to cup the berry cluster, then use both thumbs to stroke the berries. The ripe ones would just fall into your hands. Anything that didn't fall off from a simple stroke wasn't ripe.

"This is *easy!*" Jessica exclaimed with glee. Em agreed. In comparison, it took a tremendous effort to gather just a few pints of huckleberries over several hours—granted, Em was mostly busy watching for bears at the time. Today, though, at this rate, Jessica and Em would have the same number of blueberries in thirty minutes with just the two of them picking.

"I would have brought you over here a bit sooner," Martin said, "but I'd let my church youth group pick the bushes clean right before you moved into the rental house. I wanted to let the remaining berries ripen before picking again."

"No worries. This is *great*," said Em as she gathered handfuls of berries with ease. "Thanks so much."

Suddenly, Frisco, who'd been casually meandering between the rows of blueberry bushes, started growling. Em couldn't see the dog, but Martin went over to find his pet, saying, "Frisco! What is it boy?"

Em stopped picking and went to look at the terrier at the end of the second row. His muscles were taut and his canine teeth were showing as he stared outside of the fence towards the trees, which were about thirty feet away. Em looked at the tree line. The sun was very bright, making the shadows deep in the trees. Em couldn't see anything, but she trusted the dog's senses.

"Should we head inside?" Em asked Martin who was standing next to Frisco.

Martin was looking at the woods too. "Well..." he said slowly. Evidently, although he couldn't see anything either, it obviously spooked him that Frisco continued to stare aggressively at the same spot for so long.

"Maybe it's the thing from last night," Em suggested. "Maybe we should go inside." Em and Jessica had picked about six pints in ten minutes, so Em didn't feel the need to hang around any longer.

"Yeah," agreed Martin as Frisco continued to growl and then bark. The dog's hairs were standing on end. Martin added, "That might be a good idea."

Em took Jessica's hand and led her out of the blueberry patch gate, but Martin was having a hard time getting Frisco to leave the patch. Em felt torn. On the one hand, she didn't want to stay out here any longer with her daughter in possible danger. On the other hand, she didn't want to leave Martin out here alone trying to deal with his dog. Em compromised by starting to slowly walk off with Jessica while constantly looking back at Martin.

Martin didn't bring a leash, so he'd have to lean over and grab Frisco's collar to get him to move. Frisco still refused to budge as Martin verbally cajoled him.

Em decided to try calling Frisco herself on the off chance that hearing a different voice would jolt the dog into moving. "Frisco!" Em called, "Come on, boy! Come here!" Even Jessica joined in, but it didn't seem to help. Em wondered if Martin should just leave Frisco out here and get him later, but she suddenly remembered Freddie the Rooster and his grisly fate.

Then Em thought, *If it comes to a choice between that dog and my daughter, I'm picking my daughter.* She was on the verge of telling Martin that she and Jess were heading back to the house when a booming roar echoed from the trees that Frisco was barking at.

Jessica and Em screamed in unison at the sound. At that moment, they saw the damn dog zip out of the blueberry patch, pass them, and disappear out of sight around the barn. Then poor Martin began hobbling back as fast as he could with his cane. Em yanked Jess's hand as they ran from the area. Em kept looking back to make sure Martin was following. Part of her expected to see something pursuing Martin but the area behind him remained clear as they rushed past the barn toward Martin's residence.

Martin turned the corner of his house to the front door while Em pulled Jessica further on to their rental house. Martin stood at his front door to let Frisco inside while Em unlocked their front door. Jess bolted into the foyer. Em looked back to see Martin gesture for her to get in her house as he closed his front door.

After shutting and locking the front door, Em looked out the window to see if anything was prowling around outside. There was no way to see the blueberry patch from here, and Martin's house obscured most of the barn, but she saw nothing. She continued to watch for about ten minutes, but nothing came.

Em found that she was breathing hard. Jess was standing flat against a wall near the stairwell. Em realized they were still wearing the harvesting baskets around their waists, except that all of their blueberries were gone—no doubt scattered like a trail of breadcrumbs all the way back to the barn. She walked over to Jess and hugged her as they calmed down. "I'm sorry, Jess," Em said trying to calm down. "I'm sorry you had to go through that."

"Mom," Jessica said, "I don't know if I like this place."

Then Margaret came halfway down the stairs still in pajamas pulling headphones off of her head. "Are you guys okay?" she asked in confusion.

"No," Em said. "Where's your brother?"

"Uh," Margaret started, "I think he's talking to his friends online. He's got his headset on upstairs."

"So neither of you heard what just happened," Em stated angrily. "You guys can't hear a damn thing with those headphones on all the time!"

Em told Margaret to get Jason and meet her downstairs in the kitchen as she removed the empty harvesting baskets from herself and Jessica. When they were all gathered together, Em explained what had happened outside at the blueberry patch. She was sure Jason and Margaret would have heard the roar from the woods because it was so frighteningly loud—except that they were both wearing headphones.

Em could tell that her two older children were taking this seriously, especially since Jess was so obviously upset and unwilling to go outside anymore.

"Mom," Jason said, "I'm sorry I couldn't hear anything with my headset on."

"Me too," said Margaret apologetically.

"Look," Em said, "I need you two to start taking responsibility for other people in this family. To start paying attention to your surroundings. Do you get it? If we had been injured out there, would you have even noticed that we hadn't returned after a while?"

Jason and Margaret looked appropriately chastened and remorseful. Em remained dissatisfied but didn't think it would be productive to belabor the point. "I just need you to do better, okay?"

"Okay, Mom," was the response.

"I gotta call your Dad and tell him what happened. And—as if I have to say this—*nobody* is going outside right now. Understand?" Heads were nodding. Em looked at Jessica, who was still upset, and then turned to the other two, "Guys, take Jess upstairs and all of you do an activity together. Watch something funny or whatever. Just take care of your sister for me right now while I call your Dad."

Em dialed Keith and hoped to God that his phone was getting a signal at the Lodge. After ringing for a bit, Keith picked up. "Hey, hon, what's up?" he said.

Em sighed. "Keith, you're not going to believe what just happened. And, frankly, maybe something does need to be reported to the Sheriff's Station."

\*\*\*

"Here's McArthur Lake Road," Cal told Liam as they drove north on Route 95. Liam turned left onto the road and looked for the lake parking lot. The two *Eagle Newspaper* employees were going to film some video for the most important news story of the week. Liam was the "social media guy" at the newspaper and wrote short community updates for the publication online. Cal, on the other hand, wrote both hard news and features. The editor gave Cal a lot of leeway since the staff was so small at *The Eagle*. Cal also livestreamed on social media for any breaking community news, so he and Liam worked together to make sure their reporting was complementary and not redundant.

Last night, a little after 10 PM, Cal had heard on his 911 Emergency Notification Scanner that a teenage boy needed medical transport from the Everton Sheriff's Station to Everton General Hospital. Then he heard chatter on the police scanner about McArthur Lake. From the tone in the voices of the dispatchers and the Sheriff's personnel, Cal felt something big had happened. Sure enough, this morning at 7 AM, the Sheriff's Office announced that the missing teenager Steven Mahakian had been found by Jack Evers on Monday night. Jack found Steven on Route 95 near McArthur Lake.

Cal rushed over to the Sheriff's Station this morning to get details on the story. The deputies didn't really have any additional information to provide other than that the kid probably ended up on the Idaho Centennial Trail, which went past McArthur Lake. From there, Steven made it around the lake to Route 95. The deputies couldn't say why he had trekked all the way up and over to the other side of the Selkirk Mountains. People lost in the wilderness generally don't travel uphill to find civilization. From Indian Creek Campground to McArthur Lake is about twenty miles as the crow flies, but if Steven had found a trail in the woods, then it would naturally be easier to traverse the area.

Cal was sure that the Sheriff's Office was withholding information—probably trying to confirm Steven's story—but at least Cal knew where Steven was discovered and that he'd come from the Idaho Centennial Trail. Cal wanted to get some footage of Route 95 as well as the hiking trail. He didn't want to shoot a livestream for this so he had

Liam come along to operate the video camera and take photos for the report.

They shot the Route 95 footage first, which took all of five minutes. Liam captured the road on video as Cal explained that Everton resident Jack Evers had been driving south from Bonners Ferry when he spotted an exhausted Steven Mahakian travelling on the right shoulder.

Then Cal and Liam got back in the car and drove around the lake to get closer to the trail head. Cal had heard that the Idaho Centennial Trail, sometimes called the ICT, was notoriously difficult to traverse because it was one of the most remote trails in existence. It was 930 miles long in totality, traveling the entire north-south length of Idaho with few roads intersecting its path. There were no towns within easy distance for resupply, and much of it had to be bushwhacked to get through. One of the few east-west corridors of the trail connected McArthur Lake to Priest Lake across the Selkirk Mountain Range. Surely not a hiking trail for the faint of heart.

Liam found a spot to park near some public restrooms, then they walked up a gravel road for about fifty feet to find the trail. Cal was not one for hiking, and Liam preferred motorbiking on designated outback roads, so neither was familiar with this area. Cal consulted an online map on his phone and decided they were at the trail head. Liam set up the camera and starting filming when Cal was ready.

"This is the Idaho Centennial Trail near McArthur Lake. Authorities say that Steven Mahakian crossed the Selkirk Mountains between Indian Creek Campground and McArthur Lake over a period of eight days,

160

ending up around this area last night. The authorities haven't released any more information than that. The Mahakian Family has also been silent regarding Steven's experience for the past eight days. Steven was on the Cross-Country Team in high school, and he was young and healthy, so it's not a complete surprise that he was able to travel across such rugged terrain. It also helps that the weather has been warm in the mountains this summer, and that the creeks and rivers had plenty of water. No doubt, Steven was able to survive because of these circumstances."

Cal walked slowly toward the camera as he continued to speak. "It's not completely unheard of for people to survive in the wilderness without supplies or shelter. In the summer of 2020, Gia Fuda survived alone for nine days in the Cascade Mountains of Washington State. Searchers eventually found her alive near Scenic Creek. There's also the case of Lisa Theris, who, in 2017, survived for twenty-eight days in the Alabama wilderness. She was eventually found unconscious by the side of a road about four miles from the town of Midway. Both women survived by drinking water from creeks and streams, and eating berries or mushrooms. We can add Steven Mahakian to that list of miracle survivors." As he finished his report, Cal tried not to lapse into that trite reporter tone that afflicted so many in his field.

"As always, we'll be bringing you the latest updates on this incredible story as we learn more. I'm Cal Russo for *The Everton Eagle*."

Liam stopped recording and gave a thumbs-up sign before saying, "Do you want me to get some video of the trees and vegetation?"

"Please do," said Cal as he examined the dirt trail, which was framed on either side by thick woods as it continued away from the gravel road. The trail was pretty wide at this point—around ten feet across.

"I think I've got enough footage," said Liam after a few minutes. "Did you want me to get anything else?"

"No, that's good for now," replied Cal. "Go ahead and get the stuff back to the car. I'm going to walk up the trail a bit just to see what it looks like…maybe get some footage on my phone."

"Okay," said Liam as he grabbed the microphone and camera. "See you at the car." Liam was already walking back down the gravel road by the time Cal pulled his phone out of his pocket.

Cal started walking up the dirt trail. He wanted to see how difficult the terrain was around the area. After about fifty feet the trail veered left but was still easy to traverse. It even seemed that vehicles had driven up here judging from the tire tracks on the ground. Cal decided that there wasn't much point to going any further since the trail probably wouldn't get difficult for a long ways off—a longer way off than Cal was willing to travel.

Cal walked to the middle of the trail, brought up his phone to eye level, and hit the video record button. Suddenly, he heard a tree being shaken violently to his left. He quickly looked to where the leaves were still falling from a fifteen-foot tree several feet into the wood line. The shaking had stopped as he watched. He looked down at the base but there were a lot of tall bushes and shorter trees obscuring it. Cal was confused. Were raccoons or squirrels jumping around the trees? But the shaking was so violent that he wasn't convinced small mammals were responsible. A mountain lion maybe? Suddenly he felt uneasy.

Cal turned to walk back down toward the gravel road, but as he walked, he heard something large start to parallel his progress inside the tree line, crushing underbrush and branches as it went. Cal stopped and looked. The parallel movement stopped as well. The brush was too thick to see into, but he knew something was there. Cal started walking again as he stared at the trees. Cal heard branches snapping and saw bushes moving as something large brazenly paced him in the vegetation. Cal froze a second time. Whatever was following him also stopped.

Horror seemed too mild a word for what Cal experienced in that moment. He immediately felt the urge to run, but simultaneously felt paralyzed. Something was overtly stalking him and he desperately wished he could disappear. Cal had the irrational thought, *If I don't move, it won't see me.* But he already knew that whatever it was *did* see him and he cursed himself, *MOVE, Cal! RUN damn you!* Yet none of this internal cajoling motivated his body to move.

Then a piercing, guttural scream tore through Cal's world from the woods. He was finally unfrozen and ran like a spring gazelle back down the trail to the gravel road and the car beyond.

Liam was standing at the open driver's side door watching Cal barreling toward the car. Liam shouted in shock, "What *the hell* was that?! Are you okay??"

"Get in the damn car and drive!" Cal barked as he bolted into the passenger side seat. Cal immediately looked up the gravel road. *Was anything following him?*

Liam started the car and zipped forward as Cal continued to peer behind them. Nothing was in pursuit. After a few minutes, Cal allowed himself to face forward and relax a bit.

When they were back on Route 95 and heading toward Everton, Liam asked, "Okay, what the hell was that?"

Cal was mute for a while as he tried to process what had just happened. His heart was still pounding furiously.

Liam kept looking over at him as he drove, trying to assess Cal's mental state.

Eventually, Cal said breathlessly, "I don't know what it was...it stayed in the woods the entire time."

"*It?*" Liam reiterated.

"I was about to record some video when this tree started shaking violently...like I've never seen...and this thing...wait, *oh my God!*" Cal looked at his phone which he'd been clutching all this time—it was still recording. Cal screeched in elation, startling Liam.

Cal punched the stop button on his phone and shouted, "*God, yes!*" Then he turned to Liam and said, "*I got it on video!!!*"

Cal directed Liam to drive back to *The Eagle* offices so they could review all their footage. He then explained what had happened on the trail when he was alone on the ICT. Cal played back the video on his phone as they continued to Everton. The video didn't seem to show anything useful since Cal held the phone in a bunch of odd positions as he walked and then ran. It was the audio that mattered at this point. During playback in the car, when the audio played the scream, it sent chills down Cal's spine. Liam cursed out loud.

"I don't even know how to describe that," Liam said. "A woman screaming that somehow mutates into a gorilla roaring?"

"Better description than I could have come up with," said Cal.

"Should we be calling the Sheriff or something?" inquired Liam with concern. "Is this thing related to Steven Mahakian? I mean, there could be a dangerous animal out there."

"Well, those are all good questions. Here's another question: would it still even be there if we *did* get the deputies to investigate?" Cal asked. Then he sighed. "Now *I know* what it's like to be one of *those* people."

"Like what people?"

"The ones who experience something odd and don't want to report it for fear of being laughed at or ridiculed," Cal explained. "Now *I'm* the crazy one."

"Yeah, but this time we have evidence. There's the audio," Liam countered. "We should tell the authorities."

"Yeah, fine," Cal conceded. "Fine. Let's go to the Everton Sheriff's Station and let them hear the audio."

Cal reported the encounter to the Sheriff's deputies as soon as they arrived in Everton. He also played the video sound for them, suggesting that there could be a dangerous animal on these hiking trails. Liam corroborated the story.

The deputies were interested in the recording, and said they would notify Animal Control about the situation. The scream-roar was definitely frightening and unusual, but the officers felt it was probably a grizzly bear—still something dangerous that should be investigated, but probably not related to Steven Mahakian.

Cal was not surprised at the deputies' reaction, although Liam was clearly disappointed. "So now what?" Liam asked as he sat in the driver's seat and started the car outside the station.

"Back to the office," said Cal. "I want to look over our footage on the big screens there."

"You got it, boss man," Liam said as he turned onto the road. "All I know is, next time we film near the woods, I'm bringing my gun."

Cal didn't protest.

# Chapter 10

July 14 – Wednesday

Jack was sitting at his kitchen table finishing up his morning coffee when the house phone rang. Jack's home actually belonged to his parents and he only moved back in to take care of his elderly mother in 2006. When she passed away two years later, he inherited the house and decided to continue living in it. His niece Stefanie grew up in this house and Jack thought he would eventually leave the property to her. There was a single-room guesthouse in the back that Stefanie used whenever she was in Everton, but since it was detached from the main house, Jack didn't always see her, even when she was staying there.

The main house still had a land line, and the phone number hadn't changed since it was installed decades ago. Jack wondered who might be calling since he always gave people his cell phone number to reach him. *Who would be calling such an old number now?* He walked over to the old rotary telephone hanging on the kitchen wall and picked up the receiver.

"Hello," Jack said.

"Hello…Jack?" said a female voice.

"Yes, this is Jack. To whom am I speaking?"

"Jack, this is Kathy." Upon hearing her name and the familiarity with which she spoke, Jack knew exactly who was calling, although he wished he didn't. Jack was tempted to put up a pretense. *Kathy who?* he wanted to say. But Jack was too old to play games anymore.

"Kathy," he said unemotionally. "Stefanie's not here if you're trying to find her."

"No, Jack," Kathy continued. "I know Stef's not there—and I'm sorry for everything. I know you don't want to talk to me, but I wouldn't have called except that…you need to know some things about the past. It may or may not make a difference to you now, but I need to tell you if you'll listen."

Jack felt that there was nothing his two-timing, child-abandoning, weed-smoking ex-sister-in-law could tell him that he'd be interested in, but his more logical side persuaded him to listen.

"Fine," he said nonchalantly, "say what you need to say."

"Thank you, Jack," Kathy said gratefully. "To start, I don't know if you knew, but Stef and I have been in touch over the phone for about a year now. I don't deserve it, but she's allowed me to be in her life in some small way."

"Mm hm," Jack acknowledged tersely. He *didn't* know that, but he couldn't fault Stefanie for wanting to know her own mother.

"Well, Stefanie recently told me that she plans to have Tom declared deceased. And, of course, it makes sense after so long, but…the more I thought about it, the more it bothered me the way Tom disappeared."

"It didn't bother you back then," Jack said sharply. He couldn't help it.

"I know," Kathy agreed sadly. "I was in a drugged-out stupor and I really have no excuse, Jack."

*Crap*, Jack thought. He wanted to be angry with her, but her accommodating manner was making that difficult. "Fine, go on," he said.

"Jack, I shouldn't have left Tom and Stefanie. And I know there's no going back to make up for it. I wasn't happy with Tom—you know how he was, just making excuses all the time..." Kathy stopped herself short, then restarted. "Anyway, that still didn't make it okay for me to cheat on him or to abandon him and Stef. When I left, I know he went into a depression, and your mom ended up having to take care of Stefanie."

"Well, it should have been you, Kathy. Why weren't you there for Stef at least?!" Jack asked angrily. If Kathy wanted to come clean, she should at least have to answer some basic questions.

"Because by then I was hooked on so many drugs and I couldn't handle taking care of *myself* let alone Stefanie!" Kathy answered plaintively. "Look, I don't want to fight with you, Jack! *You're right!* I'm a terrible person and I should have been there for Stefanie. And I've said all this to her. I don't make any excuses to her for my behavior and I'm not trying to make excuses with you now. I'm just telling you what was going on. That's all."

"Fine, then if you're done confessing all of your sins we can end this conversation," Jack said harshly, although he didn't hang up. He might have ended the call abruptly once upon a time, but he didn't now.

"Wait, Jack," Kathy pleaded. "Just wait! I haven't told you the part you need to know yet!"

"Fine. Spill it," Jack said impatiently.

"Look, when Tom and I were dating, there was a spot we used to drive to for privacy. An abandoned logging road outside of town. After Stef was born, we stopped going there. But when our marriage was on the rocks, and we were fighting all the time, I knew that he would sometimes go to that same spot to drink, or to get away from whatever problems we were going through."

Jack listened intently as Kathy continued talking.

"So when I heard from some friends who still lived in Everton at the time that Tom went missing, I honestly thought at first that he'd just gone off like I did, just left it all behind for a new life. I went off to Florida—maybe he went off to California or Hawaii even. You know, it didn't seem crazy to me back then. It was only in the last few months, when I found out from Stefanie that he disappeared *after a fight with you*, that I thought maybe he went to that same spot. Maybe he didn't leave town after all. Maybe he just went to the same spot to drink and get away from it all for a few hours."

Jack's mind started racing. Kathy was giving him a clue as to Tom's possible last whereabouts—over a decade too late! In his mind, Jack was calling Kathy all sorts of insulting names, but instead he shouted, "*God, Kathy*, you could have told me this fourteen years ago! You know, like, *when we were searching for him damnit!* You know how hard it is to search for people in winter, Kathy?? In the snow?!"

Jack heard sobbing on the other end of the line. He hated to admit it, but part of him felt elated that Kathy was suffering over this. But after a few minutes, Jack sighed and said gently, "Okay, Kathy."

"Jack, I've been sober for three years now," Kathy continued hoarsely. "Things are getting clearer and clearer every day. And there's one thing I know for sure: Tom would *never* have left Stefanie. He was better than me." Kathy started crying again as she struggled to say, "Something must have happened to him...I know Stef was in college already, but he wouldn't have left her like that—and right before Christmas? *Never.* Maybe his car went off the road in the snow...on that logging road..." Her sobs prevented her from continuing.

Jack started to feel a little numb as Kathy cried. Maybe it was shock. "Have you told Stefanie what you just told me? About that drinking spot of Tom's?" Jack asked.

Kathy sniffled. "I tried calling her *before I called you*—I tried yesterday—but she's not answering her cell phone."

"She's out on a field survey right now," Jack volunteered.

"Yes," Kathy agreed, "she told me she'd be in the forest for a while, but I thought I'd give her phone a try anyway. I tried calling her the day before yesterday too and she didn't pick up, so I called her duty station. They said it's not unusual for field crews to lose cell signal for long periods of time, but they'd gotten a satellite phone message from her team for the standard check-in that day, so they weren't concerned. And since there wasn't an emergency, the duty station wouldn't pass along personal messages. So, I called you."

Jack sighed again. "Okay. Tell me where to find this logging road."

Jack made a few business phone calls after hanging up with Kathy. Then he grabbed a fast-food burger before trying to find this abandoned logging road she spoke of. After looking at an online map, Jack realized that the logging road Kathy described was actually on his family's land. It was probably put in when Jack's grandfather Elijah was still alive because it was located in a part of the forest that Jack hadn't ever visited. His family had hired different logging companies to harvest trees several times over the past century, and they wouldn't have necessarily recorded these temporary logging roads on any printed map. However, with the advent of satellite imaging, these man-made features on the ground can't stay hidden.

Jack took a well-known road out of town heading north that followed one of the many creeks in the area. After several miles, Jack found the road with no name and no gate. It angled steeply down for about thirty feet before leveling off. It was a gravel road about twelve feet across in most places. Kathy said he would know if it were the right road because about two miles down he should see a turnout on the left next to a large tree stump. Jack doubted that any turnout would still be evident after this much time had passed, but whatever.

It was a bright midday, so it was easy to navigate around any forest debris in the road. Despite the summer sun, Jack felt jumpy, but what did he expect? He was out here, after all, looking for his long-lost brother. Part of him didn't want to find anything. Maybe it would be *better* if he found nothing.

Jack quit thinking about what-ifs and just kept driving. Even with his F-150 truck, he couldn't go faster than about 20 mph due to the forest detritus and new growth covering the road, so the search for this alleged turnout felt like it was taking a while. Just when Jack thought that he should turn around, he hit the brakes hard.

There, on the left shoulder of the road, was a large tree stump about three feet in diameter, and parked just beyond it was a vehicle covered in pine needles, dust, and small branches. Jack was shocked. Despite the layer of dirt and leaves, Jack could tell that it was definitely Tom's silver Dodge Stratus. From his position on the road, Jack could see the rear and passenger sides of the car. The dust-covered windows didn't allow any clear view of the car's interior from this distance.

Jack turned his truck off in the middle of the road and sat for a minute. He didn't want to get out of the truck. He didn't want to see what was in that Dodge Stratus. A heaviness came over Jack as he realized he didn't want to be here at all, but it was too late. There was no turning back now.

He took another few minutes to steel himself for whatever happened next. First, he did a 360° scan of the area through the truck windows. He didn't see any movement, so he exited the vehicle and surveyed Tom's car from a distance of about ten feet. The forest had started to claim some of the turnout around the silver vehicle. Younger trees, bushes, and ferns encircled the car as though trying to hide it from Jack. Even from above, some branches were attempting to cover the car's roof.

Jack brought out his phone and decided he should take some photos of Tom's car before he disturbed anything. This was also a way to forestall looking inside the time-worn vehicle. Jack took a step closer. He captured the rusty license plate and a wide view of the car from both the rear and right passenger side. He made sure to catch the tree stump in the photos too.

After a few minutes, Jack sighed. No more delaying the inevitable. He walked along the right side of the vehicle, which faced the road. The car's paint job looked pretty worn from years of snow and sun beating down on it. The back and side windows were dirty and revealed nothing of the interior.

Jack continued to walk until he could see the front windshield. He gasped as he discovered four bullet holes scattered across the glass. The holes were positioned fairly far apart in an almost straight line. Jack started to feel anger. He put his hand to his mouth as if to stifle the emotion. He remembered he had his phone in hand and brought it up to take several photos of the windshield.

Jack didn't think anybody was in the front seat, but it was hard to tell with the web of cracks in the glass compounded by years of dust and pine needles. Jack checked his surroundings once more before walking over to the driver's side door. He was shocked to find that the door was missing altogether. It seemed that it had been torn clean off the hinges and was not in the immediate vicinity. Jack could also see that no one was in the front seat. He was about to lean inside before remembering he should take photos. Dirt and dead leaves were sprinkled around the driver's side entrance.

Jack squatted down a bit to get a better view of the interior. There was an open bottle of whisky on the passenger side floor and a gun on the floor near the brake pedal. Shell casings were scattered about—Jack saw three right away. Shattered glass shards littered the driver's seat and the floor, both in and outside of the car. A small, silver flip phone was lying on the passenger side seat. The keys were still in the ignition turned to the OFF position. Jack craned his neck to look into the back seat and saw nothing immediately apparent.

Jack stood up and tried to assess what he was seeing. *What happened here, Tom?* he thought. *Who were you shooting at?*

Jack walked around the entire car taking photos as he went. He didn't see anything more of note, so he reached into the driver's side dashboard and popped the trunk. As he neared the back of the vehicle, he was hesitant to pull up on the ajar trunk door, but then decided to just open it with a quick yank. Thankfully there was no body in there.

Jack photographed the trunk which contained some spare tools. Then he looked into the forest. It was the only place left to search for the missing car door…and Tom. Since it was summer, the forest floor was alive with ferns, saplings, moss, and various shrubs. Light was able to penetrate the high canopy above, but there were darker spots too where trees stood closer together as though plotting some secret scheme.

There was a natural opening between the closest trees and Jack figured it made the most sense to start there. He stepped in slowly and scanned the floor methodically. The most obvious thing to look for was the silver car door. Jack tried not to disturb anything as he walked. He spied a dead tree branch about two feet long and picked it up so he could use it to prod at the vegetation. The plants nearby varied in height from five inches to a foot tall.

Jack decided to search in a radius of five feet from the point of entry into the forest just to be more systematic. He didn't find anything in the five-foot radius, so he extended the search radius an additional five feet, skirting around trees as he went. Still nothing. He extended the search radius another five feet. And another five feet.

It was in this swath that he found the car door lying flat on the floor with the silver exterior side up. It was mostly covered in pine needles and loose bark. Jack took a photo and then brushed off the dirt to get a better look at it. The window was smashed up, which explained the glass shards in the car and on the driver's side. The door seemed beat up and dented around the edges and on the fiberglass surface, but he couldn't say what had caused the deformations—someone punching or kicking at it? He pulled the door upright to stand it on an edge and discovered a bunch of insects and decayed plant matter underneath, but nothing else. He examined the hinges and found that they were definitely broken—the metal had snapped. *What could pull a car door off its hinges? A man or a bear?* he wondered, but Jack already had other suspicions.

Jack lay the door back down in its original spot, then looked around the area again. He looked back toward the vehicle and saw that it was a clear shot from the Dodge Stratus to the door's resting place—no intervening trees in the way. *Even if a bear did pull the door off its hinges, it wouldn't toss or drag the thing this far away.*

Jack really doubted that a bear had anything to do with this situation, especially after his own experience at the Lodge a few nights ago, but he was trying to exhaust all conventional explanations. The car door must have weighed close to forty pounds. Does a bear have the physical ability to throw something that heavy more than a few feet? Sure, they can probably drag really heavy objects a long distance, but would a bear drag a car door away in the middle of a confrontation? Or even *after* a confrontation? Jack was sure that a bear would be more interested in the vehicle's human occupant than the door.

As Jack continued to scan the surrounding foliage for more clues, he felt inexplicably drawn to a specific spot to his left. He glanced over at an area covered in ferns. There was no logical explanation for why he was drawn there, but the feeling was undeniable. He slowly approached the spot until he glimpsed a patch of blue fabric between the fern fronds.

*No*, Jack thought to himself. After stopping for a few seconds, Jack continued to the spot and pulled back the fern fronds with his own hand. Unmistakably, underneath the plants lay a patch of blue jacket material. In his mind, Jack could still see Tom storming out of the house that night, grabbing his blue jacket as he left.

"No," Jack said weakly. He brushed away some pine needles and dirt. The jacket seemed intact. Jack touched the fabric and then pulled up on the shoulder of the garment. As he pulled it up, a jumble of bones slid out the bottom of the jacket.

Jack felt like he was going to vomit and pass out at the same time. The periphery of his vision was going dark. He dropped the coat and put a hand on his knee as he tried to regain his composure. His head was experiencing waves of pressure as though the blood flow were being disrupted. Finally, he plopped to the ground and sat there just trying to breathe.

Jack didn't move for a while. He realized he just wanted to stop looking and hand this whole endeavor over to someone else. He couldn't bring himself to continue searching the area. A small pile of skeletal remains from the jacket lay right in front of him, picked clean by insects. Jack thought he saw a couple of ribs and an assortment of vertebra. This was an abomination. He couldn't take anymore photographs. This was not clinical to him. *His brother was dead.* And no doubt more horrors lay scattered around here like Easter Eggs waiting to be discovered. Where was the rest of Tom? Jack didn't think he could handle finding more of him this way.

Feelings of nausea gave way to anger. Jack shouted unintelligibly into the forest in frustration and grief. Tom had been here *all this time—in the damn woods!* For the first time in his life, Jack felt incredible resentment and hatred for the forest surroundings of his home state. It hid things. It kept secrets that it had no right to keep.

Jack looked at his cell phone. It had a signal. He called the Everton Sheriff Station to report that he'd found the remains of his brother Tom Evers. The deputies said they were sending a patrol car out right away.

Jack hung up the phone and sat immobile. He felt numb as he stared at the ferns to his right and listened to birds chirping in the background.

When the deputies arrived on scene about thirty minutes later, Jack was still seated in the same spot next to the blue jacket. He felt drained but was able to succinctly summarize what led him to this area and how he came upon Tom's jacket and partial remains. The deputies wanted Jack to go back to his truck and wait there, but he insisted on watching the team work.

Jack stood up and walked a few paces away from the jacket, but stayed close enough to watch as the deputies continued the search. Just a foot or two from the jacket, a deputy uncovered a human skull in the dirt. Photographs were taken and notes were written down. Jack saw them uncover a boot and the remains of Tom's jeans with his wallet still inside the back pocket. He watched the team systematically bag up the evidence and put up crime scene tape. A team was also examining Tom's vehicle and the contents.

Jack looked at his watch. It was 6:40 PM. He suddenly felt very tired. The deputy in charge gave Jack his contact information and said they would call Jack when they were done searching the site. An autopsy would be conducted on the skeletal remains as soon as possible. Internally, Jack doubted that they'd ever really know how Tom died since no soft tissue remained.

Reluctantly, Jack got in his truck and headed home, but he didn't want to go back to an empty house, so he called his ex-wife Ellen on the road and asked if he could stop by.

179

Ellen was shocked at Jack's news over the phone. He arrived at her place around 7:15 PM. The sun was still out. It was hard to believe that only this morning he had spoken to Kathy about checking out a logging road. That conversation felt like a lifetime ago. A new reality had imposed itself upon him when he found Tom's jacket and had to accept the hard truth that followed.

Ellen opened the front door and, before Jack could say anything, she hugged him tightly. He almost broke down right there but managed to walk into the living room and drop onto a couch.

"All this time," Ellen said. "He was right there."

"Yeah," Jack replied weakly. "It was horrible, Ell." He described the conversation with Kathy this morning and finding the old logging road. Then he described everything he'd found, including Tom's remains.

"My poor mother," Jack said. "She somehow knew he was dead. I don't know how, but she'd insist to me that he was gone. She'd never say that to Stefanie though. –*God,* I've got to tell Stef." Jack took his cell phone out and selected the chat with Stefanie, but his fingers hovered over the buttons motionless. What was he going to say? *Hi Stef—found your dad in the woods today. Let's talk.*

No. He needed to talk to her real-time, but she probably wasn't getting a cell phone signal out in the field right now.

After a while, Ellen put her hand over the phone and took it from Jack. She said, "How about just texting Stef that you have important news and need her to contact you as soon as she can?" Ellen was typing it out for Jack. She read the text aloud and hit the send button after Jack nodded.

"Do you want to contact Kathy too?" Ellen asked.

"Yeah," Jack said. He gave Ellen the number that Kathy had given him this morning in case he needed to call her back for more information. Ellen used her own phone to call Kathy and explain what had happened. The two of them had met a few times at family events so they weren't strangers. Ellen had remained close with Jack's mother Eileen even after the divorce, so she sometimes saw Kathy and Stefanie at Eileen's house before Kathy had left Tom.

Jack could hear Kathy sobbing over the phone at the news of finding Tom's remains. He was glad Ellen was the one dealing with that instead of him. He still didn't feel very charitable towards his ex-sister-in-law.

"Does Stefanie know?" he heard Kathy ask Ellen.

"Not yet," Ellen replied. "Jack texted her that he needs to discuss something important, but we're not sure when she'll see the message."

"I don't know," Kathy said. "Maybe this counts as a family emergency. Maybe the duty station can send a sat-phone message for this."

Ellen looked to Jack for his reaction. "Yeah," he said, "I think this counts as a family emergency." Ellen told Kathy to go ahead and ask Stef's duty station about that. After discussing a few more details with Kathy, Ellen hung up.

Ellen asked Jack if he'd told Bobby and Jenny about finding Tom yet. He indicated he hadn't, so she texted them briefly about it. Jenny insisted on driving up from Coeur d'Alene the next day. Bobby was

181

thinking of moving up his vacation time so he could be in Everton by this weekend.

Upon seeing that text message, Jack called Bobby on his cell phone. "Look, son," Jack started. "I appreciate you wanting to be here right now, but I'm okay. I don't want you to rearrange your whole schedule for this. It's a long drive from Boise."

"Dad," Bobby responded, "this is obviously some screwed up crap going on with Uncle T and that *bothers* me. So don't worry about my schedule. I'm gonna come up as soon as I can, and I'll text you when I know for sure what day I can get there."

Jack acquiesced. He actually did want his kids around while dealing with the discovery of Tom's body, but he was trying to be a tough guy and not impose on them.

"How are you holding up, Jack?" Ellen asked after he finished talking to their son.

Jack shook his head. "All those years we didn't know where Tom was, it was easy to just chalk it up to his flaky personality—that he'd just up and left town like a dumbass, not telling anyone about it. It was easy to explain away because Stef was old enough to take care of herself—off to college and all. And *their* relationship had really broken down at that point because of his drinking. Stef hated it. Mom was the only one who still defended him, even though he was doing a piss-poor job taking care of her." Jack was starting to get angry. "Thank God you were here, Ell, to let me know Mom needed more help than Tom was getting her."

"I was glad to look in on Eileen," Ellen said. "She was still family to me."

"I know, but I couldn't let you be the one to take on the responsibility of caring for her. She was *my* mother. And I had no problem moving back to Idaho for that, but Tom was just a spiraling mess. Even in her eighties, Mom was still all there, you know, and pretty healthy. All Tom had to do was make sure she had her groceries and made it to her doctor appointments—maybe get a plumber to fix a toilet now and then. That's it! And he couldn't even manage *that*." Jack shook his head again in disgust.

After a minute, Ellen asked gently, "Is that what the fight was about the night he disappeared?"

Jack looked down at his hands as he rubbed his knuckles in agitation. "Yeah," he replied tersely. "I hadn't planned to unload on him that night, but Mom had both of us over for Sunday dinner, and Tom needed money...*again*. In his fifties asking his elderly mother for money. I flew off the handle. He stormed out. Mom was crying...*wow*, I was a *real jerk* starting that whole row in front of her." Now Jack was angry at himself. He should have confronted Tom when they were alone the next day, not in front of their mother. "If I'd just kept my mouth shut, then Tom wouldn't have driven off to that logging road and had God-knows-what happen to him."

"You don't know that, Jack," Ellen interjected. "According to Kathy, he went up there a lot. You don't know that *he wouldn't* have gone up there whether you had a fight or not. Maybe getting the money from

Eileen would've made him feel guilty, and maybe he would've ended up on that logging road that night anyway. Point is, *you don't know.*"

"I guess," Jack conceded. Maybe he should stop trying to blame someone for Tom's death. Stop blaming Tom and stop blaming himself.

Ellen sighed. "What do you think happened to him? Did he owe people money? Was someone after him? I mean, the bullet holes in the windshield..."

"I don't know," Jack confessed. "I wasn't exactly his confidant. I know I saw something weird at the Lodge the other day, and I *now* know that something scared the hell out of Dad up at the cabins...but...maybe *it was* a bear that got Tom. I don't want to be the guy who cries 'Bigfoot' every chance he gets."

Ellen considered Jack's reasoning for a moment before saying, "Yeah, but aren't bears hibernating by December? It was cold enough to be snowing that week. I mean, I *guess* a rogue bear may have still been running around at that time, but I don't really buy that story."

"Hmm," Jack hadn't accounted for the bear hibernating season. "Well, from the way the bullet holes were placed, he was either tracking something coming at him as he fired his gun, or he was shooting at multiple targets in front of the vehicle."

"Maybe something was crossing in front of the car toward the driver's side door," Ellen said.

"Yeah," Jack agreed. "And why would anyone tear off the car door? Even if they were loan sharks collecting on a debt, would they really bother to tear off the car door? Who does that?"

"And then throws or drags it twenty feet into the woods," Ellen added.

"Right," Jack sighed. "Then, they either yank Tom out of the car and take him to the spot where I found him, or he ran off when he got the chance and got stopped there by a bullet or something. –*God,* are we ever going to know?"

"When will they have the autopsy report?" Ellen asked.

"A few weeks from now, I think," Jack replied. "But I know the coroner personally. I'm pretty sure he'll let me know what he finds before the official report is ready."

"Well," Ellen said, "It seems that the most important thing we've learned is that Tom didn't just up and leave. Something happened to him."

"Yeah," Jack said somberly.

"When the time is right," Ellen continued quietly, "when Stefanie is back in town, maybe we can think of having a memorial for Tom."

In that moment, Jack's heart broke like a dam. He wept into his hand trying to stifle the noise. He wept for all the regrets he had and for all of the time he wasted fighting with Tom. He mourned his mother's pain over losing Tom like that. Ellen held Jack's other hand and cried for Tom as well.

His brother was dead and Jack had no emotional defense against that hard truth. There was no way to soften the blow of this loss. And, in this moment, the why's didn't really matter. The only thing that mattered was Jack would never see Tom again in this life.

*I'm sorry I wasn't there for you, Tom*, Jack wailed internally. *I'm sorry.*

# Chapter 11

## July 15 – Thursday

Jack woke up feeling like crap. He was amazed that he'd gotten any sleep at all last night. He left Ellen's house the night before around 10 PM. She had offered the guest room to him so he wouldn't be alone, but it wouldn't have felt right sleeping over at the house she had shared with her second husband Ben. Jack had nothing against the guy, especially since Ben had treated Ellen well and gave her no grief. He'd died almost twenty years ago, but it was *still* Ben's house, and Jack respected that. So Jack went back to his family home to get what rest he could.

As Jack lay in bed watching the sunlight peek through the curtains, he heard his daughter knocking at the front door saying, "Dad, it's Jenny!" and then letting herself in with her own key. Almost everybody in the family had a key to his parents' house—his ex-wife Ellen probably still had hers. Jack looked at the side table clock. It was 7:45 AM. Jenny must have gotten up early to get here from Coeur d'Alene.

"Yup," Jack called out as he got up. "I'm upstairs, Jenny. Be down in a minute."

"Take your time, Dad," she called from the kitchen. "I'll start some coffee and eggs."

A little while later, Jack was at the kitchen table eating breakfast with his daughter. They spoke about Tom and remembered all of the good times together—all of the holidays spent here at Gramp's and Grammy's house. Tom gave the best gifts for Christmas and always brought the pumpkin pie for Thanksgiving. And he got Stef any pet she ever wanted so there was always a menagerie in Grammy's backyard of abandoned animals—ducks, turtles, gerbils, hamsters.

Jack checked his phone and saw there were a bevy of text messages. Ellen had informed everyone in Jack's social circle about the news, so there were a ton of condolences in his chat queue. Even people from Gibson Drake and Eden Design had sent text messages.

Keith wrote, "Jack – Em and I are so sorry to hear about your brother Tom. Please let us know if we can do anything to help." Bill sent, "Jack, I'm so sorry about Tom. He was a good guy and didn't deserve this. Let me know if there's anything I can do." David and Leanne texted, "We're here for you, Jack."

Jack scrolled through several more messages until he came upon one from Cal Russo from last night. It read, "Jack, I heard the news about your brother Tom. I can't tell you how sorry I am. I also know the circumstances of his disappearance are nebulous. I found something that I want to show you. I know this is a bad time, but it might be related to Tom's death. Can we meet some time in person? I'll understand if you can't."

Jack wondered what Cal could possibly want to show him, but if it were really related to Tom, he should check it out. Jack typed in response,

"Cal – I'll be at the Lodge around 11 AM this morning. We can meet there." Cal immediately replied that he'd see Jack then.

Jack was disappointed to find no messages from Stefanie. Jack cursed under his breath and then said to Jenny, "I hope nobody texts Stefanie about her dad until I get a chance to talk to her."

"Where *is* Stefanie anyway?" asked Jenny.

"She's out in the field. This trip was going to be a bit remote—north of Upper Priest Lake I think," Jack answered.

"Should we be worried?" Jenny pressed.

Jack sighed. "We should be concerned. But you know Stef—she's no dummy. She wouldn't take unnecessary risks. And I've tried to reach her in the forest before on previous trips and gotten no response for a day or two."

Jenny frowned at that. "Things can go south pretty fast in the backcountry, Dad."

Jack considered his daughter's comment for a moment. "Yeah. Let me check with Kathy."

Jack texted, "Kathy, have you heard anything from Stefanie? Did her duty station pass on the message about a family emergency?"

Kathy texted in response, "Stef's supervisor tried to pass on the message to Stefanie that there's a family emergency last night, but they're not sure that the message went through. They did get a sat-phone text earlier this morning from one of her teammates for check-in. None of the crew is answering their sat-phones right now though. Her supervisor is checking with the satellite company to see if there's a problem with the signals. He said they've had problems with previous companies regarding the firmware in the past. Sometimes messages are successfully sent one way, but not the other, which may be why Stef didn't get the message about a family emergency."

Jack wondered if he should be worried. *Could it be related to the strange happenings around the Lodge? Or was Jack imagining connections that didn't really exist?* In the safety of his own thoughts, Jack could postulate anything, but saying it out loud was another matter altogether. Maybe it was really just a technical problem with the phones.

"What's the matter, Dad?" Jenny asked.

Jack said, "Stef's duty station is having a hard time connecting with the field crew. They're checking with the satellite company about the phones."

Jack texted Kathy asking her to keep him updated.

"Are you worried?" Jenny asked with concern.

Jack shook his head. "*Not yet* anyway."

"You know, I can help stay on top of this," Jenny offered, seeing her father's distress. "Give me Aunt Kathy's phone number and I'll keep in touch with her about it."

Jack readily complied and then checked the time on his phone. It was 9:25 AM. "Jenny, I have to get to the Lodge this morning to meet Cal Russo. Can you keep me informed?"

"Of course. I'll let you know the moment there's any update. –Also I was thinking of seeing Mom for a bit. I was planning on staying the night either here or at Mom's."

"Of course, baby girl. You know this is your home too," Jack said plainly. In these moments, it felt like forty years ago, when Jenny was a teenager. After the divorce, since Jack lived in California while the kids were growing up, he'd have Bobby and Jenny stay at his parents' house with him during the summer months for visitation. Breakfast in the summer with his kids was always so great. His mom would make everyone pancakes and sausage, and it was like no one was ever in a bad mood in those days.

"Also, I was thinking," Jenny started, "maybe you, me, and Mom can have dinner together later? I can make something. We can reminisce more about Uncle T while waiting for info on Stef."

"Sure," Jack smiled wanly. "Sounds good. Just text your old man what time we're eating."

Jack showered and changed his clothes before heading out to the Lodge. He arrived around 10:45 AM to a bustling construction site. It looked like the outdoor landscaping was underway and lodge signs were being positioned around the property. Meanwhile, a contractor was hauling rolls of carpeting into the lobby for installation in the guest rooms.

Just then, to Jack's happy surprise, Em drove into the parking lot and stopped her car next to Jack's truck. Apparently, Keith had left all of his reading glasses at the house again, so Em was bringing two pairs back to the Lodge. Em hugged Jack and expressed her sorrow over the loss of his brother Tom.

"I can't even imagine what you're going through, Jack," Em said.

"Well, we always knew that this was a possibility—that maybe he had died in a car accident or something and we just couldn't find him. But, nothing can prepare you for it really."

"Do you have any idea of what may have happened?" Em inquired.

"In my opinion, someone—or something—attacked him, and it ended in Tom's death." Jack thought Em had a good head on her shoulders, so he disclosed to her almost all of what he'd seen at the logging road.

"Do you think it was maybe...um...an animal of some type?" Em asked keenly.

"Well, sure," Jack said. "It could totally be...nonhuman. I mean, the car door was ripped off and thrown twenty feet away, so...anyway, on top of finding Tom...I just learned that Stef's duty station can't get a hold of her team in the field today."

Em frowned. "What? Is it serious?"

"That's the thing. I'm not sure," Jack said. "After finding Tom that way...I can't help but wonder if..."

"If what?" Em gently prodded when Jack said nothing more.

"If there's a connection," Jack finished. "Tom was in the woods when he died and Stef is incommunicado in the woods right now. Maybe I'm jumping to conclusions. She's been out of touch before on these field surveys, and I never worried about it then."

Em seemed about to say something and then stopped herself.

Normally, Jack wouldn't coax people into talking if they'd made a choice not to, but this time, he did. "Were you about to say something?"

After a second, Em seemed resolved and spoke without hesitation. "Jack, I'm just going to say it. I don't mean to make you feel worse, but *there are strange things in the woods around here*. I don't know if it's related to Stefanie's team, or Tom's passing, but I know it's *not normal*." She was very firm about her statement.

"Tell me what you're talking about," Jack said with curiosity.

"Three nights ago, we had just finished dinner at the house. It was around dusk and I heard police sirens outside, but when I looked out the window, there was nothing. Yet the sirens continued, and it was coming from the woods. *Inside the woods*. I checked the map later on and there's no road where those sounds were coming from. *Then...*" and now Em was getting very emphatic with her statements, "there were whooping noises calling to each other from different parts of the woods...and finally a *shriek like from a woman dying* rang out. That is *not normal*, Jack."

Jack felt some relief that he wasn't the only one experiencing strange things lately and was about to comment, but Em wasn't finished.

"*Then*, the next morning, I went out with Jessica and Martin to the blueberry patch on the grounds to pick berries. Well, Martin's dog Frisco suddenly starts staring at the woods nearby and growling loudly. The dog is so worked up over this that he eventually starts barking nonstop at something in the woods. We couldn't see anything, not from where we were standing anyway. At this point, I'm getting really nervous and suggest we just leave—especially after Martin told me earlier that his rooster got taken by some predator a few months ago. Well, the damn loudest screaming roar came from the trees and *I thought we were going*

193

*to die*. We all ran back to our houses and I kept looking back to see if anything was chasing us, but thank God nothing came."

"Oh geez," Jack said with surprise. "What did you do then?"

"I called Keith at the Lodge and told him what had happened, and then I called the Sheriff's Station to report some large animal in the woods—but Jack, it's not like a bear or a wolf. And I know that coyotes and mountain lions can make strange sounds, but whatever made that scream at the blueberry patch was *big*. And the calls going back and forth from different locations the night before? That means *there's more than one*."

"Well, it's funny you say that," Jack started. "I don't know if you're aware that I saw an intruder at the Lodge last weekend—"

"*Yes*, I am," Em interjected.

"And…it wasn't…" Was he really going to admit this to Em? Were they really on the same page?

But she finished the sentence for him, "…*human? It wasn't human*?" Em seemed angry.

Jack grimaced. "Right. It wasn't."

"Yeah, I'm tired of pretending there isn't something strange in the woods, Jack," Em said indignantly. "My kids' safety is the highest priority to me, and I just don't feel safe letting any of them anywhere near the woods. I hate to say it but it's true. Every time I'm near the forest, I feel like I'm being watched. When we were huckleberry picking, there were trees snapped in half at the first spot—what is up with that? Then, when we were blueberry picking, something screamed at us. Even at Bill's

Fourth of July Party…I got creepy vibes from the trees in his backyard." Em shuddered. "At first I thought it was just me, that maybe I was imagining things, but too many strange things are happening at the same time. What about all of the missing animals? Is that *normal* for here? Or what about the missing teenager? Why did he run into the woods instead of returning to his friends? I mean, is this a normal summer for Everton, Idaho?" Jack didn't think he'd ever heard Em say so much at once. During conversations, she was such a good listener that it was easy to just talk her ear off and never let her get a word in edgewise.

Just then Cal walked into view from around Jack's truck. "Hey, guys," said Cal somberly, "Did I just overhear you talking about something in the woods?"

"*Yes*," Em replied immediately. She was apparently not interested in beating around the bush on the topic. "Do you know something, Cal? I've watched your reporting online and I know you must hear things."

Cal snickered. "Oh, believe me, I've definitely heard things. Jack, I've got something to show you. Um, I don't know if you want to do this privately or…" Cal looked toward Em.

"Well, I don't know, does it involve a dead hooker?" Jack quipped dryly. "Because I don't know anything about that." Jack felt he had nothing to hide that a reporter might accuse him of.

Em stifled a giggle.

"Fine," Cal said unfazed. "I was examining the photos that Liam and I took around the Lodge on Monday—after the interview—and we found something odd."

Jack and Em looked at each other. Cal held up a manila folder and asked, "Where can we look at these?"

Jack scanned the parking lot, then said, "Let's use the Bike Shack. It has a small office."

"Jack, do you want me to hang back?" Em asked, although she was clearly interested in what Cal wanted to present.

Jack looked at Em and said, "Nah, come on," then gestured with his head toward the Bike Shack, which was isolated at the south end of the parking lot, away from the rest of the Lodge. It contained a large bicycle garage and a small office for managing the equipment.

Once inside the office, Cal opened up the manila folder and held several 8x10 photos in his hand. He placed the first photo on the desk. It depicted Jack standing next to Keith and Andrew near the Bike Shack, where they'd done the interview. It was a wide shot that captured the forest beyond. The nascent bike trail was evident behind them that led into the forest. The trail clearly needed more work.

"Okay...?" Jack said.

Without comment, Cal placed another photo next to the first. It looked almost identical, except that Andrew's arms were positioned slightly differently in this one.

"Yeah...?" Jack said.

Cal pointed to a patch of trees in the first photo where the bike trail entered the woods. It was hard to discern anything of significance there.

"Okay," Jack said, "What are we looking at?" Jack turned to Em for a clue but she shrugged, seeing nothing either.

"Now look at that same spot in the second photo," Cal instructed them.

Jack's eyeballs nearly fell out of his head.

"*Holy crap*," Em blurted.

Where there was previously nothing in the first photo, the second photo depicted a large, dark silhouette in the woods peeking out from behind a tree. There were bushes and saplings growing in that area, so mainly the head, one shoulder, and the torso were visible. It didn't seem to have a neck. Even with the figure being off in the distance, you could tell it was taller than a normal human being and definitely more massive. If you weren't looking for it, you could easily miss the figure in the tapestry of the forest.

Cal placed a third photo on the desk. "Here. I've blown it up for you."

"Oh God," Em whispered. "You can see the eyes." Jack saw two red dots where the eyes should be—definitely unsettling.

Jack's first thought was, *Did this kill Tom?—And my Dad?*

"This thing…" Em started, "It's in the woods…*near my house.*" She was obviously uncomfortable and worried.

"What do you mean?" Cal asked. So Em repeated her experiences at the house hearing the strange calls and screams in the woods, including Frisco's aggressive reaction to something in the trees.

Cal took a folded paper out of the manila file and opened it up to reveal an area map with certain points highlighted in yellow marker. He pointed to the trail head near McArthur Lake, saying, "Two days ago, I heard a similar scream at this trail where Steven Mahakian came out of the woods. –And I have an audio recording." He took out a yellow highlighter.

"My son recorded some of the whooping from my house too," Em added.

Cal said, "Can I get a copy of that?" Em nodded. Then he continued, "Where's your rental house, Em? Here?" Em corrected Cal by pointing to an area a couple of inches away from his original guess. Cal marked it. Then he said, "The Lodge is here," and pointed to another highlighted spot. "This is Indian Creek Campground, where Steven Mahakian went missing…unfortunately, I haven't been able to get an interview with Steven, and his family and the authorities are being tightlipped about it…"

"He was chased," Jack said. "When I found him on the highway, he said they weren't human and that they herded him through the woods. He never saw them but the kid was terrified for sure."

"I was hoping that you knew something," Cal said to Jack. "Did he say why he left his friends that night? Why he didn't go back to the campfire?"

"He said something was in between him and his friends and it scared him so bad that he ran the other way—into the woods. The kid was a little delirious from exhaustion so it was hard to get clear answers from him, but he was definitely traumatized by something…or some *things*."

"Why aren't they releasing that information to the public?" Em asked.

"The family probably doesn't want any stigma on the kid," Cal explained. "Steven is set to go to one of the Federal Academies—the U.S. Merchant Marine Academy in New York—and you need a Congressional Nomination *in addition* to being accepted by the school. He was supposed to report to campus last week—when he was still missing—so I don't know what the status of his Appointment is now. But if he needs to reapply next year, I bet his parents don't want any stories of Sasquatch to screw his chances of acceptance."

"Ah," said Em. "As a parent, I get it."

"Anyway," Cal continued, "that campground area where Steven went missing is also where a fisherman and his son reported being followed in the woods near Indian Creek...the *same day* Steven went missing."

"I didn't hear about that," said Em. "What about the Nielsens' missing goat and their neighbor's missing dog? Where are *they* located?"

Cal pointed to a spot he had already highlighted.

Jack pointed to another spot and said, "This is where I found Tom."

Cal said somberly, "Right," as he highlighted that area. Then he said, "The majority of these encounters have happened in the past two weeks, not counting Tom."

"Or my Dad," Jack said. Em and Cal looked at Jack in puzzlement, so he explained what he'd recently learned about the day his father had a heart attack nearly thirty years ago—that something scared the hell out of him. It was at this same area where the Lodge now sat. Both Em and Cal were stunned.

Em was shaking her head as she said, "Well, you two are the natives here. Is this activity normal?"

"You hear stories," Cal said. "You know, a cousin's best friend's uncle once saw a hairy man in the woods for two seconds. That sort of a thing. Nothing to record in the history books and certainly nothing I ever considered seriously. I'm a reporter and I need facts to write a story. But *now?* Not only have I witnessed something personally, but I'm seeing photographic evidence and hearing audio evidence of something real in the woods."

"Heck, I have video of this thing at the Lodge last weekend," Jack said.

"What?!" Cal exclaimed.

"Don't get all hot and bothered," Jack cautioned. "The Sheriff's deputies looked at it and wouldn't commit to it being more than maybe a big guy in a fur coat. The video wasn't great because it was at night and badly lit. But I saw it from about fifteen feet away—*it wasn't a guy in a fur coat.* We've had a night watchman on duty since Tuesday and he's been reviewing all of the surveillance footage we had of the prior days. He hasn't seen any other activity so far."

"Jack," Cal began, "Like I said, I'm a reporter, and there's definitely a story here. If you look at the map, there are incursions going further and further south from Priest Lake, all coming closer and closer to Everton. For some reason these things are moving south now. So what I want to know is, what are you going to do about the Lodge? I'm not trying to ruin your business—heck, I'm actually in favor of the Lodge being built

200

here—but this thing in the woods…this Lodge is firmly located in its perceived territory. If you consider that something scared your father here almost thirty years ago, and that this photo shows one of those things right here on the property *this week*…well, I think we can assume they live here. And they're going to keep coming."

Jack actually hadn't even been thinking about the consequences for the Lodge project. He'd been fully consumed with figuring out Tom's and his father's deaths. Part of him didn't care about the Lodge at all in this moment, but he knew he'd have to consider how to move forward with this venture. He'd need to talk to Bill and David again…soon.

"Jack," Cal continued, "I'm going to approach my editor about doing a story on this thing in the woods. I consider it a public safety issue. I'm giving you advance warning because it's going to affect your business."

"Give me a few days, Cal," said Jack. "I need to figure this out with my business partners."

Cal replied, "I'll tell you when it goes to print—if I can even get my editor to approve it—but even if he doesn't approve, people need to know about this. I'm committed to making the community aware of this issue. How many people have to get hurt before we do something?"

"What about local law enforcement," asked Em. "Can't they do something about this?"

Cal was shaking his head. "I reported my incident to them just like you reported yours. I even played my audio for them."

"What did they say?" Em inquired.

"The same answer. It's a bear or someone playing pranks. Jack had video and they didn't put much credence in *that*."

"Well, what about *these* photos?" Em continued. "They're real enough for me."

"I'm done going to the deputies," Cal replied. "They'll just say the light and shadow are playing tricks on the eye—or that it's a publicity stunt by the Lodge. No. This is where journalism has to force the issue with the authorities. I've got to get the public interested and aware so that there's pressure for the Sheriff—and maybe the Mayor—to look into this seriously."

"By the way, Cal," Jack said. "You'll probably want to know about this—"

"About what?" Cal asked as he started picking up the photos.

Jack continued, "Stef's duty station is having a hard time reaching her team on the satellite phones today. They're checking with the satellite company for problems."

Cal stopped picking up the photos. "So they think there's a problem with the phones?"

"They don't know what the problem is," Jack clarified. "It sounds like they're starting with the satellite company for answers. It seems that Stef's team can send messages out but doesn't receive messages. Her team has sent daily check-in text messages, but when the duty station tries to contact them, they don't respond."

Cal was silent for a moment as he stepped away from the desk. "That's not okay," he said as he started pacing in the small office. Cal was clearly upset with himself and clearly convinced that this had something to do with the large creature that all three of them had had encounters with. "We need to go out there."

From Cal's reaction, Jack wondered if he and Stefanie were more than just friends. Stefanie hadn't mentioned dating Cal, but that didn't mean anything. She was a very reserved person—cautious to a fault. She didn't want to get hurt and kept herself emotionally isolated, which was probably the result of having such unreliable parents.

"Well, wait," Jack said as he held up his hands to calm Cal down. "We don't know yet what's wrong. Could just be a problem with the phones." After speculating internally himself that it *was* Bigfoot, Jack found it strange that he was now trying to dissuade Cal from assuming that very same thing.

Cal came back to the desk. "Stef was supposed to be north of Upper Priest Lake." Cal held the highlighter above the map as he looked for the vicinity.

"Yeah," Jack nodded. "I don't know the exact location for her team at this point though."

"I know where she's supposed to be," Cal said as he chose a specific spot in the area above Upper Priest Lake to highlight. "I talked to her last Saturday when she and her crew were in Coolin to resupply and grab a shower."

Jack perked up at that information. "Really?"

"Yeah," Cal replied. "The field crew drove into town to charge their batteries and get some wi-fi to upload data. Coolin is an easy point to resupply. The drive from Coolin to wherever they were going was about two hours, some of it on Forest Service roads. They park on the road and hike in the rest of the way, but they come back to town on the weekend."

Jack thought if Stef and Cal were talking during her down times from her work trip, then they were definitely more than just friends. Jack asked, "Did she say anything on the phone? About anything weird happening?"

"No," Cal started, "but I wouldn't doubt that she hides things from me so I won't nag her about being more careful. I was very adamant that she not go on this trip right now. After weeks of missing animal reports, I figured that a lot of grizzlies or something were coming into the area this summer.—And I know she can handle herself in the woods, but this was *a lot* of missing animals, okay? Like *eighteen* in three weeks at that point. Now it's more."

"I didn't hear about that," said Jack.

"My editor put it in the print and online editions of the paper, and I did a social media post about it," Cal explained. "The Sheriff's Department also posted warnings about predators in the area on their social media accounts." Cal shrugged.

"When was this?" Em asked.

"Around the last week of June," Cal replied. "Like they say, if you're not looking for something, you probably won't notice it. It's just background noise to you if it's not an immediate issue in your life right then."

Cal began picking up the photos and the map when Jack asked if he could have copies. Cal let Jack keep the 8x10s since he already had the digital originals, and said he'd be in touch if there were any new developments in the story. Jack promised to let Cal know any news on Stefanie.

After Cal left the office, Em asked, "What are you going to do, Jack?"

Jack leaned against the desk in thought. "I don't know. The most important thing to me right now is getting in touch with Stefanie. Hopefully I'll hear soon that they've fixed the phone problem."

Em was nodding in agreement.

"Beyond that, if we're talking about the Lodge, this is my family's legacy. It's not the money that's at issue for me at this moment—though I'm sure my business partners, Bill and David, will feel differently—but these things have haunted my family for generations, and I was completely unaware."

Just then, the office door opened and Keith stuck his head in saying, "Em, there you are—where are my glasses?"

"Keith," Jack said. "I need to have a meeting with Bill and David first, but after that, we're probably going to have a discussion with you and Andrew on possible changes to the project."

Keith furrowed his brow in confusion. "Okay…"

Jack said, "I'm sure Em can fill you in. I've got to make some phone calls. Can I have the office?"

Em and Keith left while Jack rung up his business partners asking them to meet at the Lodge this afternoon. Unfortunately, Bill and David were both out of town, but could be back in Everton to meet tomorrow morning. It would have to do.

Jack checked his text messages and saw that Jenny planned to make dinner at his place tonight. In all of this turmoil, he looked forward to spending time with Jenny and Ellen.

He decided to call Kathy to get an update on the search. "Kathy, any word yet on finding Stef?"

"No, Jack," Kathy replied anxiously. "I'm worried. I know she's done field work in remote locations before, but I've actually reached her by cell phone a couple of times in those remote spots. That's why this time bothers me."

"Has Jenny contacted you yet? I have some meetings scheduled for the next day or so, but Jenny can help with calling people if I'm in the middle of something." Jack said.

"Yes," Kathy replied. "I already spoke with her. –You know, Stefanie's supervisor kept telling me earlier that there's probably nothing to worry about, that it's not unusual to lose satellite reception in the forest. Even satellite phones experience spotty coverage. Or they might have let the battery run out on their sat-phones."

"Well, I certainly have no faith in technology," Jack said.

"Same here," Kathy said in frustration. "I don't know what to do, Jack. I don't know if I should be worried or not."

"Just keep on top of the duty station. That's all we can do for now. Let me know what happens either way and we'll go from there. I'll drive anywhere to look for her myself if need be."

"Thank you, Jack," Kathy said before they hung up.

Jack looked at his watch. It was already 2:15 PM. Jack decided he wanted to go home and rest.

He left the Bike Shack and stood outside on the adjacent bike trail, which was simply a dirt path at the moment. At some point, a work crew would be laying asphalt into the forest to form a 2-mile loop that circled back to the Lodge. Jack stared at the trail's entrance into the woods, steeling his nerves in case he saw any shadowy figures lurking among the trees. He didn't see anything, but that didn't mean something wasn't watching him.

*What was he going to do about the Lodge? And was Stef okay?*

Later that night, after dinner, Jack got a call from Kathy saying that a firmware update had happened recently, which was probably causing the glitches with the satellite phone. Stef's supervisor said that three of Stefanie's crew came back in from the field late today and called the duty station from Coolin. The crewmembers indicated that they hadn't realized there was a problem with the satellite phones because all of their outgoing messages seemed to transmit just fine, but they admitted that their phones didn't receive any incoming messages while in the field during the last day or so.

Apparently, Stefanie and another crewmember had stayed in the field while the others came back to town tonight to upload data. Stef and her partner were to hike out to the last site, camp overnight, and collect data there tomorrow—Friday. In fact, Kathy said with some relief, Stefanie had transmitted a sat-phone message to her supervisor just this evening. Stef communicated that they had successfully set up camp and would send another message in the morning before starting their survey. They were scheduled to return to town tomorrow afternoon.

Since Stef and her partner were able to transmit outgoing messages, her supervisor was inclined to let them complete their survey without interruption—unless Kathy insisted that the family emergency was dire and that they needed to send someone in the field to get Stef. Kathy told the supervisor that their news could wait until Stefanie returned.

"I hope you don't mind, Jack," Kathy said with trepidation. "I just thought that one day wouldn't matter at this point. You know how much she cares about her work."

"No, that's fine," Jack replied. He too was extremely relieved that Stef was fine. It suddenly didn't seem so urgent to tell her about finding Tom. Let her finish her survey in peace. Telling her right this second wouldn't change what had happened to her father. "We'll tell her when she comes back tomorrow."

Jack silently thanked God that Stef was safe. She would finish her survey tomorrow and he could talk to her about finding Tom then. Now he could turn his focus back to the problem at the Lodge.

# Chapter 12

## July 16 – Friday

Jack woke up to his cell phone ringing. He looked at the clock on his nightstand—the time was 6:42 AM. He picked up his phone and saw that Andrew Colgan was calling him. Jack usually woke up on his own by about 5:30 AM, so it was strange that he'd slept in this long, but it was probably related to the emotional toll he was suffering from both finding Tom and not knowing if Stefanie was okay. The project manager for Gibson Drake must have something important to say if he was calling this early.

"Hello," Jack said with a frog in his throat. He tried to clear it.

"Jack, it's Andrew. I'm sorry to bother you at this hour, but I thought you'd want to know that some vandalism occurred at the Lodge about two hours ago."

"What?" Jack was fully awake now.

"Yeah, the security guard—Fred Cross—was in the Security Office reviewing the backlog of surveillance footage around 4:30 AM when he heard a crashing noise out front. When he got to the lobby, he saw that a large rock had been thrown through the glass door. It was a dangerous mess."

"Oh damn," Jack commented.

"Fred didn't see anyone through the lobby windows, but no other rocks were thrown. He called 911 right then and deputies arrived around 5:15 AM. I'm at the Lodge now. If you look at the Lodge from the outside, it's the right side Lobby door that needs to be completely replaced."

Jack was getting out of bed as Andrew talked. "Can you leave everything the way it is until I get there? Don't clean it up. I want to see it."

"Sure, Jack."

"What about surveillance footage?" Jack asked.

"Bill had the security company install additional cameras in the parking lot a few days ago, and the lighting around the Lodge is much brighter now since we installed the permanent light fixtures, but we still didn't catch the perpetrator on video."

"How is that possible?!" Jack asked as he put Andrew on speaker to pull his pants on.

"Because the rock was thrown from beyond the parking lot lights...it was thrown from the woods...south of the Lodge." Andrew spoke without emotion, but Jack could tell that Andrew was wound up pretty tight from this development.

"So, the rock was thrown from eighty to a hundred feet away? Beyond the Bike Shack on the other side of the parking lot?" Jack asked in amazement.

"Yes," Andrew answered. "I watched the parking lot camera footage myself with the deputies. The cameras didn't capture the perpetrator because we don't have cameras in the woods."

After a moment of silence, Jack asked, "How big is the rock?"

Andrew replied flatly, "It's about fourteen inches across. Weighs about…fifteen to twenty pounds." The information was so stunning that Andrew didn't need any histrionics to convey the extraordinary circumstances.

"What did the deputies say?" Jack inquired sullenly.

"They didn't say anything other than they'd write up the report."

"No speculation on who did this?"

Andrew actually snorted then. "No speculation whatsoever, Jack."

Jack ran a hand through his hair and shook his head. "Okay, I'll be there in thirty minutes. Hold the fort."

"Yes, sir," Andrew replied tersely before hanging up.

After washing his face and brushing his teeth, Jack knocked on his daughter's bedroom door and poked his head in. "Jenny?" Jack said quietly.

"Mmmnn," Jenny turned over to look at her father through squinty eyes. "Dad?"

"Jenny, there's been some vandalism at the Lodge. I'm gonna go check it out. I'll call you if anything happens."

"Geez, Dad, what is going on with that lodge?" Jenny asked in irritation. "Is it really Bigfoot like Mom says?"

"Eh, she told you about that?" Jack asked with some embarrassment.

"Of course she did," Jenny replied. "You know, Dad, I won't think you're crazy. You can tell me this stuff too."

"Yeah…okay," Jack conceded. "Look, I'll call you later."

Jenny mumbled an "okay" as Jack closed the door.

Jack made it to the Lodge around 7:30 AM. Work crews were present but the mutilated front door caused some disarray in everybody's work flow. It wasn't really safe to enter through the lobby so workers were using side entrances. Jack saw Andrew standing out front with Keith.

"Guys," Jack started as he glanced at the shattered glass on the entryway pavers. The front doors were eight feet tall and mostly glass so there were a lot of shards scattered about. "Still no footage of the perpetrator?"

Keith spoke up. "None so far. Fred left at the end of his shift at 6:30 AM after giving his statement to the deputies, but I reviewed some of the footage before and after the event. Nothing."

"Any guesses?" Jack asked.

"I would assume," said Andrew, "that the suspicious intruder from last weekend is involved."

"Were any of the props damaged?" Jack inquired.

"No," Keith answered confidently.

"I want to see that rock and the video," Jack stated. "After that, we can have people clean this up. I assume you've got photos for insurance?"

Andrew said he'd text the pictures to Jack right now.

Jack got inside through the restaurant entrance and easily found the offending rock at the foot of a coyote prop in the lobby. Jack took a few of his own photos and then picked up the rock. It was damn heavy. Jack brought the rock with him to the Security Office and sat down to review the video.

Sure enough, several cameras captured the rock whizzing through the air and striking the lobby door. Then the lobby video showed Fred rushing out from the Security Office holding a baton as he looked out the front windows. Jack rewound the parking lot footage to the point at which the rock emerged from the woods. He gauged the position in relation to the Bike Shack, then left the Security Office to find the project managers.

"Andrew," Jack said when he found him still out front talking to several crew leaders. "Did you or the deputies search the area in the woods where the rock was thrown from?"

"Yes, they searched and I accompanied them." Andrew was shaking his head. "We didn't find anything."

"Take me to the spot. From the footage, it seemed to be right over there," Jack said as he pointed to an area beyond the Bike Shack.

Andrew walked Jack over to the area he and the deputies had previously searched. Jack surveyed the foliage and the dirt for clues. The ground was covered in bark and pine needles, so no footprints were evident. He even tried looking for tufts of fur or broken branches but saw nothing.

Jack turned to look at the Lodge from this vantage point. Whoever threw the rock all the way to the Lodge's front doors must have been a record-breaking shot-putter. Jack would have liked to talk to the security guard, but the guy had just finished a 12-hour shift, so he probably wouldn't be too keen on Jack calling right now. Jack decided to talk to Fred Cross when he came back to the Lodge for his security shift at 6:30 this evening.

Jack returned to the Security Office to review some of the footage backlog while he waited for Bill and David to show up for their meeting at 9 AM. There was nothing on the video that Jack could find other than the two established incidents on record—the intruder that Jack witnessed in person and the rock thrown early this morning.

Jack's business partners arrived on time bearing coffee and doughnuts. After Bill and David inspected the vandalized front door and viewed the video footage, Jack suggested they move to the Bike Shack to talk. Jack grabbed a folder from his truck as they walked through the parking lot to his de facto office.

Once they were in private, Jack said, "Guys, this thing at the Lodge is getting serious now."

The other two agreed.

David stated, "You think it's our hairy friend from the weekend."

"Yes," Jack replied. "And *Cousin It* is escalating the conflict. A nighttime Peeping Tom is one thing. Throwing projectiles through the front door is war." Jack hadn't meant to frame it that way, but after he said it, he realized he meant it.

"Are we sure this specific instance isn't a human?" Bill queried.

214

Jack snorted. "Well, then I guess we have an unknown Olympic shot-putter living in Everton who *hates* the Lodge. And just to make it clear what we're dealing with..." Jack opened the folder he'd grabbed from his truck to show his business partners Cal's photos of the dark figure in the woods.

David was amazed that the thing was caught on camera fairly clearly. "Is that the bike trail into the woods? Right near this office?" David asked as he pointed through the Bike Shack's wall to the nearby forest.

"Yup," Jack said.

Bill scowled. "Well, now we *really* have to do something about this. It's real. It's making trouble."

"Yes," said David, "but is it all that surprising? It obviously considers this area its territory—going all the way back to Jack's dad if not earlier than that. No one has been up here for generations, and then suddenly we're building a major structure in its home. How would *you* react?"

Bill retorted, "I'm not saying I wouldn't do the same thing in its place, but what are you suggesting we do, David? Pack up the whole operation and leave? That *is not* an option."

"I'm not sure what we should do, Bill," David replied in irritation, "but do you honestly think we'd be able to operate a Lodge here with families in residence? *For God's sake*, there's a bike trail going into the woods! Are we just going to advertise that as part of the experience?"

Then David mockingly assumed the air of a circus showman and said, "Do you like *jump scares*, boys and girls? Well you're in luck! Take a bike ride into the unknown and see Bigfoot scare the living snot out of you and your whole family! It's just like the Yeti on the Matterhorn Ride in Disneyland!—Except *this* Bigfoot *is real!* Hope you make it out alive! He's so unpredictable!"

Jack sat with his arms crossed listening to the exchange. In all honesty, he wasn't sure what they should do, but he was convinced that eventually these encounters would result in someone getting injured…or worse.

"It's an *animal*," Bill stated. "So we treat it like an animal. We run it out of here just like we would an errant bear or a mountain lion. *We* are the dominant species and the dominant species always pushes out competitors in its territory."

"I'm not so sure that we're the dominant species, Bill," David returned. "Sure, there are probably more of us humans, but perhaps we're like the wildebeests in Africa. Their sheer numbers ensure the wildebeests' overall survival, but in a one-on-one confrontation with a lion, who wins? From what Jack has said about his encounter, it sounds like Bigfoot wins—*every time.*"

"We have the technology and we have the brains," Bill countered. "We send out a team of hunters to push this thing out of the area back to wherever it came from and to cow it into submission. This is, after all, Jack's land. Is he supposed to just abandon the idea of ever using it?"

"Of course it's Jack's land," David agreed, "but those things also think it's *their* land. And we have to be realistic about the chances of eradicating their presence here."

"Then we build out even more than we've done now," Bill suggested. "We push this project to make a commercial village up here with *triple* the human presence. Do you think these things weren't visiting the lakes and rivers around Everton a few hundred years ago? When no humans were around? But the more people that settled here, the more pressure there was for them to leave. *I* certainly haven't heard of Bigfoot walking through downtown Everton in *my* lifetime. Pushing them out *works*."

"Maybe," David said. "Or maybe they're like bears that never completely leave an area. Their presence may wax and wane, but bears certainly don't see boundaries when it comes to raiding trashcans."

Bill looked to Jack in exasperation. "Jack, you've been awfully quiet. You wanna chime in here?"

Jack sat quietly for a moment. They both made valid points and Jack wasn't getting a good gut feeling one way or the other on what to do. Bill's approach seemed pretty heavy-handed with no guarantee of positive results. On the other hand, David's advocacy on the creature's behalf was somewhat off-putting. Jack was a conservationist, but he also wanted to develop the land for the prosperity of his family and his town. Letting animals have all of the wilderness and never pushing into new territory was a ridiculous notion. There were still vast tracts of land that no human had ever set foot on in America—and particularly in Idaho. Jack didn't feel guilty about using roughly two square miles for the Grizzly Bear Lodge and its activities.

Jack finally spoke. "I agree with you both in part. I'm with David in that I don't think this issue is easily solved. But I'm also with Bill in that we need to push back on these incursions. Remember, these things have seemingly had a hand in the deaths of both my father and my brother, and that doesn't sit well with me. I don't recall any of *us* killing one of *them*. And this *is* my land. I'm not ceding it to a hairy wild man. If they were just coming around to look—maybe steal a sandwich or two—I wouldn't really care, but that's not what happened this morning."

"So it sounds like you're *with me* on this," said Bill.

"Well, I like your passive-aggressive option, Bill—building up even more out here," said Jack. "The problem is *it'll cost even more*."

David was shaking his head. "Assuming that plan actually solves the Bigfoot problem—and that's a *big* assumption—we wouldn't see any profit for *years and years*. Not to mention the added time to fund, design, and build this so-called village. I kind of wanted to still be alive when this project started putting out some cashflow. –What about if we repurpose the site from an entertainment proposition to a scientific endeavor?"

"What do you mean?" Jack asked. "A place for studying Bigfoot?"

David shrugged. "Sure, why not?"

Bill rolled his eyes. "Oh for crying out loud—can we get some serious suggestions here? Since when has studying Bigfoot ever turned up anything solid? And who's going to pay to come traipse around the woods hoping to get a glimpse of Sasquatch? Seriously, who?"

"*I don't know*—I'm just brainstorming!" David retorted. "Sure, it'll require some research. Doesn't mean it won't work."

"Right," Jack said, "what we need is more information. Maybe we should hire some experienced hunters to scope out the surrounding area and see if they find any evidence of Bigfoot. See if they can give us real information like nesting sites or prey animal caches. Maybe they can put up trail cams. Once we have more information, we can make better decisions. *Meanwhile*, we continue construction and increase security measures."

"What do you mean?" asked Bill. "Like add more security guards? Maybe *armed* security guards?"

"Sure," Jack answered. "More guards, more shifts…"

"Great," David said sarcastically. "Sounds like the warden has the prison completely under control. Now we just need to add some guard towers with search lights—and gun turrets—then we'll be *all set!* I mean, what family wouldn't *love*—"

Bill interjected snidely, "Oh stop being so melodramatic, David!"

"Guys, look," Jack said with his hands up as a peacemaker, "my son is coming up tomorrow from Boise. I'll ask him to scope out the area and see what he thinks—see if he can find any signs of them. Meanwhile, we *should* add more guards. Maybe have two men at night since that's when they seem active. Agreed?"

Bill and David both acquiesced. Bill said he'd get the security company to send another guard for the night shift as soon as possible, but he didn't think it would happen for a few days.

219

Jack decided to stay at the Lodge while the other two left. He went around talking to random workers, asking if they noticed anything unusual on the job site. Other than the incident with the safety fencing that Frank Tiller had mentioned on Monday, no one else came forward with a story.

Jack remembered that he needed to update Andrew and Keith about the decisions from the meeting with Bill and David. Unfortunately, both of them were in the middle of supervising important installations, so he asked them to stay for a little bit after the work crews left for the day. They agreed.

Jack's phone rang and he saw that it was the coroner's office. The coroner called to let Jack know they had the results of the autopsy. As Jack told Ellen earlier, the official report wouldn't be ready for a few weeks, but Jack knew the coroner personally through community organizations. The coroner knew that Jack's family had suffered a lot from Tom's disappearance and wanted to let Jack know unofficially what he'd discovered.

First, dental records confirmed that the remains belonged to Tom Evers. Second, the bones had been exposed to both freeze-thaw weathering and wet-dry weathering. This caused some disintegration of the bone matter, however, they were still able to determine that the skull—which had been partially buried under detritus over time—had experienced blunt force trauma on the back of the head. Basically, after studying the fracture pattern, the coroner determined that a hard, flat object impacted the back of Tom's skull. Someone could have hit him with the flat part of a shovel blade, or Tom could have fallen to the ground and landed on a large rock. It wasn't clear if the impact was the ultimate cause of death, but it was a definite possibility if it resulted in severe bleeding to the brain. Third, they didn't have a full skeleton to work with, which was attributed to animal scavenging, therefore, they weren't sure if Tom sustained any other injuries. Tom's jacket was still zipped up and intact when he was found, which lent credence to the theory that he was not attacked by a wild animal—he probably wasn't killed as prey.

Jack also learned that they didn't find any blood on Tom's clothing, which further supported the theory that it wasn't a wild animal attack. Jack didn't think it was a bear or a mountain lion that got his brother. He thought it was something just as wild but more calculating and intelligent than any predator he'd heard of.

Jack thanked the coroner and asked when the family could take the remains for a proper burial. It sounded like they could make arrangements for next week. Jack really didn't want to make any decisions without Stefanie.

A food truck was in the parking lot when Jack came out of the Bike Shack from talking to the coroner. His growling stomach told him he should grab a burger, so he hung out with some of the crew for lunch.

Afterward, Jack went to the Security Office to watch more security footage in the backlog. The nightwatchman Fred Cross was trying to get through it all but it was a lot, even on fast-forward. The monotony of the footage was broken by an occasional deer or mountain lion wandering around the premises—in color at that.

After Jack's encounter with the hairy intruder last Saturday, Bill had insisted on updating the cameras with color night vision and infrared. In low light, the cameras would still see in color. If there were zero illumination, the cameras would turn on infrared lighting in the immediate area and the video would switch to black and white. Unfortunately, anything further away than ten feet would not appear very clearly. These updated cameras were installed around the Lodge a couple of days ago, as well as in the parking lot—sixteen cameras total for inside and outside. Who would have guessed that they should have installed cameras in the surrounding woods too? Anyway, sixteen cameras recording 24/7 generated a lot of video.

Jack had been watching for about two hours when his cell phone rang from a number he didn't recognize.

"Hello," Jack answered.

"Hello, Mr. Evers?" asked a voice cautiously. It sounded like a young guy to Jack.

"Yes, speaking."

"Mr. Evers, this is Steven Mahakian. You found me on Route 95 a few days ago."

That took Jack by surprise. "Hello, Steven," he replied lightly. "How are you? I haven't heard anything in the news. Are you okay?"

"Yes, sir," Steven replied nervously.

"I'm glad to hear that. What can I do for you, son?"

"Well, Mr. Evers, as you know I...I was really out of it when you found me, and I'm not sure what I said, but I wanted to ask you not to tell anyone about it."

Interesting. "Well, Steven, I'll certainly respect your wishes, but I'm just curious as to why you don't want me to talk about it."

"My parents are concerned that it would reflect badly on me...when I go to the Merchant Marine Academy...my parents don't want any stories to follow me there."

"Ah...Are you going there soon?"

"The Academy is allowing me to defer my entry until next year because of what happened."

"Well that's good," Jack responded. "But I don't think you have anything to be ashamed of, son."

"I...I don't know what to think about it, sir," Steven said with discomfort.

"Have you told anyone about your experience? Your parents? Or the deputies?"

"Yes...they...they uh..." Steven trailed off. "They think it was probably bears or something."

"Is that what *you* think they were?" Jack asked evenly.

"I..." Steven didn't finish his sentence.

"Steven, when I found you, you said you were being chased through the forest, and that the things that were chasing you weren't human. And *I* believe you," Jack said sincerely. "I believe some type of creature, or creatures, chased you through the forest. And do you want to know why I believe you?"

"…Why?" Steven asked tentatively.

"I believe you because I saw one of them myself a couple of days before I found you on the road."

"*You did?*" Steven asked in surprise.

"Yeah," Jack said, "at the Lodge I'm building near town. And I was *scared out of my wits,* kid. I can't imagine what it was like for you, being chased like that for days."

"What did it look like?" Steven asked quietly.

Jack sighed. "It was about eight feet tall, probably taller actually— and it was *massive.* It had hair all over its body. And it had red eyes that shone in the dark. I was frozen in place. It was about fifteen feet away and I thought I was a dead man. I'm lucky I didn't fall over trying to get away—damn might have broke my hip."

"Did it chase you?"

"No, son, *thank God* it didn't. It just looked at me for a bit before heading back into the forest."

"Then why did they come after *me?*" Steven asked in exasperation. "What did *I* do?" Jack could hear the pent up emotion in Steven's voice, asking why he deserved what had happened to him.

"I don't know why they picked on you, Steven. Look, I need to figure this out too," Jack explained. "They're visiting my property and I'm scared someone's going to get hurt. I won't go public with anything you told me that night, or anything you tell me now, but I'd *really like to know* everything that happened to you. I need to know if they're dangerous so I can figure out what to do. Can you help me?"

Steven hesitated for a minute. "Well…if you promise not to repeat it—because I'll deny it in public—"

"I swear," Jack said. "I won't make any public statements about whatever you tell me."

Steven was silent for a bit, and then he said, "That night, I went off to…to take a leak in the woods. Everyone was laughing and being loud at the campfire and I wanted to hurry up and get back to them. I only went to the other side of the cars—they were parked on the other side of the turnout—I didn't even go into the trees. When I turned to go back, I saw something crouched down between the two parked cars. It was too dark to see clearly, but I could also sense that it was there, if that makes sense? I don't know if I made a noise or stepped on a twig, but suddenly it turned its head back and looked at me. I…" Steven stopped talking for a bit.

"What happened then?" Jack probed. He knew the kid was traumatized, but Jack really needed to know what happened.

"Sorry…it's hard to talk about. It was probably the scariest thing I'd seen in real life at the time. I…I saw its eyes. They were yellow…but like…predatory…or angry even…" Steven started breathing hard. "I was scared. I ran the opposite way without really thinking. I just wanted to get away. Before I knew it, I was in the woods and clueless about the direction I was heading in. I wanted to get back to my friends and could still hear them and see the fire, so I tried to circle around and exit the woods directly next to the campfire, but…" Jack heard Steven struggle.

225

"It's okay, Steven. Take your time." Then Jack asked himself yet again if he was a bastard for making the kid re-live this stuff, but he ignored the thought. He *needed to know everything.*

Steven got his breathing under control and continued. "I tried to head back to the fire, but something growled at me from the tree I was heading toward. The sound came from *up in the tree,* so I looked up there—something must have been sitting or standing on one of the lower branches—I saw red eyes looking down at me. *God, I was so scared.* I ran the other way again. And I kept running.

"I don't know how long it was before I stopped. I tried to use my phone then, but it wasn't in any of my pockets—I don't know when it fell out. I tried to get a sense of which way to go, but it was really hard with all of the trees blocking the sky, and there was almost no moon. It was so dark. I got tired after a while. I tried to rest because it was pointless to travel with it being so dark. At some point, *they* found me...and this time, they were...screaming at me. I ran to get away from them." Steven took a moment to collect himself again.

In a more normal voice, Steven continued, "I *tried* to get back to the campfire a couple more times, but something always blocked my way. So I ran the opposite way—stopping sometimes if I got winded—all the way up till sunrise. Then I'd try to find somewhere to rest in some thick brush or something.

"That's pretty much what the days were like. I'd run until I felt like I'd gotten away. They seemed to leave me alone during the daytime, but I don't think they ever stopped watching me. I'd be lucky enough to run into creeks and get water that way. I tried to follow the creeks because I knew they'd eventually lead to a lake or back to town, especially if I just went downhill. But sometimes I didn't have a choice which direction to go—I always went *opposite* from them...from their screams and growls.

"It was mainly at night when they would harass me. That was *their time*. They wouldn't tolerate me staying in one place at night. I finally found a hiking trail—I found out later it was the ICT. I just followed it. I can't remember exactly which day I found the trail. There were plenty of berries along the dirt path, so that's what I ate the entire time. Even when they screamed at me when it was dark, or threw rocks in my direction, I just tried to stay on the trail. I thought I would die out there. When the trail ended at McArthur Lake, I couldn't believe it. I had almost given up hope. I didn't know what lake it was, but I saw a few houses and streetlights nearby. And then I found the highway and started walking toward what I hoped was south. I guess that's when you found me."

Jack was a little surprised that Steven had told him so much. It must have been somewhat cathartic to let it all out to someone who believed you, someone who didn't question your sanity. Someone who'd encountered the same thing you did and knew the fear.

"Thank you, Steven, for sharing that with me," Jack said. "Can I ask you something? Do you think they're intelligent? Like us?"

"Like us?" Steven thought for a second. "I don't know if their minds work like ours, but they definitely had a goal... they were trying to get me to move from one place to another. But I don't think they want to be friends if you're asking that. They're not like dogs or dolphins—or even

227

gorillas. Humans can sort of hang out with gorillas and chimpanzees—I've seen the movies and the documentaries. I don't...I don't think we can hang out with these things."

"Yeah," Jack said glumly. "I'm not sure if they'll stay away from the Lodge or if they'll keep coming—even after we get a lot of visitors and guests. But I don't want anyone to get hurt."

"Well, I can tell you this, Mr. Evers," Steven said with confidence, "they're not afraid of us."

"Why do they hide then?" Jack asked, genuinely curious. To date, Steven was the only person he knew who had spent so much time in contact with these things.

"My guess is that they know our numbers make us stronger. I mean, maybe they see our houses and our cars and they know we can make things that they can't. Maybe that scares them a little. But when we're alone, they know we're weak...that we don't have a chance against them. You know, all those stories about seeing a lone Bigfoot here or there? After what I went through, I don't think there's ever *just one*. If you see one, there's probably more that you *don't see* hiding and watching. But that's just my opinion."

"Well, your opinion counts for a lot," said Jack. "So, I gotta ask, do you think they would ever kill one of us?" Jack was thinking about his brother Tom.

"I..." Steven sounded like he was thinking it over. "I don't know, but I definitely felt like I was in danger the entire time I was out there."

Jack sighed. "Okay. I appreciate you talking about it. I know this wasn't easy for you."

"You're welcome, sir."

"You know," Jack said, "if you ever want to talk about it, feel free to call me."

"Thank you, sir," Steven replied.

"Can I ask you for another favor, Steven?"

"Sure."

"If I ever need more answers, if I have more questions, can I call you? You're pretty much the expert here, and I have a feeling this problem won't go away for me."

"Yeah, you can call me, sir. I don't mind."

"And I want you to know, there's more of us who've witnessed strange things than you realize. There's just not a place for us to talk about it."

"Yeah, tell me about it," Steven said. "All I know is, I'm not going into the woods ever again. I know the Merchant Marine Academy has slightly different training than the other academies—like there's an abbreviated boot camp—but if they make us go into the woods, I don't know if I can do that now. Not...not now..."

"You know what, Steven? You just take it one day at a time. One step at a time. If they want you to do something you don't want to do, then don't do it. You've already proven yourself in my book."

"Thank you, sir, but I don't think my parents see it the same way."

"Well, parents are parents. They love you and I won't ever tell you not to listen to them. I just want you to know that you're no coward for not going back into the bush."

"Thanks, Mr. Evers." After a pause, Steven said, "You know what doesn't make sense to me?"

"What's that, Steven?"

"I've been going to Priest Lake pretty much my entire life. My friends and I have hung out on those backroads *dozens* of times during high school—especially in the summer. We'd used that same turnout *at least* two times before. I *never ever* saw or heard *any* of these things before that night. *Not once.* So why now?"

"Hm," Jack thought. "Well, someone I know—who's also had an experience—thinks that they're moving further south right now for unknown reasons. They're even roving around on the edges of Everton stealing pets and livestock. But specifically why now? I don't know."

Steven was quiet for a bit. After a few beats he said, "I have nightmares about it. Sometimes I can't stop reliving it." Steven sounded scared and desperate.

"Me too," Jack admitted.

Steven was struggling to maintain his composure, but Jack could hear him breathing raggedly. And then Jack heard some sobs.

"It's okay, son. It's okay. You went through something that any tough guy would be having nightmares over. You did okay—you understand? You're a survivor. There's nothing to be ashamed of. If anyone tells you different, don't listen to them because they didn't go

230

through what you went through and they don't know crap. Seriously." There were more sobs on the other end, so Jack continued. "You did okay. If it takes a little while to get over it, then that's what it takes, Steven. There's nothing wrong with you. And you call me *any time* to talk about it, if you need to get things off your chest, *you call me.* I'll be there for you, Steven. You understand?"

"Okay, Mr. Evers," Steven replied with a sniffle. After exhaling a few times, Steven said, "I can hear my Mom parking in the driveway— she's back from the store…I'd better get off the phone before she gets in the house. They don't really want me to talk to you."

"Okay, Steven. You take care of yourself, son. And if you ever need anything, you let me know."

"Thank you, sir."

Jack was glad that Steven had called him. That kid had been through hell and lived to tell the tale, except that it was a tale most people didn't want to believe. There was no proof of what Steven experienced, so people would rather he just kept quiet about it. That's the mindset. The problem with that is, if you never acknowledge the problem, you can't ever formulate a solution. And Jack needed a solution for the Lodge.

Jack continued watching the camera footage for another couple of hours until he noticed on one of the active monitors that work crews were finishing up for the day. He left the Security Office to check the progress on the Lodge. He saw that Roy was positioned in a corner of the lobby so that guests could take pictures with him without impeding the through-traffic at the entryway. A lot of the rolled up carpeting was still piled up in various places.

There were three coyotes in the middle of the lobby that needed to be installed in their final positions on the side of the Security Office. Work crews had yet to finish the wall scape and raised platform, which would be fashioned into a forest floor for the coyote pack.

Jack walked past the front desk to the Great Room which housed a big, stone fireplace at the far end and antler chandeliers hanging from the vaulted ceiling. There were going to be mounted elk and deer heads on the walls here eventually. For now, the animal heads were propped against the walls. Scattered around the room were the moose element, two elk, a mountain lion, and a mother bear and cub. The last two would remain in this room to provide a family atmosphere. Who couldn't relax sitting next to a cozy fire while watching a mother bear playing with her baby cub?

A small pack of wolves also inhabited the Great Room as you entered from the lobby. There were four individuals in the pack, which stood on a raised platform fashioned into a rock outcropping. Two of them had animatronic heads that would rear up and howl every now and then during waking hours. The installers had already connected the wolf pack element to the control panel, so they were good to go. All one had to do was flip a switch and the wolf howls would sound off every hour on the hour during the day. The staff could even hit a hidden button to activate the wolves off the cuff for guests.

Jack felt that these animatronics were tasteful and enhanced the Lodge's peaceful atmosphere. The hidden button was located on a control panel near the Great Room's entrance to the Security Office. Jack walked about twenty feet into the Great Room to look for that unmarked button on the wall. The crew had placed a small tree element with some shrubs in front of the panel, forcing Jack to crouch against the wall in order to reach behind the tree.

"Really, guys?" Jack muttered as he bent down to feel for the control panel. Jack finally pressed the square button. The wolves raised their heads and howled. It was awesome.

Jack looked at the other elements in the high vaulted Great Room. The moose would probably end up in the rock climbing room, and the elk and mountain lion would probably move to the Falcon Micro Brewery. The falcon elements were already hanging from the ceiling over there. Bill had found an existing successful microbrewery in Sandpoint that was interested in establishing a second location, so he struck a deal with them to place it here. NSI gave them a great rate on the lease. Despite the large space in the Great Room, it felt cluttered and cramped with all of the animals in here—after all, moose are *huge*, and this one had antlers. It was almost like trying to move through a labyrinth to get around the room. But even the clutter was inspiring to Jack. Everything was coming together so perfectly...except for a certain intruder.

Jack walked back toward the lobby to assess the repairs there. Since they had to wait for a new right-side door, they screwed plywood to the front and back of the damaged door until its replacement arrived. All of the glass had been removed from the area.

"See you on Monday, Jack," said Frank Tiller as he passed Jack on the way out of the building.

"Heading out a bit late, Frank?" Jack returned.

"Yeah," Frank replied. "Andrew wanted us to finish something before the weekend."

Before Frank was out the door, Jack asked, "Where *are* Keith and Andrew anyway?" Jack started looking down the hallways adjacent to the lobby. He didn't want to keep them too long on a Friday night.

"I think they're in the Rock Climbing Room," Frank answered.

Jack headed to the western hallway which opened into the Rock Climbing Room. Andrew and Keith were discussing how to adjust a certain section of the installation with a vendor representative from the rock climbing wall company, which was taking longer than expected. They told Jack it would be another hour until they were free. Jack didn't mind waiting.

In the meantime, Fred Cross arrived for his night shift. This was the perfect time to ask Fred what he saw this morning.

"How are you, Fred?" Jack asked as Fred walked in the front door.

"Hey, Jack," Fred answered. "I'm okay. I see they patched up the door."

"Sort of—it'll take a while to get the replacement. Anyway," Jack continued, "I wanted to ask you about this morning. When you came out of the Security Office to investigate the broken glass, did you see anything through the lobby windows? Or through the glass doors?"

"No, sir," Fred answered as he shook his head. "I looked pretty hard but there was nothing out there."

"You didn't see some movement maybe?" Jack pressed. "I get that you didn't see anyone specific, but maybe you saw some shapes moving outside?"

Fred thought about it for a second, trying to recall the moment. Then he shook his head again. "Sorry, Jack. There was just nothing out there when I looked."

"Okay, then did you hear anything?" Jack asked. "Anything at all? I mean, even something seemingly insignificant or unconnected? Like a dog barking or whatever?"

"Well, I was holed up in the Security Office at the time watching the backlogged surveillance footage, and the door was closed—you know how it won't stay open because it's got the hydraulic door closer on it, right? And the Security Office doors on each side of the room are metal, so it's hard to hear anything through them at all, let alone anything outside of the building. I literally didn't hear anything until the rock came through the glass. –Even that was a little muffled. I guess those security doors are pretty thick."

"Yeah," Jack said absentmindedly. This interview was like trying to get blood from a turnip.

"And you heard nothing after you came out of the Security Office?"

"No, nothing," said Fred. "Sorry, Jack."

Jack nodded. "Well, you know we're looking at getting a second security guard for the night shift, so you shouldn't be going solo for too much longer here."

"Yeah, I heard—but whichever way is fine with me," Fred said, trying a little too hard to be nonchalant about it. He was a young guy in his early to mid-twenties. He probably didn't want to appear nervous about the incident, especially since it was his job to guard the place, but who wouldn't be unsettled? There were no people around for miles at night while the Lodge was under construction. And cell phone coverage was spotty until Jack could figure out how to get another cell tower built close by—or a landline all the way up here.

Jack let Fred start his shift since there were no more details to be had and decided to see how the various rooms in the Lodge were coming around. He started with the back management offices and saw that they were pretty far along. In fact, one of them had a comfy-looking desk chair that Jack rolled out to the lobby and sat in for a spell. He realized that he was pretty tired from running around non-stop talking to people since 7 AM. He tried to enjoy the view through the floor-to-ceiling lobby windows in front of him.

*Idaho really was a beautiful place*, he thought as he sank into the comfortable chair. *I'll just close my eyes for a second.*

236

# Chapter 13

## July 16 – Friday Night

Jack hadn't meant to doze off, but he suddenly found himself being nudged awake. Andrew and Keith were standing over him and it was almost dark outside.

"Hey, Jack," said Keith. "Sorry it took so long working on the rock installation."

Jack sat up straight as he stretched out his back. "What time is it?"

"Almost 8 o'clock," Andrew answered. "The rock climbing guy left a while ago, but we needed to hash out some things with the artists."

"Wow, late work day," Jack commented as he got up. "Are the artists still here? What were you working on?"

"Actually, I sent the artists home fifteen minutes ago," Keith said.

"Keith and I had to discuss scheduling for a bit. Sorry it took so long, Jack," Andrew apologized.

"If you want, we can show you what all the hubbub was about in the Rock Climbing Room," Keith offered. He and Andrew clearly looked tired, but also satisfied that they'd worked things out.

Just then Fred entered the lobby from walking a perimeter outside.

"Hey, Fred," said Jack, "You wanna come see the Rock Climbing Room?"

"Sure," Fred responded lightheartedly.

The four of them walked down the west hallway to assess the progress. Jack was impressed with the realism of the rock texture at the base of the column.

"We're going to continue this texture all the way up to the top," Keith explained. "The issue was that we didn't want the realism to interfere with the safety considerations."

"Well, it looks great," said Jack. "You guys are doing a great job."

Fred agreed that the Lodge looked amazing so far.

"Okay," Jack started, "so I don't want to keep you two here too much longer since it's late already, but I just wanted to talk about how the vandalism has affected this project."

Keith and Andrew were nodding. Fred was starting to excuse himself from the group when they were all startled by a loud crashing noise in the lobby. It sounded like glass shattering.

"*Holy*—" Jack uttered involuntarily. He turned to look down the hallway toward the front entrance and couldn't believe his eyes.

"What the…" said Keith peering down the hallway. "Is that *a tree?*"

They all looked at each other and then cautiously walked toward the lobby. Sure enough, lying on the floor was a gosh darn tree—maybe eighteen-feet tall, when it used to be upright. Its roots were still sticking out of the left-side lobby door, having crashed through the glass like a battering ram. The trunk was about eight inches in diameter, though most of its branches were missing, like they'd been snapped off beforehand. The tree seemed to have been yanked out of the ground while it was alive. They all stared at it dumbfounded for a minute.

Andrew said in amazement, "This doesn't make any sense. There aren't any trees this large near the front doors. How did this tree get here even if it *did* fall over?"

Everyone's mouths were agape. No one could properly digest what had just happened. It was as if time stood still.

Jack looked out of the large lobby windows but couldn't see anything moving outside. The sun hadn't set just yet, but the tree canopy surrounding the Lodge had already started blocking much of the light, creating deepening shadows in the nearby woods with every second that passed.

Fred took out his security baton and cautiously walked around the tree to the other lobby door, which was boarded up due to the glass being shattered this morning from the thrown rock. Jack followed him.

Fred pulled the large door ajar and peered outside. "I don't see anything," he said to them quietly.

"Lemme get out there," Jack said as he tried to move past Fred. The rest of them trailed Jack outside.

They fanned out about six feet from the front doors to look around. The parking lot was devoid of life under the bright overhead lights, but Jack knew they were being watched. Despite his suspicion that they were under surveillance, Jack felt that there was safety in numbers, which is why he didn't hesitate to investigate outside.

The four men scanned the surrounding woods before them but could not detect any movement in the hundred-foot-tall trees. Jack thought that it was eerily quiet, and the bravado he felt a moment ago began to fade. The sun wouldn't set for another hour or so, but for all intents and purposes, it was already dark around the Lodge.

"We should check the security footage," Andrew suggested as he moved back toward the front doors.

Suddenly, one of the further parking lot lights blew out. Then another light exploded. And another. The four of them froze and watched in confusion.

"What the hell?!" exclaimed Keith.

Jack realized that the lights were systematically being destroyed by rocks. "Someone's throwing rocks at the lights!" he shouted.

Then, before any of them could respond, a large rock whizzed past Jack's chest, striking Andrew in the lower leg as he stood near the open lobby door.

"*Arrhhh*," Andrew grunted in pain. Everyone's gaze shot to Andrew crumpling down on the ground as he grabbed at his injured leg. A rock the size of a baseball lay next to Andrew's foot. Keith, Fred, and Jack immediately looked around the parking lot for the threat.

"Uh, guys," said Fred nervously. "Something's heading towards us from the road." Jack glanced at Beverly Road and saw a dark mass moving towards them from a few hundred feet away.

Then Keith interjected, "From the forest near the Bike Shack too!" Keith pointed to the other side of the parking lot a couple hundred feet in

240

front of them. Although it was too dark to see details, plainly something large was moving in that area.

"Get inside!" Jack yelled. Keith and Fred ran over and dragged Andrew through the front door as Jack followed. He quickly looked back in horror to see a large, dark figure in the distance already moving swiftly through the dim parking lot toward them.

"*Move!*" Jack commanded, ready to push them into the lobby if needed. "*It's coming!!*"

They stumbled into the entryway as shattered glass hit the outside pavers. Jack shut the right-side door, which was temporarily girded with plywood, as more outside fixtures were being destroyed. The exterior lights were sputtering as debris and rock fragments rained into the lobby through the shattered glass of the left-side door. The outer wall sconces finally exploded, plunging the exterior into darkness.

"Get into the Security Office! NOW!" Jack barked as they all ran through the lobby, past the prone tree trunk, to the metal door at the back of the room.

Once inside the Security Office, Jack locked the door while Fred keyed up the lobby camera on Monitor 1. Keith dumped Andrew onto one of the chairs against the wall and checked his leg.

"*Arrhh*," Andrew grunted as he held his right lower leg. He said through gritted teeth, "God, it might be broken…"

On Monitor 2, Fred keyed in the camera positioned outside the front doors with a fisheye view of the outer walkway and now dark parking lot—the same camera that caught the intruder with Jack the other night.

The lights in the front area were out—destroyed by thrown rocks, just like the parking lot lights no doubt. The camera, however, had the ability to emit infrared light up to about ten feet away in zero light, providing black and white video in this mode. Nothing seemed to move on the camera feed.

"Damnit," whispered Keith as he frantically punched buttons on his cell phone. "I can't reach 911! There's no damn signal in here!"

"If only we had a security alarm in place," Fred muttered. "Like a panic button…"

"Yeah—that's getting installed two weeks from now," Keith said dryly.

"Please tell me there's a landline!" pleaded Fred as he also frantically tried to call 911 on his cell phone.

Jack looked annoyed as he whispered violently. "It was in the works! Do *you* have a landline at *your* house?" Jack sniped.

Fred shut his mouth.

Jack scanned the monitors for movement. On Monitor 2, his eyes were drawn to a dark shape almost gliding into view outside. As the shape became more defined, an object flew out of the darkness toward the camera. The feed went dead.

"*Oh God,*" cried Fred, "they took out the camera!"

Jack looked at Monitor 1, which had an interior view of the lobby from near the Security Office. The boarded up, right-side door was slowly opening, but since plywood was affixed to the door to cover the hole where the glass used to be, whatever was opening the 8-foot tall door remained unseen. After a minute, something was flung at the lobby chandelier from the open door, plunging the area into darkness.

"Holy crap! This *can't* be happening," Fred whispered as he put a hand over his mouth.

A tiny bit of light was streaming into the lobby from the western hallway—to the left as you entered the lobby doors—which is where they'd been assessing the rock climbing column earlier. The lobby camera was positioned at the corner of the room near the Security Office so that it could capture both the front door, the western hallway, and some of the front desk. In the low light, the open lobby door appeared as a rectangular, black shadow on the monitor. Then a huge, silhouetted shape emerged from the door and stood erect—although still partially obscured by the door, it stood *taller* than the door after entering the lobby.

There were gasps in the Security Office but no one dared speak a word. Jack hoped that the metal doors were sealed up tight so that no light shone at the seams to betray their location. He couldn't believe this was happening. Why was it pursuing them now? Surely the creature wouldn't venture into the building any further. It had made its point, right?

Jack couldn't see a face, and he couldn't see the eyes, but he sensed that the thing was scouring the lobby for its prey. Jack could hear his heart pounding in his ears. He could feel his awareness slipping into a paralysis of fear and struggled to come back to his senses.

As Jack mentally clawed his way back from the brink, a blood curdling scream tore through the Lodge, shaking Jack to his core. It wasn't so much that the scream could be heard through the door, but rather that it caused *everything*—the walls, floor, and ceiling—to shudder. It felt like the Lodge itself was afraid.

Jack suddenly felt very small. If he were in a bed right now, he'd pull the covers over his head hoping that the monster didn't see him and just go away. Fred exhaled audibly and looked like he was about to throw up. Jack saw that Andrew and Keith were frozen against the opposite wall in the Security Office, trying to keep it together.

Then Fred whispered violently, "*It's coming towards us.*"

Jack whipped his gaze back to Monitor 1 and saw a hulking, dark figure purposefully glide in the direction of the Security Office. There was no up-and-down bobbing motion in its step. It was stalking its prey through the dark lobby with deliberation. Strangely, even though the camera had color night vision, and there was even some light from the hallway behind the creature, Jack couldn't see any detail in its face. Somehow, the figure swallowed the light.

Then the camera lost sight of the creature, which meant that it was probably right outside the Security Office door. Jack looked at the others with anticipation. The four of them glanced at the door. All was silent.

Jack was stunned out of the moment by a thunderous slam to the Security Office door. They all cried out in surprise and horror to see a huge dent in the middle of the metal door. Before anyone could think, the door was pounded again and again. The whole room seemed to shudder from each blow. The metal was buckling. The hinges were coming undone.

A horrifying shriek from the other side of the door preceded another round of pounding on the metal barrier. That door wouldn't hold much longer.

"Out the other door!" cried Jack as Keith pulled Andrew out of the chair. They all escaped through the back door of the Security Office, which led to the Great Room in the back of the Lodge. Jack was last out of the room as he slammed the door shut.

Fred was in the lead as they hurriedly maneuvered between animal elements and other items haphazardly stored in the Great Room. Only a tiny bit of light was streaming into the room from its connection to the lobby. Other than the green lit exit sign above the back door, the darkness engulfed them, which was fine with Jack. The foursome had to navigate around the elk, moose, and bear props still waiting to be placed in their final stations. Jack heard what must have been the creature finally busting into the Security Office.

Fred found a spot for them against the wall behind the elk and some shrubs. They were midway through the room. Andrew grunted quietly as Keith placed him on the floor, although stealth didn't seem necessary at this point as they heard the sound of equipment and furniture being smashed to pieces in the room they had just abandoned.

"Maybe we should get out of here while we can!" Keith whispered urgently. "The exit door is right there—"

"Are you kidding?" Fred responded incredulously under his breath. "There are more of them outside! I saw something moving on the road!"

Jack was amazed that anyone could still have a logical conversation at this point. He heard himself whispering in desperation, "Maybe it'll leave if it can't find us..." He found himself clinging to the hope that this was just an animal that couldn't remember much of anything beyond what happened in the last few minutes. They were like apes, right? He'd seen documentaries on gorillas. Didn't they have limited problem-solving abilities? *Out of sight, out of mind, right?*

Suddenly, the Security Office door violently blew open as terror gripped the foursome. There were no longer any lights illuminating the Security Office but Jack could still sense something emerging from that small space into the Great Room. As black as their surroundings were, this creature was darker, and its mass was palpable, as though it pushed air molecules like a wave into the room.

Jack watched from behind the legs of a 5-foot tall elk as the creature slowly creeped into the room, gradually becoming silhouetted by the residual light from beyond the lobby. Jack couldn't believe his eyes. How did this thing fit into the Security Office? It was like an industrial-sized refrigerator on legs paradoxically gliding through the room with a reptilian fluidity...searching.

*It hadn't forgotten about them at all.*

As the creature invaded the Great Room, Jack felt himself hunker down tight against the wall, wishing he were an inanimate object incapable of experiencing emotions. Jack found it unnerving that what was once so thunderously loud only a second ago was now so calculatingly quiet. The massive figure moved ever so slowly toward the center of the room, merging its shape with that of the centrally located moose so that Jack couldn't distinguish between the two. The creature must have been about twenty feet away. The further into the room the thing moved, the harder it was to see. It could easily come upon them against the wall as it played this perverse game of hide and seek. And then they'd be dead.

Jack surreptitiously scanned the room but could no longer locate the creature. Maybe this thing had excellent night vision. Perhaps it had already seen them and was now merely toying with its food. Seconds felt like hours. *Where was it?*

Then Jack heard slow, heavy breathing from somewhere near the fireplace. It felt like something the size of an elephant was nearby...and it was moving closer. Jack couldn't take it anymore. He knew they needed to get out of this enclosed space. He almost couldn't breathe. His mind was reeling as he tried to think of a distraction to get that thing to look somewhere else...to *go* somewhere else. The room was so silent that Jack was convinced everyone could hear the sweat dripping off of his face onto his shirt.

Without further thought, Jack slowly slid across the floor toward the control panel on the wall. He felt Keith grab at his shirt in the dark but there was no way to discuss this or to explain his actions. Jack tried to move quieter than a mouse as he reached up behind the tree element. He felt for the square button and pushed it.

The howl of wolves broke the silence and Jack felt monstrous footsteps run toward the wolf pack near the wide doorway to the lobby.

Jack kept pressing the button over and over to keep the howls going. Suddenly he heard growls and something angrily being torn apart at the wolf pack platform.

*This is our chance!* Jack thought as he scurried back toward the others on the floor. They must have all had the same idea because the others were already stumbling toward the exit door to the right of the fireplace.

The foursome quietly erupted out of the back exit onto the outdoor walkway that connected the pool house to the outdoor event space. Jack attempted to control the closing of the exit door, hoping that the creature didn't notice their escape—though how could it not? *Some* light must have spilled into the Great Room from outside as they egressed.

Fred urged them to follow him to the left, toward the grassy area for weddings and outdoor parties. Andrew was leaning heavily on Keith as they ran.

Jack kept looking back at the exit door in case the creature punched it open in pursuit, but amazingly it never did. Had it been *that preoccupied* with the wolves? If so, Jack counted it a miracle.

"We need to get to my truck around front!" Jack whispered hoarsely to Fred so that the young security guard would know where to lead them. The outdoor lights were still functional on this side of the Lodge.

"We can go around past the restaurant and hit the parking lot that way," Fred replied, gasping for breath as they quickly crossed the grass and rounded the corner of the building that housed the rock climbing column. Andrew was really struggling to keep up even with Keith's help.

Fred grabbed Andrew's other arm as he and Keith tried to carry most of Andrew's weight. Meanwhile, Jack reached into his pocket to get his keys ready.

Once they rounded the corner of the microbrewery, Jack was stunned to see the parking lot so dark, but then he remembered that the creature had destroyed most of the lights here earlier. The foursome kept running as Jack fumbled with his keys. He finally clicked the truck key fob to locate the vehicle in the dark and unlock the truck doors. Everybody headed for the lit vehicle.

Every nerve was frayed as Jack and the others scrambled into the vehicle. Fred jumped into the front seat and Andrew yelled in pain as Keith shoved him into the back.

"Move, Andrew!" Keith ordered as he tried to scoot into the back seat next to Andrew and shut the door.

Jack started the truck and the headlights lit up the lobby doors about fifty feet away. Jack could see tree roots protruding from the smashed, left-side door at the entrance. The right-side door was open, and to Jack's horror, he saw two giant, yellow eyes glaring menacingly at him from inside the dark lobby. Jack was terrified.

Without warning, the creature charged out of the front doors. Jack reflexively hit the gas hard and jerked the wheel to the left. The tires squealed in protest as the truck bed spun sideways to align with the motion of the front wheels. Everyone felt the vehicle slide to the right as the truck pivoted towards Beverly Road. As the truck screeched forward, Jack straightened the steering wheel and aimed for the exit.

Fred turned around to look through the rear windshield. "*Oh God*, go faster! *He's chasing us!*"

Jack hit things in the parking lot trying to negotiate around piles of landscaping supplies while still maintaining some speed. He couldn't afford the luxury of checking the rear view mirrors to confirm Fred's statement while trying not to crash. Fred must have been telling the truth because he heard Keith screaming a stream of expletives.

The truck's tires screeched and squealed as the passengers were jostled side to side. Jack heard an angry roar somewhere behind them as the truck fishtailed onto Beverly Road and away from the Lodge. He finally looked in the rear view mirror to see a dimly lit, massive figure run out onto the road behind them. Jack sighed in relief when it didn't chase them.

*Thank God*, he thought as they headed toward town.

Jack realized that Beverly Road is a dark and scary place when you're traveling fifty miles an hour at night with only the truck's headlamps to light your way. Not to mention the fact that you've just escaped the most frightening creature you've ever seen.

Everyone was breathing hard in the cab. Fred seemed a bit catatonic in the front seat as he blankly stared ahead. Andrew seemed to have passed out from the pain in his leg. Jack feared Andrew might have a broken tibia or something. Meanwhile, Keith was trying his cell phone again with no luck.

"*You've got to be kidding me!*" Keith complained as he still got no signal to call 911.

Jack had just switched the setting on his headlamps to bright when he saw multiple downed trees piled up like a dam across the road ahead. He barely hit the brakes in time to slow the vehicle somewhat before slamming into the obstacle and scattering the trees forward.

"What the hell," Jack exclaimed as he gripped the steering wheel to maintain control. The truck jolted up and every other which way trying to traverse over the pile of fallen trees and branches. There was no way that Jack was stopping the truck, but their forward progress had slowed to a few miles per hour as the wheels tried to find traction on the uneven terrain. Jack cursed the fact that he didn't have 4-wheel drive.

Above the sound of the truck's engine and the crunching of the trees under the tires, Jack and the others heard a loud whooping call from the trees to their right. Fred turned his head to the sound in panic.

Jack looked to the right but could discern nothing in the darkness beyond the headlight's illumination, so he concentrated on the terrain ahead. The high-beams on his headlamps revealed that debris of all types—rocks, uprooted bushes, and saplings—lay in the road ahead of them as far as Jack could see. It was almost as if a hurricane had passed through the area.

*There's no way the road was in this state when the last of the work crews left the Lodge, right?* Jack thought to himself.

As the truck tires grappled with the fallen saplings, suddenly something crashed against Fred's side window. Fred shouted in response as everyone looked at the cracked glass, which amazingly had not shattered.

"They're throwing rocks!" cried Fred as another object impacted his car door just below the window.

"We've got to go faster!" shouted Keith as he frantically scanned the area from which the rocks were thrown.

"You're welcome to get out and push!" Jack yelled as he increased the pressure on the gas pedal and they cleared the last sapling. Their speed increased to about fifteen miles per hour but Jack still had to maneuver around uprooted bushes and other debris in the road.

As Jack began to pick up speed, he saw bushes and rocks actively being thrown onto the road ahead of them. "Damn it all to hell!" Jack shouted as he swerved to miss the obstacles.

After clearing another sixty feet of debris, suddenly the road seemed clear of obstructions and Jack hit the gas, hoping that they were home free. Before he could celebrate for more than a second, a creature ran out of the forest onto the road just ahead and Jack reflexively swerved to avoid hitting the figure. The truck went off the road into the dirt but didn't hit anything. Jack tried to swerve back toward the road, which caused the truck to spiral. Jack pumped the breaks as he turned into the spin, trying to regain control of the vehicle.

Finally, the truck stopped and Jack knew instantly that the truck was turned around in the wrong direction—back towards the Lodge. Everyone was breathing hard and Andrew moaned in pain. The headlights illuminated the road ahead and all Jack could see were some smaller rocks and dirt. Despite the empty road, Jack didn't believe for an instant that they weren't being watched. After a few seconds of scanning the road,

Jack shifted the truck in reverse to initiate a Y-turn to get them pointed back towards Everton. He looked behind and maneuvered the truck into the first part of the turn, then he shifted into drive and hit the gas to go forward.

Jack immediately noticed that the truck was not moving forward, and the tires sounded like they were spinning in place. He looked in the rear view mirror, trying to adjust his eyes to the darkness behind the vehicle. The rear lights seemed incredibly dim.

"Why aren't we moving?" Fred wailed.

Everyone except the unconscious Andrew looked out the rear windshield and saw nothing discernable, but as they continued to stare, suddenly large, glowing, yellow eyes slowly descended into view from the top of the rear window. Nobody in the cab could utter a sound after realizing that the creature was at the tailgate, bending over the truck bed to peer inside the cab.

*It's holding onto the truck so we can't move forward!* Jack thought in despair.

The terror in the truck was palpable as the yellow eyes moved closer and closer to the glass. Jack couldn't think anymore. The nightmare was consuming him and he was being eaten alive by those yellow eyes of hate.

Out of the blue, Fred gargled a scream that snapped Jack out of paralysis. Jack slammed on the horn, which must have surprised the creature and made it lose its grip because the truck jolted forward. Jack jerked the steering wheel to the right to get them in the correct direction as the truck pulled away. Immediately, the truck was dealt a massive blow from behind and a thunderous roar echoed after them as they sped away. Jack caught a glimpse of the rear view mirror and saw a dark figure chasing them. Jack put the pedal to the metal until the figure seemed to stop of its own accord.

Jack realized he hadn't been watching the road ahead. He was amazed that he hadn't crashed them into the trees while he was watching the creature in the rear view mirror. Jack focused on the road in front of him as he accelerated the truck. He wasn't going to stop for *anything*. And he would run over *anything* that got in their way.

It felt like only an instant later that Jack was slamming on the brakes *again* as he saw two cars—possibly three—stopped in the middle of the road ahead. One of the vehicles was on fire. The cars had collided somehow and were facing in odd directions, as though they had all spun out and then crashed into each other. Everyone in the truck had to brace themselves to keep from coming out of their seats as the truck screeched to a halt—Andrew yelled in pain as he was jolted back into consciousness.

"No!" cried Fred as they came to a halt.

Keith leaned forward between Jack and Fred to get a better look at the crashed vehicles ahead. "My God, is that Frank's car?" Keith said.

There were no downed trees in the road that Jack could see, no rocks or uprooted bushes anywhere. Jack couldn't tell what had caused this mess. He looked at the car windows lit up by the truck's headlights but couldn't see any people in the vehicles.

Jack exhaled and said, "We should check the vehicles for injured people." He quickly scanned the side and rearview mirrors for any sign of pursuit from the creature.

"*I'm not getting out of the truck*," Fred said adamantly in terror.

After a heartbeat, Jack said, "Fine, I'll go."

"Wait," Keith said, "even if we find people, where are we gonna go? The cars are completely blocking the road—I don't think your truck can push them out of the way."

"Well, actually, I think my truck *can* push these cars out of the way one by one, but I don't want to be anywhere near these cars with one of them on fire like that." Jack thought for a second. "There are logging roads intersecting Beverly all up and down from the Lodge to the break in the trees south of here. We passed several of them already. We need to turn around and take the one that reconnects with Beverly further south. Some even connect to highways on the east side of Everton. I'd prefer trying to find the one that connects back to Beverly again though."

"But you don't know which one to take?" Fred exclaimed.

"I have a pretty good idea—and, at this point, it's our only option." Jack's main concern was that the logging roads might be in severe disrepair in some spots, meaning maybe even impassable, but he thought it was best not to mention that, seeing how everyone's sanity was stretched thin, especially Fred's.

"Either way," Jack continued, "we need to get the hell out of here—that car could blow at any time. I'll go check the cars for survivors."

"No, old man," Keith interjected as he put a hand on Jack's shoulder. "I'll go. You stay in the truck. We need the truck's headlights to search the cars, but be ready to turn it around once we're back inside. –*Frickin honk if you see something.*"

"Don't dillydally with that fire out there, Keith," Jack commanded. Then he reached into the glove compartment and grabbed a flashlight. "Here, take this. If you don't see anyone, just get your ass back in here."

"Yeah," Keith said before turning to Fred, "*You.* Get the hell out and help me." Keith didn't wait for a response from Fred. He scanned the surroundings before getting out of the truck and shutting the door.

Jack looked at Fred, who hadn't moved an inch. Jack sighed and started looking around the vicinity, trying to watch for movement while also trying to watch Keith hurriedly walking toward the cars. He saw that Andrew had completely passed out again in the back seat.

"Damnit!" Fred muttered as he was finally motivated by enough courage—or shame—to exit the truck and head for the cars. Keith was shining the flashlight in the first vehicle and not seeing anyone.

Fred ran over to the second vehicle with Keith, both of their heads bobbing up and down as they bent to look inside the cars from all angles. Every so often they'd turn to scan the trees nearby. Jack's truck was raised up higher than the cars so he could see the other two run over to a third car and then sprint back to the truck. It felt like forever waiting for them to return.

"Nobody anywhere," Keith said quickly as they shut their doors. No one speculated aloud on the reasons for that. Keith added, "There's a large, fallen tree blocking the road on the other side of the cars—too big for cars to drive over. Probably what caused the crash."

Jack shook his head in disgust. Keith looked at his cell phone again and announced dejectedly that there was still no damn signal.

Jack turned the truck around and headed back toward the Lodge with the intent of turning down one of the logging roads on the left— toward the west—long before they ever reached the Lodge. He was sure that one of the back roads reconnected to Beverly further south, but he hadn't mentioned the fact that the logging road forked *at least* once. Jack glanced at the small, electronic compass screen above his rearview mirror. It currently indicated that they were traveling north.

"Guys," said Jack as he drove, "once we're on the logging road, watch the compass up here to make sure we're heading west to start. In the dark, in the backwoods, it's easy to get turned around. The logging road might fork a few times. We just need to keep to the left and eventually head south."

Jack wasn't traveling that fast—maybe 35 miles per hour at most— because he didn't want to miss the logging road. Everyone intently scanned the path ahead for a break in the trees indicating a turnoff.

"There!" shouted Fred as he pointed up to the left.

Jack turned off of Beverly onto the dirt road. It was surprisingly smooth driving at first, but there were some serious rocks jutting out of the dirt along the way. Jack tried to avoid them where possible, but the truck jolted up and down as he ran over others. It was a terror ride trying to maintain speed while evaluating the dirt path in front of them. Jack had a death grip on the steering wheel as much to control the truck as to control his fear.

At one point, Fred muttered an expletive out of nowhere.

"What's wrong?" Keith asked from the back seat as they were jostled.

"I thought I saw something," Fred explained frenetically as he scanned his side of the truck through the front windshield and then back toward Andrew's passenger side window. Fred ignored his side window because it was a web of cracks from being hit with rocks earlier.

Jack kept focusing on the path in front of him, looking for that left fork, hoping he hadn't already missed it. He glanced at the compass LED display and it showed "W" for west. So far so good.

Jack had to decrease speed to about 15-20 miles per hour once they turned onto the logging road, which seemed more and more like a hiking trail that was getting narrower and narrower by the minute. Jack silently thanked the ATV enthusiasts and off-roaders for taking their backroad adventures on his land without permission all these years. He was convinced that those activities must have kept this road cleared of new tree growth.

"Up ahead," Keith said as he poked his head up front and pointed forward.

Jack saw a fork in the road and veered to the left. "That's one down," said Jack. "Probably one more to go." He looked at the compass and it indicated that they were heading southwest. So far, their trip on the logging road had been downright peaceful, and Jack hoped beyond all hope that it would be the most boring truck ride back to town from here on out.

Then, from an unseen herald in the night, they heard a soul-shattering scream in the distance, as though a woman were being murdered in the woods. Blood drained out of Jack's extremities at the sound, causing his fingers to tingle. And the sound didn't stop. Ten seconds. Twenty seconds. Thirty seconds. Whatever was screaming never took a breath.

Jack looked over at Fred, who sat petrified as white as a corpse, like rigor mortis had already set in. In the rearview mirror he caught Keith wearing a look of intense trepidation as he leaned forward between the two front seats watching the road ahead. The scream finally ended but tension remained high.

Jack had been considering increasing speed for a few minutes but the fear of blowing a tire on an unseen boulder made him hesitate. The sound of a rock hitting the rear windshield stunned Jack out of his thoughts. Keith and Fred turned to look backwards. Jack looked in the rearview mirror and saw a crack on the glass in back. Then Jack heard what sounded like trees cracking, as though something large were pushing its way through the forest near the back of the truck on his side.

"Something's following us!" Keith exclaimed as he looked out of his side window towards the rear.

"*Go faster!*" Fred pleaded, coming out of his catatonia.

Jack added pressure to the gas pedal just as a huge thwack hit the back of the truck. Everyone exclaimed in surprise.

"*God*, go faster!" Keith shouted as he looked behind.

The sound of trees being knocked over and pushed aside continued, accompanied by a *thud thud* sound of something massive stomping through the woods, keeping pace with the truck on Jack's side. Jack looked at the speedometer and saw that they were going 30 miles per hour. Jack increased speed to 40 miles per hour.

*Please, God, don't let us crash*, Jack prayed as he worked to keep the truck on the uneven road. He could hear snorting and breathing outside of the vehicle to his left, just outside his side window. He didn't take his eyes off of the road to inspect the horror on his left, which he felt was daring him to look.

"Jack!" Fred screeched as he frantically pointed to the left up ahead.

Jack was concentrating so hard on not looking to his left that he almost missed turning left on the second fork in the road. The turn was so hard that everyone in the truck was thrown to the right side. The compass showed they were heading southeast, which meant they should be cutting back toward Beverly Road.

Their speed was back down to 25 miles per hour from taking the last left turn, so Jack hit the gas a bit more to get back up to speed. As he watched the road, the high-beams on the truck's headlights illuminated something large and black standing on the right side of the road about a hundred feet ahead.

"*What is that?*" Fred whispered.

*"Don't stop!"* Keith urged as they all stared at this thing becoming larger and larger in their view. It was like being in a rocket ship being pulled toward the fatal surface of the sun.

For his part, Jack had no intention of stopping, even if it jumped in front of the truck to block their path like a concrete wall. He had no more nerve for this game. He just wanted it to end.

Time slowed down even as the truck picked up speed. Jack saw the creature in great detail, but in the moment, what really destroyed Jack were the yellow eyes of hate. That thing wasn't looking at the headlamps. It was looking *above* the lights, directly into the truck at Jack. It *knew* Jack—had perhaps been watching Jack for weeks. Or longer.

This thing looked like an ugly man with light grey skin and black hair. Its eyes were amber like an animal's and the whites were not visible. Its body was covered in hair, except for its chest, which was muscular like a bodybuilder hopped up on steroids. It certainly was a male and he was not young. His face had scars and wrinkles, and his expression was a scowl of hate. Teeth were showing but not like humans show teeth—it was how a wolf would bare its weapons.

The creature, still staring at Jack, crossed the logging road in an almost arrogant manner, daring Jack to try and hit him. The creature had reached the other side in a mere two steps and then positioned itself on the left side of the road, waiting.

In that moment, Jack knew that it *hated* him with a passion. As the truck got closer and closer, the thing menacingly bent down lower and lower so that its eyes were level with Jack's. That look was seared into

Jack's mind. Jack's body didn't want him to get closer. Self-preservation was kicking in. His mind was being hijacked. *Going toward the creature was wrong,* his body explained.

Jack's senses told him, *This is not an animal. This is a* monster. *Go away from the monster.*

Jack fought back against his animal brain and hit the gas harder when they were within twenty feet of the creature. They needed to go *toward the monster* to get out of this place.

Moment of truth. The thing was so massive and powerful that the possibility of it shoving the truck into the trees and killing everyone on board seemed like a given. Twelve feet tall. Four feet wide. Black wall of muscle and hair. Raw power beyond believing. The intelligence to chase and harass in a calculated fashion. An apex predator in every respect. In a moment, this charade of an escape would end, and Jack and the others would be dead.

Strangely, death didn't come. But in that instant of passing, the monster leaned down to look into Jack's side window at him. And Jack looked back. A nanosecond of time that lasted an eternity.

Those yellow eyes were seething with murderous hate. It was up close, personal, and terrifying. This was no generic sentiment. It was specific and sentient. In that look of hate and evil, Jack was eaten alive. His soul became food for this creature. Jack was just a meal on two legs and he only just now realized it. Was it seconds or hours that passed as Jack felt his soul being consumed?

Then suddenly the moment was gone and Jack saw the dirt path ahead, starkly illuminated by the truck's headlights. Jack didn't know how far they had driven before he was abruptly making a hard right onto Beverly Road.

Everyone seemed to exhale at the same time. They weren't out of the woods yet, literally, but they were close. They passed a sign on the road that said the Everton city limit was only eight miles away. Jack realized there was only about a mile left to go of thick woods before the terrain changed to low brush and sparse trees the rest of the way.

Jack didn't dare slow down and remained on high alert, eyes scanning the dark road ahead for the slightest movement. In shock, he slammed on the breaks hard as he saw several figures wearing clothing hobbling down the middle of Beverly Road. The people started to lunge for the road's shoulder when they heard the screeching tires behind them.

"It's Frank and the rest of the crew!" Keith exclaimed as he got out of the truck. Fred got out of his own volition to help as well.

Frank and three other men started walking toward the truck on Jack's side wearing relieved expressions. There were no explanations given from either party except that Frank said they should put Patrick inside the truck because his ankle was busted.

Jack could hear Frank saying, "Thank God you guys showed up! It was gonna be a long walk back to town!" Before Keith could protest, Frank and the rest happily proceeded to get in the truck bed, leaving Keith and Fred to get back in the cab.

Jack sensed some weird disconnect between Frank's group and theirs. Frank seemed incredibly jovial considering the night's events. Surely these guys had seen the creatures when they abandoned their crashed cars on Beverly Road, right? There was that fallen tree blocking their path. Surely they were attacked at that point?

"Holy—" cried Frank from the truck bed in surprise. "What happened to your rear windshield, Jack?"

"Dude," said another guy in the truck bed, "what have you guys been doing at the Lodge?"

The guys in the truck bed laughed.

Jack turned around in his seat to find Keith in the cab. Keith was back in his seat behind Jack. They exchanged a look of bewilderment. It seemed like the new passengers weren't scared at all. They weren't in a state of shock over anything.

Jack faced forward again and continued toward town, careful of his driving since human cargo sat in the open truck bed. He checked every shadow and gripped the steering wheel in anticipation of an ambush.

Keith turned to Patrick, who was seated in the back between him and Andrew—still unconscious—and asked, "What happened on the road after you guys left the Lodge?"

"It's all kind of sketchy to me too," Patrick started. "I was driving my car, and Eddie was up ahead of me with Mike. They carpooled today so Eddie was gonna drop Mike off at his place. We were turning a bend and all of a sudden Eddie's car slams into a car stopped in the road, and then I hit Eddie. Turns out, it was Frank's car. He had stopped in a blind

264

spot because there was a downed tree in the road ahead—it was too heavy to move without equipment. Man, as hard as we hit Frank's car, I'm surprised he didn't get seriously hurt. It felt like a Hot Wheels smash up."

Keith was puzzled. "But didn't Frank leave an hour or more before you guys?"

"Uh well, when I was leaving the Lodge, Frank was outside talking to Eddie, so I guess he stuck around for a bit." Patrick shrugged.

"What happened then?" Keith questioned.

"We all got out of our cars, but my ankle couldn't support much weight. I knew it didn't feel right when I got out of the car. We couldn't drive back to town because the tree was too big to move. Nobody was getting a cellphone signal so we decided to walk to Everton. We figured that we'd have more chance of getting a signal once we got clear of the woods—we planned on calling you guys too to warn you about the car pileup once we got a signal."

"One of the cars was on fire when we found them," Keith said.

"Man, really? How'd you get around the cars and the tree?" Patrick asked.

"Logging road," said Jack as he looked in the rearview mirror. "Did you see anything out there? While walking on Beverly Road?"

"Like what?" Patrick asked.

"*Are you serious?*" Fred interjected as he turned around to glare at Patrick.

Patrick looked shocked at Fred's outburst.

Keith gave Fred a look and then turned to Patrick and said calmly, "Did you maybe hear anything odd while you were walking on the road? Maybe you saw some strangers on the road…or in the woods?"

Patrick crinkled his brows as he considered the question. "Um, we did hear some strange shrieks from the woods…off in the distance. I couldn't tell what it was, but I'm not from around here. I'm not really sure what kinds of animals live here. We only have stray cats meowing in the alleys back in Santa Monica."

After some silence in the truck, Patrick added, "I was mostly trying to cope with my ankle while we were walking back to town. Did something happen?" Patrick looked from Fred to Keith.

Fred turned back forward.

Patrick then looked at Andrew and asked, "Is Andrew okay? Is he just sleeping?"

Keith finally said tersely, "We were attacked at the Lodge."

"*What?*" Patrick replied in disbelief. "Who attacked you?"

Keith opened his mouth to respond but couldn't seem to find the words.

"Suffice it to say," Jack answered blandly, "I think you guys will have Monday off…maybe the rest of the week too."

"Is that why Fred's window is cracked?" Patrick asked, apparently just now noticing the damage. "And the rear windshield?"

Fred was shaking his head in disbelief as he stared ahead.

"Yeah," Keith replied wanly. "That's why the window is cracked."

Patrick was obviously confused over everyone's belligerent attitude, but decided not to press the issue. He said nothing else for the rest of the ride.

Jack noticed the city glow of Everton in the distance and felt himself start to relax as they entered the town limits. After passing a lone gas station and a closed auto mechanic shop, Jack realized he didn't know where he was going. He quickly decided to head to the hospital because Andrew was in bad shape, still unconscious in the back seat. And Patrick was obviously injured from the car accident.

Keith asked where they were headed and Jack explained his intentions. Keith then dialed 911 on his cellphone, which finally got a signal, and informed the emergency responder that they were heading to the Emergency Room at Everton General Hospital. He also asked them to alert the Sheriff that they were attacked at the Lodge and had just come from there. Keith didn't provide any more detail than that over the phone.

At the hospital, Andrew was rushed in for an examination. The ER nurses wanted to examine Jack as well, but Jack insisted that he was fine and that the staff should look at his companions first. Keith called Em and explained that he was at the hospital. Keith asked her if there was any disturbance at the rental house, and she said nothing had happened tonight. Jack called his daughter Jenny and ex-wife Ellen to have the same discussion. Jenny and Ellen also indicated that it had been a quiet night so far.

A couple of Sheriff's deputies arrived about fifteen minutes later to take the report from Jack, Keith, and Fred. Jack hadn't discussed with the others beforehand what they would tell the deputies, but he decided not to beat around the bush.

As the three of them stood outside of the hospital with the deputies, Jack said outright, "We were attacked by Bigfoot and I don't really care what anyone thinks. It's the truth."

Keith and Fred backed him up. They explained everything that had happened at the Lodge earlier that evening, starting with the tree thrown through the lobby door, up to the mad escape in the truck, and finally finding Frank and the others on the road walking back to Everton.

The deputies didn't scoff. It was hard to read whether they believed the account or were just so jaded from listening to people's stories that they no longer reacted at all. Either way, they said they would send some deputies and fire trucks up Beverly Road to check on the crashed vehicles tonight. They didn't want the car fire to spread to the trees.

"We should check the surveillance footage from the Lodge," said one of the deputies.

"We can try," said Jack, "but if the internet isn't working up there, we'll have to go back to the Lodge and retrieve the hard drive in person—if it's not destroyed." Jack shook his head at that. It would be so predictable if that hard drive were smashed to bits in the Security Office. How could it possibly be intact when Jack heard the creature rampaging in that room like a bull in a China shop?

The deputies said that they probably wouldn't be able to reach the Lodge until morning since they had to first clear the three-car accident on

Beverly Road tonight. Jack insisted that he accompany the deputies to the Lodge come first light. The deputies didn't object.

Jack, Keith, and Fred remained outside of the hospital after the deputies departed, still in shock over their ordeal.

Fred broke the silence. "Why do you think Frank and the others didn't get attacked when they were walking on the road? I don't get it. They were out in the open. That downed tree on Beverly Road was obviously meant to stop any vehicles from getting back to town. I mean, Patrick acted like it was just a Sunday stroll in the park for them—other than having a busted ankle. I mean, *what the hell?*" The young security guard was obviously upset.

"I agree," Keith said soberly. "It doesn't make sense. Maybe these creatures just attacked whichever group was most convenient at the time. Bad luck for us, you know?"

"No," Jack stated. "Not bad luck. It was me. He was after *me*. Maybe it was bad luck for you guys that you happened to be with me when it all went down. I'm sorry for that."

Keith shook his head. "You didn't do anything wrong, Jack. What makes you think it was interested in *you*?"

"My family has owned that land for generations, and those things have probably been on that land for even longer. It knows my family. It was present at my father's heart attack at the old cabins, and I'm pretty sure it was involved somehow when my brother died in the woods on that logging road. And now, what's been going on at the Lodge...it's all been happening on my family's land, and those things have been watching my family for generations."

Keith's brow wrinkled in thought. "Yeah, but Em was telling me that Cal—the reporter, right?—that he thinks there's some sort of predatory migration into the area. All the missing animals—even what happened with that kid Steven Mahakian—that's all recent. And none of that was on your land."

"Maybe there are two things going on," Jack said as he shrugged. "Maybe both are happening. I just know that those creatures have been haunting my family for generations. That's not just a recent development. That thing..." Jack paused a second as he shuddered. The memory of that monster looking straight at him on the logging road disturbed Jack beyond words. His truck hadn't really felt like much of a barrier at the time. "That thing," Jack repeated, "It knew me. It was looking straight at me on the logging road."

"Then why didn't it attack us?" Keith asked, trying to figure it all out. "It could have killed us all, Jack. No question."

Jack didn't have a definitive answer for that. It was true. The creature *could* have easily killed Jack, Keith, Fred, and Andrew on that logging road—truck or no truck. Jack felt that he knew the answer—that the creature had a calculating nature, that it considered who to kill and when to kill, like a human would, and had decided that it didn't benefit it in the moment to kill them all—but there was really no way to confirm that notion.

After a moment, Jack said, "I don't know why it didn't kill us, but I don't think it spared us out of the goodness of its heart." There was *nothing* good in those yellow eyes. Dan Meeks had it right. Those were eyes of hate.

"What's going to happen to the Lodge?" Keith asked.

Jack frowned. "I don't know. I'll have to talk to Bill and David about it. Keith, can you communicate with the Eden and Gibson Drake people? Tell them...um, tell them..." Jack didn't know where he was going with this. He was losing the threads. God, he was tired.

Keith put a hand on Jack's shoulder. "Don't worry about it, Jack. I think this might fall under 'Acts of God,' or something, in the contracts. I'll tell the crews tomorrow that the Lodge suffered some damage, and to wait for word on whether to show up on Monday or not. Just let me know by Sunday what you want to do."

Jack nodded.

"Jack," Fred said, "I hope you don't take this the wrong way, but I can't work up there anymore. I'm not...I can't..." Fred was shaking as he tried to collect himself.

"I don't blame you, son," Jack replied with a smile. It was Jack's turn to reassure someone. "This isn't your problem anymore, Fred. Just...be safe."

In due time, Em arrived at the hospital with the kids to pick up Keith—she wasn't about to leave anyone home alone at night after hearing about the attack. The deputies said they'd give Fred a ride home since his car was still up at the Lodge. Jenny also arrived at the hospital

271

to see her father, insisting that the doctors look Jack over before they went back to the house.

After receiving a clean bill of health, other than his blood pressure and pulse being pretty high for *some odd reason*, Jack followed Jenny back to the house in his truck. He didn't talk when they got back home and Jenny didn't push.

Jack headed straight to bed and promptly passed out.

# Chapter 14

July 17 – Saturday

Jack woke up in a cold sweat. He opened his eyes and saw Jenny standing over him saying, "Dad! Dad, wake up! You're having a nightmare." Jenny turned on the light at his nightstand.

"Unh," he moaned as he sat up and wiped drool from his mouth. He looked around as he tried to calm down. He felt a chill on his skin from the sweat.

Jenny sat down on the side of his bed. "You were having a bad dream, Dad."

Jack rubbed his face and ran a hand through his white hair, trying to shake off the dregs of the dream from his mind. Jenny got up and went to the bathroom to get him a glass of water. He gladly took the glass from her and downed it. He was parched.

After a few minutes, Jenny said, "Are you okay, Dad?"

He stared at his daughter, trying to anchor himself in the present. "Yeah...I guess I'm pretty shook up from what happened—what time is it anyhow?" he asked as he looked at his side table clock. It seemed to still be dark outside since no light was coming into the bedroom window.

"It's 3:50 AM," she said. "You were yelling something like 'we have to get out of here.' I heard you from my room."

"Oh," said Jack weakly. Then suddenly his dream came back to him. He was in his truck driving like a madman in the dark, but the truck didn't seem to be moving. Fred was screaming in the passenger seat next to him. Keith and Andrew were in the back seat, unnaturally calm, but also agreeing that they should leave. And the entire time in the dream, he felt a dark presence off to his side. Lurking. Seething. Waiting.

Jack heard its ragged breathing—like a monster that didn't care about hiding anymore. He didn't dare look back there. He didn't want to see the eyes. He could almost feel the monster reaching out to grab his shoulder.

That's when he must have started yelling out in real life. Now that he was awake, he realized that he had been having that same dream over and over again the entire night. This must have been the third or fourth iteration. He truly was in hell.

"Do you want to talk about it?" Jenny asked.

Jack was silent for a few seconds. He tried to strip his emotions from the events of the evening so that he could explain to his daughter why he was so unnerved. It had been fairly easy to rattle off the chain of events to the Sheriff's deputies at the hospital, but now, in the quiet of the night, finally safe at home, the true trauma of the encounter emerged.

Jack started slowly, "The creature chased us all night, you know. I told you that much over the phone, right?"

"Yeah. Before I drove to the hospital, you told me all of that. The thing actually came out in the open."

"I've never been so scared in my life. I've been in war, I've done some crazy stunts on movie sets where I'm pretty sure I was a hair's breadth away from a stupid death, but...I've never been terrified like that."

"Dad, thank God you and the others made it out alright. I know some people were hurt, but no one died." Jenny sighed. "Dad, I never liked that campground."

"Yeah, you hated being away from your friends," Jack smiled, trying to lighten the mood. "You'd rather be at your friend's house, right?"

Jenny remained serious. "No, Dad. That's not why I didn't like that place."

"Why then?"

"When I was little, and we used to go there sometimes, before you and Mom got a divorce, I would see...shadows...moving through the trees." Jenny seemed upset. "I didn't know what they were. All I knew is they were dark. I thought they were *shadows* moving in the trees."

"When was this?" Jack asked, concerned at his daughter's discomfort.

"I must have been maybe four or five."

"Did they ever come near you? Did they hurt you?"

"No," Jenny replied. "Mom kept me and Bobby close to her all the time up there. I don't think she liked being there either."

"No. She didn't."

"Dad, please promise me you won't go up there alone anymore." Jenny was serious and uncompromising. "You don't go up there without armed security, Dad."

"I promise. I won't," Jack said genuinely. He certainly had no intention of going into the forest alone or unarmed ever again—and that included the Lodge. He patted Jenny's hand and said, "I think I'll try and rest some more. I want to go with the deputies when they head to the Lodge in a few hours." Jenny gave her father a hug before leaving the room.

Jack left the light on and stared at the wall. He felt numb and tired, but he didn't want to go to sleep again. He was afraid of being trapped in another nightmare loop. Unfortunately, his mind went back to that last moment of horror when they passed the creature on the logging road. The thing seemed poised to end them as the truck whizzed by.

Keith's question came back to Jack's mind. Why didn't it attack? Why didn't it swipe at the truck like it did earlier in the evening? Jack was pretty confident that this same creature was the one that hit the truck as they screeched out of the Lodge parking lot. The same one that chased them around the Lodge.

Then Jack realized that the creature knew it didn't have to kill him because it knew it had already dominated him. It knew that Jack and the others had no fight in them. They were running like scared rabbits. It probably thought that Jack and his companions would never come back again. Jack even speculated that the creature knew killing them would bring too much attention to the area. Better to leave them alive and terrified.

*Could it be that smart? Could it be that calculating?* Jack wondered again. *Was this thing an animal? Or was it...something else?*

Jack couldn't handle anymore speculation. All he wanted was peace. He pulled the nightstand drawer open and grabbed the old Bible inside. He turned to Genesis, Chapter 1, and began to read to himself.

*In the beginning, God created the heavens and the earth. The earth was without form, and void; and darkness was on the face of the deep. And the Spirit of God was hovering over the face of the waters. Then God said, "Let there be light," and there was light.*


Jack sat in the front passenger seat of Bill's truck as they followed the deputies up Beverly Road towards the Lodge. It was 7 AM on Saturday morning. True to form, Ellen had notified Jack's business partners Bill and David of the prior night's events. Both of them met Jack at the Sheriff's Station around 6:30 AM.

Jack showed his partners the state of his vehicle at the Sheriff's Station. To any stranger passing by, Jack's truck might have looked like it'd been off-roading in the worst—or best?—way, but the smashed side and rear windshields told a darker story. Jack pointed out the spot where the creature must have thwacked the truck bed as they sped off. It was a sizeable dent.

Bill insisted on driving the three of them up to the Lodge in his truck as they followed the Sheriff's motorcade. They passed the spot where Frank's car had been on fire. There were still a few fire trucks hanging around making sure no foliage was burning.

Just further up ahead, the road had obviously been cleared of debris by front-end loaders. Fallen tree trunks were pushed to the side of the road along with loose brush and rocks. Jack felt that it was all so surreal to see the forest debris in the morning light.

Finally, the creature's dirty little secrets were being presented to everyone in plain view, yet, so far, the evidence lacked the marks of a true crime. Broken branches, displaced rocks, and fallen trees didn't really convey the feeling that a crime had been committed. Anyone could simply say that a localized tornado must have appeared.

*Yeah. Tornado Bigfoot*, Jack thought to himself.

Jack didn't know what to expect up at the Lodge. Their escape had been so dark, frenzied, and haphazard at the time. He didn't have to wait long to find out.

David and Bill gasped as they turned into the parking lot behind four patrol SUVs. They couldn't drive more than twenty feet in because the lot was a mess of debris from the smashed up office trailers. Trailer windows were broken and the trailer walls had holes punched in them. Neat piles of pavers and landscaping materials were now strewn about the parking lot.

Jack got out of the truck and they all followed the deputies to the front doors. The sergeant told Jack and his partners to hang back about twenty feet while they cleared the building. The deputies had guns drawn as they entered.

A few deputies scouted the outer perimeter while one deputy remained with Jack and the others. Jack looked at the tree line trying to discern any figures in the shadows, but he didn't see anything. That didn't dispel his concern.

Jack looked at the scattered building debris and tried to retrace the mad dash to the truck, then the harried chase dodging construction materials in the lot as they exited onto Beverly Road. The sun ascending in the sky seemed to ridicule Jack for his trepidation. Despite the obvious destruction at the site, the sun seemed to patronizingly say, "Poor, addled Jack. See? There's no monsters."

Jack had tried to download the security footage this morning from home, but the files had failed to upload again. Jack feared finding that the hard drive storing the surveillance videos was destroyed beyond repair, or that the footage would be inconclusive. The night vision cameras emitted infrared light only so far, and the creatures had demonstrated a knack for obliterating lights and cameras. If these things were merely animals, like gorillas or lions, how did they know to destroy cameras? How did they know to destroy lights?

Eventually the deputies came out of the Lodge giving the all-clear sign. One of them came up to Jack and said, "We didn't find anyone inside, but the place is pretty torn up." Then the deputies escorted Jack and the others into the building.

The lobby was a mess. The right-side front door with the temporary plywood repair was hanging askew by one hinge. There were still shards of glass and an eighteen-foot tree trunk on the floor. Pieces of the lobby chandelier were strewn about. The worst part of it all was that Roy had been ripped apart and scattered. The head was in the corner and the arms were by the front desk. The coyote elements weren't spared either.

Jack dejectedly looked over at the Security Office door, which had been smashed open. On the wall above the metal door, slightly to the left, Jack saw that the security camera had been obliterated. The creature must have destroyed it at some point after eradicating the wolf pack.

Jack picked his way through the debris and braced himself for the scene inside the Security Office. It was dark inside the room since there were no windows here, and the creature had shattered all of the ceiling lights once it broke through the metal door. Jack wasn't too shocked to find all of the monitors cracked and torn off of the walls. One of the deputies came up and shined his flashlight around the space.

Jack said, "I need to find the external hard drive that stored all of the security video." The deputy assisted in the search, which didn't take long. Jack took the black box from the deputy and inspected it. Thankfully it had been sitting in an inconspicuous spot under some corner shelving and office supplies on the desk. It appeared to be intact, but he'd need to plug it into a laptop to know for sure.

"Let's get this back to your truck, Bill," said Jack. "We can plug it into my laptop and see if it got anything."

"Don't you want to look around the Lodge a bit more to see if anything else was damaged?" David asked.

"Not right now," Jack replied. "I'm sure *there is* more damage, but I really need to see if there's anything on this hard drive."

Back outside, Bill pulled down the tailgate of his truck to serve as a makeshift table. Jack opened his laptop and attached the cables to the external hard drive. Thankfully, the hard drive was still functional and Jack was able to open the folders in it. The real question would be whether the cameras caught any useful video.

Jack found the folder labeled with the time stamps from last night. He found lots of videos from each of the sixteen cameras around the Lodge. He also noticed that the files stopped being created after about 9:17 PM from all of the cameras. He clicked on the lobby camera folder and viewed the last two clips. It was the video they had watched in real time while cowering in the Security Office last night.

There was no denying that something large entered the lobby after the chandelier was damaged, but once the creature moved to the door of the Security Office, that was the last of it on video. It destroyed the lobby camera without being filmed—not hard to do if you were positioned under it or off to the side when you emerged from the Security Office or the Great Room.

Jack sighed in disappointment.

One of the deputies was present when Jack played the video. He asked if they could examine the hard drive. Jack said he would give them copies of the videos—he somehow felt that it wouldn't be wise to give up the hard drive to the authorities. Anyway, the footage and the drive belonged to him and his partners.

The deputy left Jack, Bill, and David and returned to surveying the rest of the property. Bill folded his arms and said, "What do you want to do at this point? Obviously, this changes everything."

David said, "I never doubted your story, Jack, but this destruction is undeniable. It's violent beyond all expectation. And I don't know how we can possibly open a Lodge here now."

Jack looked at Bill. "No objections to that, Bill?" Jack asked, stunned that Bill hadn't immediately countered David's statement with an option to keep the Lodge open.

Bill shook his head slowly. "I don't want to lose money, but I don't want people killed at my Lodge either. Don't worry, I'll think of something to turn this around somehow. It won't be a Lodge, but, like David said, maybe some scientists with big grant money would be willing to spend some bank to come up here and study Sasquatch." With a twinkle in his eye, he added, "Or maybe some big game hunters would be willing to drop beaucoup bucks to hunt Bigfoot in these woods. I've been doing research online. Some people would pay to see this thing for sure. Either to hunt it or, I don't know, hang out and braid its hair."

Jack couldn't argue against either notion, and he felt no urge at all to protect a creature that gave him nightmares. Even David didn't argue with Bill about the prospect of killing the creature, and that was saying something.

"Like I said, Bobby should be arriving this afternoon, and I'll talk to him about having a look around," said Jack dispiritedly.

"Are you okay, Jack?" David asked with concern. "You've been through a lot."

"I'll be fine," Jack replied. "But I'm not ever going in these woods alone again. I feel like these things have been plaguing my family for years and I never even knew it. I owe it to my dad to do something about it. I owe it to Tom."

"Do what, though?" Bill asked.

"I'm not sure yet," said Jack. "I'll have a better idea after I discuss it with Bobby."

David folded his arms in thought. "Jack, why do you think the encounter last night was so different from your previous encounter a week ago? When you saw the creature last Saturday night by yourself, all it did was look at you and then walk off, right? But last night, it was all out war. Why?"

Jack considered the question for a second before saying, "I don't think they were the same individual. The eyes were different—the first one seemed more curious, and the red eyes were probably eyeshine from the parking lot lights. Also, I don't think he was as massive. The one last night..." Jack shuddered to remember. "Last night was a different creature. The first one was big, but this second one was bigger. I actually think there were probably several of them harassing us on the road, but the one we actually saw was probably the same one that Dan saw years ago. The one that hates us. I don't know what their social interactions are like—if

283

they're pack animals or solitary—but I think this bigger guy is definitely dominant." Jack hated remembering his encounters but also felt compelled to parse out the horrible experience.

Jack's phone buzzed. He saw that Kathy was calling him and immediately felt a sense of dread. "Kathy," he answered, "what's wrong?"

"Jack," Kathy said worriedly, "I just found out that Stef's Duty Station sent people to pick up Stef and her partner at the designated spot yesterday, but no one ever checked back in from the pick-up team *or* from Stef and her partner." Kathy sounded on the verge of tears. "Her supervisor said he already contacted the Bonner County and Boundary County Sheriffs and that they tried looking for them around 7PM last night, but there was an unexpected storm in the area that hampered their search. They're going to start searching again this morning. *Jack, what are we going to do?*"

*No*, Jack thought to himself. *You probably got my dad and my brother. You're not going to get Stef too.*

"Kathy," Jack replied, "can you get up here to Idaho?"

"Yes," she said without hesitation.

"Do it," Jack instructed. "Talk to Jenny if you need help with travel arrangements, but get up here. If I have to go out there to look for her myself, I will."

Kathy agreed that she would catch a flight immediately and would call Jenny about it.

"What's wrong?" David asked after Jack hung up.

"Stef hasn't come back from the woods," said Jack. "She was due last night but she and the others haven't come back."

Bill and David looked at each other with concern. Bill asked, "What are you going to do?"

"I'm going to find her," Jack replied resolutely.

# Epilogue

## July 17 – Saturday

Bobby drove straight to the Lodge to meet his father. His mother Ellen had told him everything that had happened the night before as he drove up from Boise on Saturday morning. He was stunned at the mention of Bigfoot and almost thought it was a joke until he heard the quiver in his mother's voice. His son Jake was riding along with and was shaking his head in amazement as they listened to her over the truck's speaker system.

Bobby called his father after hanging up with Ellen. Jack had even worse news for him—Stef hadn't come out of the woods last night from her surveying trip. A search team was going out to find her and the others this morning. Kathy was flying in from Florida later today. They were all going to head up to Coolin as soon as everyone arrived.

Bobby's hairs were up at hearing the string of bad news. After hanging up with Jack, he looked over at Jake, who sat staring out the window trying to make sense of it all.

*"What is going on, Dad?"* Jake finally asked incredulously. "Does this even compute to you?"

Bobby's memories were spooling up. Images. Feelings. The forest. The sounds. Ancient memories made new again. Things that were once confusing to Bobby were now starting to make sense. Connections were being made. The story was becoming whole.

"Son," Bobby started. "Let me tell you something about those woods…"

LOOK FOR BOOK TWO IN THE SERIES

# UNHEARD

# Author Notes

This story is set in the fictional town of Everton, Idaho. The Evers Family land is also fictional, however, many of the towns, counties, trails and geographical locations in the story are real. For instance, the Idaho Centennial Trail (ICT) is an actual hiking trail. Bonners Ferry is a real town in Boundary County, Idaho. Priest Lake is located in Bonner County, Idaho. Indian Creek Campground is really located on the eastern shore of Priest Lake. I decided that the fictional town of Everton should be situated on the northern banks of the Pend Oreille River in Northern Idaho—between the real towns of Priest River and Sandpoint.

All of the characters in the story, including Jack Evers and his family, are fictional, except for Gia Fuda and Lisa Theris, both of whom were reported missing in the wilderness and were eventually found alive.

Bigfoot, in my opinion, is real.

# Acknowledgements

I would like to acknowledge the help of my husband, John Morales, my sister Eliza David, my daughter Phoebe Morales, and my mother, Sisenanda Cicone. They were the beta readers and proofreaders for this book. My husband and sister also helped me edit the book for logic and pacing. Additionally, my daughter Diana Morales and son Bruce Morales helped bounce around ideas on plot development.

Finally, I want to thank my wonderful husband, John, for always encouraging me to continue writing and for being a huge fan of my work. Thank you for the life we have together.

# About the Author

I was born and raised in Southern California. I graduated from UCLA with a Bachelor of Arts in Near Eastern Languages and Civilizations (specializing in Egypt) and then a Master of Library and Information Science. I also completed an Advanced Paralegal Course through UC Santa Cruz.

I've been a stay-at-home mom, a military wife, and worked in several technology start-up companies. I grew up reading a lot of science fiction and fantasy novels. Some of my favorite authors are Isaac Asimov, C.J. Cherryh, Anne McCaffrey, and Robert E. Howard. I have always enjoyed writing and often considered writing a book, but it was only during the COVID-19 pandemic and subsequent quarantine (2020) that I finally channeled my energies towards this endeavor in a serious way. I thoroughly enjoyed writing *Unseen* and hope that the reader was satisfactorily entertained.

What I enjoy doing most is spending time with my husband and three children.

# Other Works by the Author

*Reign of Pigs: A Poem in Verse and Art* (2020) (Paperback) (Kindle eBook)

    This is a picture book for grownups. It is *not* a children's book. It depicts the frustration and anguish that an adult experiences when outside forces negatively impact the family.

## Coming Soon in *The Unseen Series*

*Unheard* (Fall 2021)

*Unknown* (early in 2022)

Made in the USA
Monee, IL
30 April 2023

32717926R00164